Popular Temptation author Kate Hoffmann was thrilled at the opportunity to set her second Weddings by DeWilde book in Paris. She felt it called for a research trip, which she willingly undertook. Result: our intrepid Wisconsin-based author is contemplating a return trip, possible residence, and is busily pursuing French lessons! *Terms of Surrender* demonstrates delightfully how thoroughly Kate took France to heart. Impeccable research has made for another completely engaging DeWilde story, and a romance much more pleasant to contemplate than another Wisconsin winter!

"The battle isn't won yet," Phillip said.

As he expected, Megan rose to the challenge. "Oh, I can beat you, all right. In a fair fight."

"I'll fight you and I'll do everything I can to win. Two businesspeople, no holds barred. And between us, we'll make a pact."

"A pact?"

"Once the sale of the property is finalized, we'll meet back here under these cherry trees and declare a winner. And no matter who wins, you and I will start again. No matter what our families have to say about it, we'll give each other a chance. We'll forget this damn fight and everything that goes with it and we'll become…friendly competitors. Very friendly."

Megan bit her lower lip as she considered his offer. "I'll win, you know. Will you be able to handle that?"

"I can handle anything you throw my way." Phillip grinned. "And I'm sure you'll do your best."

With that, he drew her against him and covered her mouth with his, kissing her deeply. If he could have, he would have made the kiss last forever.

"*À bientôt*, sweet Meggie," he murmured, caressing her cheek with his fingertips. "And may the best man win."

Weddings by De Wilde™

PREVIOUSLY AT DeWILDES

Mallory Powell, of the San Francisco Powells, calls off her wedding!

- Mallory Powell, Grace DeWilde's niece, has plunged beyond the safe boundaries of life within elite San Francisco society and her own successful restaurant, Mallory's.

- Her politically correct engagement to her father's right-hand man is off, replaced by a passionate relationship with writer Liam O'Neill, and spiced with the imminent arrival of their baby.

- Grace, meanwhile, has been fending off the pleasurable advances of Alex Stowe, who'd very much like to help Grace take her mind off her painful separation from her husband, Jeffrey.

And Nick Santos, dead-ended in his pursuit of the missing DeWilde heirlooms again, is making his way to Paris, where he can harass Megan DeWilde for a change....

Peggy Hoffmann is acknowledged as the author of this work.

ISBN 0-373-82544-7

TERMS OF SURRENDER

Terms of Surrender
KATE HOFFMANN

Harlequin Books

TORONTO • NEW YORK • LONDON
AMSTERDAM • PARIS • SYDNEY • HAMBURG
STOCKHOLM • ATHENS • TOKYO • MILAN
MADRID • WARSAW • BUDAPEST • AUCKLAND

Jeffrey DeWilde
CEO, DeWilde Enterprises

Dear Mr. DeWilde,

I've completed my investigation and
have enclosed a detailed report of
my findings regarding the Villeneuves'
involvement in the DeWilde jewel theft.
I am sure you will be surprised, as I
was, to discover your daughter Megan's
connection to Phillip Villeneuve. I
have included all I know of their
relationship and recent activities.
I'll leave you to question her in
greater detail.

Nick

Nick Santos
Private Investigator

CHAPTER ONE

THE BALLROOM SPARKLED with light, glittering chandeliers reflecting off gilded mirrors and beaded gowns until it seemed as if the entire room had been sprinkled with a dusting of diamonds. The magical atmosphere was the stuff of little girls' dreams, but as Megan DeWilde stood atop the grand staircase, her only concern was whether she'd be able to make it down the marble Matterhorn without tripping on her hem.

All Monaco had turned out for the social event of the season—the Baron and Baroness Waldheim's annual masked ball—and there was even rumor that Princess Caroline would make an appearance. A vivid image sprang into Megan's mind, and she saw herself making her entrance, tumbling bustle over teakettle, skirts flying, until she came to rest at the princess's royal feet, tiara askew and face flushed with mortification.

She knew what would happen next. They'd all stare and whisper what a shame it was that the venerable DeWilde family had been cursed with such a clumsy and socially inept offspring. Once they turned back to their own conversations, she'd finally be able to crawl off and spend the rest of her night nursing her bruises behind a potted palm.

"Don't look so worried, Meg. You look absolutely stunning. That costume has got to be the most beautiful thing I've ever seen. I can't believe the opera theater actually let you borrow it for the night."

Megan glanced nervously to her left and forced a smile for her sister-in-law. "I guess it pays to have connections," she murmured. "But the dress won't look so elegant once it's in a heap at the bottom of these stairs. I'm not sure I can make it. All this beadwork weighs a ton. And I can't see a thing through this damn mask." She looked down at the ornate ecru costume, adjusting the mask until she'd regained at least part of her vision. But it was no use. She couldn't see her feet or the stairs in front of her. "Maybe there's a side entrance we could use. One with a nice ramp."

"Not to worry, little sister." Megan's twin brother, Gabriel, quickly stepped in between her and Lianne, playing the part of Romeo to Lianne's newly pregnant Juliet with easy aplomb.

Megan had been thrilled when Lianne had told her of her pregnancy. She couldn't have been happier for her brother and his wife. The baby was due in August, and Megan held a secret hope that the first DeWilde grandchild might help to bring her fractured family back together.

Gabe offered Megan his arm. "If you go down, you'll be taking me along with you," he said. "After all, with what that dress weighs, you'll need someone to break your fall."

"And what about me?" Lianne teased.

Gabe smiled at Lianne as she slipped her hand through his arm. "I'm not worried about you, darling. Before too long, you'll be so round you'll just roll down the stairs without a care."

Lianne giggled and slapped at his hand playfully. Megan shot her brother a sarcastic smile, meeting the hazel eyes behind his mask. "I bet you didn't know you'd married such a gentleman, did you, Lianne?" she commented. "Maybe Gabe should wear tights more often."

"He does have cute knees," Lianne joked.

Megan drew a fortifying breath and clutched her brother's elbow. "Well, let's get this over with." The trio stepped closer to the head of the stairs and Lianne handed the majordomo their invitation.

"Gabriel DeWilde and Lianne Beecham DeWilde," the liveried servant intoned to anyone who might be listening. He waited for them to begin their descent into the crowd. Lianne leaned over and whispered something to the servant. He raised a brow and cleared his throat. "And Megan DeWilde," he added haughtily.

Megan sighed. Security for the Waldheims' ball was airtight, and no one was allowed entry without an invitation. Even though Gabe had easily been able to obtain a verbal invitation for her, there had been an awkward moment with the security guards at the front gate. Now, once again, she was reminded that she had not been on the original guest list.

"I knew I shouldn't have let you talk me into tagging along," Megan whispered. "I feel like I'm crashing the party."

"Relax," Gabe said as they started down the stairs. "You're the one who wanted an introduction to the baroness. Besides, it's about time you got out and socialized a bit. You can't stay cooped up in your office for the rest of your life."

Megan cursed her acceptance of Gabe and Lianne's invitation at the same moment her toe caught the hem of her gown. Her fingers bit into Gabe's arm and she steadied herself. Her brother was probably right. Since being deserted at the altar a year ago last summer by her fiancé,

Edward Whitney, Megan had become even more obsessed with her career, to the exclusion of all else.

Just the thought of Edward brought with it an acute flood of regret and an overwhelming sense of failure. She had thought she loved him, was certain she would make a perfect wife. Her family had been thrilled about the engagement, and they were as sure as she was that Edward was the right man for her. And Megan had always tried to please her family.

But as the wedding day approached, she had come to suspect that he wasn't the right man for her—more succinctly, she was not the right woman for him. He wanted a woman who could do it all and with astounding aplomb—a woman who could maintain her own professional life while running his personal life. A woman who could entertain at the drop of a hat and who would choose to spend her free time working for charities. A woman who would take care of the children and have a firm hand with the household servants.

What he didn't want was the kind of woman who hadn't found the time to memorize the seating charts for the wedding reception . . . a woman who didn't give a fig what color candles adorned the altar . . . a woman who didn't mind being two hours late for her own wedding rehearsal due to a business emergency.

A sliver of regret shot through her. She had tried so hard to be the woman Edward wanted, certain that she could accomplish it all if she just worked hard at it, unwilling to accept such failure in herself. But now, with the benefit of time, she knew that marrying Edward would have been a mistake. Perhaps her tardy arrival at the wedding rehearsal had had nothing to do with business and everything to do with forcing Edward to make the decision to call off the wedding.

She sighed inwardly. Or perhaps he had never really loved her at all. She'd never know for sure. But from that day on, she had been certain of only one thing—she wasn't meant for marriage or commitment. For one brief, blinding moment, she had simply wanted what her mother had, the love of a man, happiness within her own family, *and* a satisfying professional life. Only later, long after the wedding fiasco, would she learn that no one, not even Grace DeWilde herself, could have it all.

So she worked, harder than she ever had, in part to make up for the humiliation she'd caused the family, in part to convince herself that work was all she needed in life. Every hour of the day and a considerable portion of the night were dedicated to DeWilde's Paris operation. There were times she didn't even bother to go home to her boulevard du Montparnasse apartment, instead spending the night on the sofa in her office. If she couldn't be the perfect wife, then she'd damn well do her best to be the perfect DeWilde.

Even her attendance at the ball could be written off as business. The invitation had been sent to her father and mother, but the current state of her parents' marriage had precluded their attending. Grace and Jeffrey DeWilde had lived apart for almost nine months now. Megan's father had insisted that Gabriel and Lianne attend in his stead as representatives of DeWilde's exclusive Monaco store, and the pair had convinced Megan to accompany them.

It hadn't taken much convincing, since Megan had been determined to wangle an introduction to Opéra Monaco's most generous benefactor, the Baroness Waldheim. Surely a woman who hosted one of Monaco's most important social events of the season could lend a small portion of her considerable wealth to the Théâtre de l'Opéra in Paris, as well.

"Megan DeWilde," a voice said warmly, interrupting her thoughts. "What a pleasure to finally meet you."

Megan blinked, surprised to find herself standing at the bottom of the stairs, all limbs intact, and shaking hands with the Baroness Waldheim. Megan curtsied and returned the baroness's warm smile. "The pleasure is mine, Lady Waldheim."

"I have heard of your work with the Théâtre de l'Opéra and the Ballet Paris," the baroness continued. "We share a fondness for the arts, *n'est-ce pas?* We must speak of this at greater length, I think. Maybe over lunch on one of my trips to Paris." The baroness patted her hand, then turned to Lianne and graced her with a lovely smile.

Megan murmured a quick, "That would be nice," then hastily added, "my lady," before she turned and made her way down the line. She stole a glance around the room and mentally multiplied the number of guests by the "donations" they'd paid to attend. Opéra Monaco would not be cutting any corners on their productions in the coming season.

She envied the baroness's ease with fund-raising. Until a few years ago, the Théâtre de l'Opéra had only been a building near DeWilde's rue de la Paix store. It wasn't until her great-aunt Marie-Claire had insisted Megan accompany her to the theater for a season of "cultural enlightenment" that she learned it was home to the world-renowned Ballet Paris. She'd been entranced by the costumes and the dancers and the elegant surroundings. And she'd decided the Théâtre de l'Opéra could benefit from the DeWilde family's largesse.

It had been a perfect marketing marriage. Night after night, DeWilde's upscale customers flocked to the elegant building to see the latest ballet productions. And each night they were reminded that DeWilde's had played a small part in mounting the production, underwriting the cost of original costumes for a new ballet or financing the renovation of one of the lovely salons or purchasing something new for the museum.

"It's a pleasure to meet you," she murmured, shaking the next hand offered to her. "A pleasure to meet you." After a few more introductions, Megan finally found herself at the end of the line. Anxious to find a quiet place in which to retreat for the rest of the evening, she swiftly made a beeline for the open French doors that led to the terrace. She shot a quick look over her shoulder at Lianne and Gabe, then rushed right into the back of a tall masked gentleman who stood just inside the doorway.

He slowly turned, placing the fluted glass he held on a nearby window ledge and wiping the spilled champagne from the front of his costume. *"Excusez-moi,"* he said, his French perfect, his tone smooth and sophisticated.

Megan stepped back and her heel caught on the hem of her dress. As if in slow motion, she felt herself listing backward, unable to regain her balance with her foot planted squarely on the hem of her skirts. Just as she was about to give up the ship, the stranger reached out and grabbed her elbow to steady her.

"Ça va bien?" he asked.

"I'm fine," Megan said, replying in English.

"Vous êtes certaine?"

"Absolutely. I'm sorry for bumping into you. I—I wasn't watching where I was going." Lord, she'd been at the ball only a few minutes and already she'd made her first blunder. She reached up and straightened her tiara, then plucked at her mask until the holes lined up with her eyes.

Her heart skipped as he smiled down at her. Though most of his features were hidden behind his own mask, she sensed that she was looking into the face of a startlingly handsome man. "You must not apologize," he said, his English as perfect as his French.

Her fingers clutched her skirt and she tried to keep her nerves from creeping into her voice. "But—but it was my fault. At least allow me to get you another drink."

He shrugged at her offer. "I don't care for another drink," he said. "But I would like to dance." Placing one hand behind his back, he held out the other.

Megan stared for a long moment at his outstretched fingers. "You want *me* to dance with you?"

He reached down and took her hand into his. "I always make it a point to dance with the most beautiful woman at the party," he said. He pressed his lips against her fingers, then steered her toward the dance floor. "And tonight will be no different."

A flush warmed her cheeks as he easily pulled her body toward his. He moved with the music, drawing her into a waltz. Megan blinked in amazement. She'd never been much for dancing, but in this stranger's arms she suddenly felt graceful. She also felt breathless and dizzy and her mind seemed unable to put together a coherent sentence.

At first she was sure the whalebone bodice of her gown had cut off her circulation. She now understood why a lady might find use for a fan. At this moment she'd sell her soul for a cool breath of air to clear her head. But then she realized that the gown had nothing at all to do with how she felt. The man dancing with her had stolen her breath away.

"So, do you have a name, or must I call you Queen of the Night?" he said, his words soft against her temple. She could hear the smile, the warmth in his voice, and her nerves began to subside.

Megan drew back and looked up into the brilliant blue eyes behind the mask. "You recognize my costume," she said. "I'm surprised."

"Mozart," he replied. "*The Magic Flute*. But as I remember, the Queen of the Night is swallowed up by an earthquake at the end of the evening."

"I plan to leave this party in the limousine that brought me here," Megan said. "The driver's waiting out—" The words were barely out of her mouth when she realized how inane they were. She'd never been much for dazzling conversation. In fact, she usually thought of her clever comebacks twenty minutes after she'd walked out of the room.

"Ah, we've just met," he said. "And the night is still young. It is too early to talk about saying goodbye."

Megan arched her brow and glanced up at him suspiciously. He spoke to her with all the ease of a man expert in making women feel comfortable in his presence. She couldn't help but wonder how many nervous tongues he'd untied before he'd happened upon hers. "Now I recognize your costume," she said. "You're Don Juan, aren't you. I'd say your choice of costume is quite appropriate."

A grin curled his chiseled lips. "You wound me, your highness. I speak from my heart."

"As I remember, Don Juan was not ruled by his heart but his—" Megan drew a sharp breath and cleared her throat. "Well, you know as well as I, don't you."

He tipped his head back and laughed, a deep, rich sound that washed over her like a cool summer shower on a scorching cobblestone street. "*Tu es très charmante, ma chère reine,*" he said. "Why have we never been introduced before?"

A shiver ran down Megan's spine at his words. His use of the intimate form of French, reserved for lovers and close friends, was almost like a caress. "And you are very charming as well, *monsieur,*" she replied, trying to keep her voice aloof and her words light.

He pulled her close again. "Enough with these hidden identities," he said. "Tell me your real name."

"But this is a masked ball," Megan replied, beginning to get the hang of the flirtatious game they played. "It would spoil the night if we revealed ourselves too soon, don't you agree?"

"Then you will remain my queen," he replied, "until the moment we are alone and I unmask you."

For the first time since her scuttled wedding, Megan felt a small measure of confidence in herself as a woman. Behind the mask she could be anything she wanted. She could be mysterious and alluring...even sexy. She could be the type of woman who could attract a man simply with a seductive gaze or a beckoning smile. She could be a woman who was able to completely captivate a man...so much so that he'd ignore her failings as a potential mate and prefer her as a lover instead.

Still, this game she was playing was dangerous, for Megan knew all too well the consequences of letting her heart rule her head, of letting impulse overwhelm common sense. She'd done that once before and it had ended in disaster.

Since then she'd kept her distance with the opposite sex, hoping that by avoiding men altogether she might avoid the sense of failure that always marked the end of a relationship. And it hadn't been just Edward. He'd simply been the last in a line of promising companions who had begged off for some reason or another, leaving Megan bewildered and baffled.

She had finally come to the conclusion that some women simply weren't meant for marriage or commitment. Or for happily ever after. Or even for a long-term "relationship." And she was one of those women.

But tonight, for the first time in a long time, she felt differently. Dressed in such an elaborate costume, hidden behind her mask, she was no longer Megan DeWilde, corporate executive and resident expert in unfulfilled relationships. Instead she felt…very French, sensual and alive, and just a bit naughty. She wanted this game between them to go on and on, the danger be damned.

"And what shall I call you?" Megan asked, smiling her most tantalizing smile. "I suppose I could call you Don. Or would you prefer Juan?"

"Don will be fine for now," he said, his breath warm against her ear. "But mark my words, I will know your identity before this night is through."

From that moment on, Megan felt as if she'd stepped into a fantasy world, a place where her insecurities and shortcomings didn't matter and where the real world was kept at bay, where a man more intriguing and exciting than any other man she'd ever met held her in his seductive spell.

He led her from their first dance out to the wide terrace, and they danced in the moonlight, alone, with the music drifting on the cool night air and light spilling out of the tall French doors. She came alive in his arms, trading *bons mots* with him, laughing and teasing, leading him on then drawing coyly away. They spoke of inconsequential things, yet every subject seemed to bring them back to this strange but instant attraction they had for each other.

She'd felt these wonderful stirrings before, long ago, when she was young and infatuated with the notion of romance—before her practical nature replaced foolish teenage dreams. But now she felt reckless and uninhibited. Her heart beat faster every time he spoke, her breath catching in her throat, heightening her senses until the stars seemed brighter and the night air sweeter.

"Tell me, what are you doing here?" he asked, gracing her with a devastating smile.

"I'm dancing with you," Megan said.

"Have you come here alone?"

She knew what he meant, but wasn't sure how to answer him. Did he really care, or was this all part of the game they played? "What if I didn't?" she teased. "What if my husband is inside looking for me at this very moment?"

"Then we'll stay out here for the rest of the night," he replied smoothly. "And avoid your husband."

Megan frowned, oddly disturbed by his reply. "So, it would make no difference to you if I were married?"

"None at all," he replied.

"And do you make it a habit to charm married women?"

He stopped dancing and looked down at her. "Never," he replied in a tone that indicated he was telling the truth. "But then, I'd never met you. I've never in my life experienced a *coup de foudre.* I'm not certain how to proceed."

Megan struggled with the translation, sure it was an idiom she'd never heard before. "A flash of lightning?" she asked.

"Love at first sight," he replied. He grabbed her upper arms and his gaze locked with hers. "Tell me you're not married," he demanded. "Tell me what I already know."

"I—I'm not married," Megan said in a shaky voice.

"Engaged?"

She shook her head, for the first time truly glad Edward had missed their wedding.

A satisfied smile curled his lips as he pulled her back into his arms. "Then there is nothing to keep us from spending the rest of the evening with each other," he murmured.

He danced with no one else, talked to no one else, looked at no one else but her. When they moved to the strains of a waltz, he held her close. And when they strolled along the terrace and gazed down upon the twinkling lights of Monte Carlo, he held her hand or splayed his fingers across the small of her back, as if by breaking their physical contact he might break the spell that had descended over them.

"It's beautiful, isn't it," Megan said, staring down at the lights that outlined the Côte d'Azur, the coast where Monaco met the azure Mediterranean. Luxury yachts bobbed in the harbor in a soft golden glow spilling from the city. From where she stood she could pick out the Casino and the Palace of Monaco.

He cupped her cheek in his palm and turned her gaze to his. *"Tu es belle,"* he murmured. *"Ton rayonnement m'éblouit."*

I'm beautiful, Megan translated silently, sure that her French classes at the Sorbonne had suddenly failed her, then realizing she knew exactly what he was saying to her. *I overwhelm him with my radiance.* She felt a blush warm her cheeks and turned away, not sure how to react. Was he telling her the truth, or was he merely using some well-rehearsed come-on? Could she take his words seriously, or would it be more appropriate to laugh his remark away? Her gaze wandered along the harborfront until it stopped at her hotel.

Oh, hell and damnation. Right now she didn't really care what his motives were. If he was bent on seducing her, who was she to object? Since she'd eliminated both marriage and commitment as unacceptable options for her, maybe a brief affair with a profligate playboy was the only option left to her.

She'd made a vow on the day she moved to Paris that she would live life with greater abandon, like a French woman and not the conservative British-bred girl she'd been most of her life. That vow had resulted in her botched attempt at marriage. But this was different. This was just one night of pleasure. Certainly the risk was worth the reward, wasn't it? After all, she couldn't be expected to swear off men for the rest of her life, could she?

Megan took a deep breath and looked up into his eyes. "Do you have a car?" she asked.

He seemed taken aback by her odd question, but nodded.

"Then let's get out of here," Megan said. "I'll meet you out front in five minutes."

With that, Megan scooped up her skirts, readjusted her mask and made her way back inside, her mind already forming a plausible story for Gabe and Lianne. She found them both inside near the edge of the dance floor, arm in arm as they watched the dancers whirl in front of them. Megan stared at them for a long moment, wondering how Gabe had been so lucky to find love. He and Lianne were a perfect match, so sure of the feelings they shared, so content in their life together.

But then, Gabe led a charmed life. He took risks but he always came out on top, never losing confidence in the notion that he would triumph in the end—both personally and professionally. Megan closed her eyes and bit her lower lip, trying to dispel the flood of envy that rushed over her. Maybe there would never be a Mr. Right for Megan DeWilde. But Mr. Right Now was waiting outside and she wasn't about to let him get away.

"Meg! Where have you been?" Lianne asked the moment Megan stepped to her side. "I saw you dancing, but then you disappeared."

Megan placed her palm on her forehead. "I've been getting some fresh air. I have a simply splitting headache," she said in a voice that sounded properly pained. "I'm going to leave now."

Lianne frowned in concern. "You don't look well at all, Meg. Your face is flushed and your eyes seem a bit glazed. Gabe, why don't you fetch the car and I'll help Meg to the door."

"Oh, no!" Megan cried. She swallowed convulsively. Lord, she'd never been adept at lies and now she was making a total hash of this, too. "I—I don't want to spoil your evening. I've already called the hotel. They're sending a limo."

"Don't be silly," Lianne said. "You don't need to ride home alone. We'll leave with you."

"Please," Megan pleaded. "I feel badly enough already. You stay and enjoy the party. After the baby comes, you'll have precious few opportunities to dance the night away."

Lianne sighed, acquiescing. "All right. You're sure you can get back to the hotel on your own?"

Megan gave her sister-in-law a quick hug. "I'm a big girl. I'm sure I can handle a limo ride on my own." But even as she said the words, Megan wasn't entirely sure she'd be able to handle this particular limo ride.

Gabe gave her a kiss on the cheek, then stared down at her with a penetrating gaze. Her twin brother knew Megan better than any person on the planet. He had sensed her doubts about her relationship with Edward and he was the only family member who wasn't furious with rage when the groom didn't show up for his own wedding.

Gabe had always been able to tell when she was skirting the truth. From the time she'd thrown his lucky football down an old well at Kemberly, the DeWilde family estate in England, to the time she'd set him up on a blind date with a mousy school chum who she claimed had a "drop dead" body, he'd always known what was going on in her head. He most likely knew she was lying now.

"Are you sure you'll be all right?" he asked.

"I'll be fine," Megan said, avoiding his hazel eyes. "You two have fun and I'll see you tomorrow morning." She forced a smile. "We'll have breakfast before I take the TGV back to Paris."

Megan decided to beat a quick retreat before Gabe had a chance to question her further. She hurried through the crush of guests, her skirts held high, then raced out the intricately carved portal to the circular drive in front of the mansion. Breathless, she glanced along the line of limos, searching for the black-and-white costumed man with whom she would spent the rest of the evening.

Suddenly, a limo door opened in front of her and a man stepped out. Megan's breath caught in her throat and she knew it was him. He'd removed his hat and mask and the striped doublet he wore. Now, his face exposed, he was dressed in just his ruffled shirt, tight black satin breeches and knee-high boots.

Megan couldn't draw her gaze away from his face. She'd imagined that he would be attractive, but in no way was she prepared for such a devastatingly handsome man. His features were striking in their masculinity—a firm mouth and chiseled jaw, an aristocratic profile with a perfect nose, brilliant blue eyes and raven's wing brows.

Faced with his blatant sensuality, Megan was tempted to turn and run. All her earlier confidence drained out of her as she realized she was hopelessly outclassed by this man.

A man who looked like this was used to having any number of worldly and sophisticated women fall at his feet. What could he possibly want with her?

Megan winced inwardly. She knew exactly what he wanted, and what she wanted as well. Lord, she'd never in her life gone to bed with a man she'd just met! And she couldn't believe she was actually considering the possibility now. Megan DeWilde, last of the red-hot wallflowers, bedding a complete stranger—a stranger who probably had a revolving door installed in his bedroom to handle the crush of women eager to slip between his sheets.

He held out his hand. "Come," he urged. "You can't run back inside. There's nothing for you there."

Megan drew a shaky breath. "Listen, Don, or Juan, or whatever your name is, I really don't think that I—"

He covered her lips with his fingers. "Don't," he murmured, drawing her near with a suggestive smile. Slowly, he lowered his head and pulled his fingers away. "Don't."

His mouth covered hers and he drew her body along the lean length of his. Megan's knees buckled beneath her, but he slipped his arm around her waist to steady her, not breaking their kiss for even an instant. The kiss seemed to last for hours, and Megan barely realized when he pulled away, so numb with desire was she.

"If you want to go back inside, go now," he said. "Because in a few more seconds, I'm not going to let you out of my arms."

"I—I don't want to go," Megan replied in a small voice. "I'd rather stay here with you."

He turned her around and pressed her back against the side of the limo. His hands drifted up along her arms then across her shoulders. Her eyes widened as he carefully pulled off her tiara and the ornate turban that hid her hair. Dark waves tumbled down around her shoulders. Slowly, he reached for her mask. She held her breath and closed her eyes, not wanting to witness the look in his eyes, certain she'd see disappointment there when the face behind the mask was revealed.

She knew she wasn't beautiful, not in the classic sense. Her complexion was too pale and her mouth too wide. Her nose had nothing to recommend it, though it was straight, and her eyes were a wishy-washy shade of hazel, neither green nor brown. At least her hair could be counted as a good feature, now that she'd changed the color. In her quest to be more French, she'd transformed herself from mousy brown to rich, dark mahogany at Jean-Louis David, one of the most famous hair salons Paris had to offer.

"Beautiful," he whispered.

She opened her eyes in surprise and he kissed her again.

"Are you ready to leave?" he asked.

She nodded and he helped her into the limo, taking care not to sit on her costume. The voluminous skirts kept them a few feet apart, and the ride down the mountainside and into Monte Carlo was passed in an uneasy silence on her part.

Before long, the driver negotiated one last hairpin turn and the limousine approached the bright lights of Monte Carlo.

"Would you prefer my hotel or yours?" he asked.

"I'm not sure," Megan said, shooting him a sideways glance. "I've never done this before."

He raised his brow. "Never?"

"I—I mean, I have, but not this way. I just don't want you to think I'm—you know. I've just never—I'm not a promiscuous woman."

He gently reached over and pulled her against him. Megan pressed her hands to his finely muscled chest and looked up into his face, her eyes wide and wary.

"Who are you?" he murmured, brushing his mouth against hers. "Who are you that you've stolen my heart in just one night? We're alone now. Tell me your name."

"Megan," she murmured. "My name is Megan."

He kissed her again, long and deep, his tongue probing against hers until he knew her mouth as intimately as he'd soon know her body. "Ah, Meggie. My beautiful Queen of the Night. *Nous sommes faits l'un pour l'autre.* We are made to be together."

A delicious shiver ran down Megan's spine and she realized that there was no turning back. She wanted this man as much as he wanted her. She needed to lose herself in his arms and in his body and forget the woman she was by the light of day. "Tell me your name," she said.

"It's Phillip," he replied. "Phillip Villeneuve."

At first his words didn't register through the haze of passion that clouded her mind. "Phillip Vill—" Her voice died in her throat and she blinked hard. "Villeneuve?" She forced a light laugh. "For a moment, I thought you said Philippe de Villeneuve."

"Actually, I prefer Phillip," he murmured, seeking out her mouth again. "And my family hasn't used the 'de' before our name in years. Yes, I'm Phillip Villeneuve." He kissed her softly. "Now that we've introduced ourselves, perhaps we can get to know each other—"

"The hell we will!" Megan shoved away from him and scrambled to the other side of the wide seat. She reached out and banged her fist on the smoked glass partition between her and the driver. "Stop the car!"

An expression of concern flooded his face. "Megan, what's wrong?" He reached out to touch her, but she slapped at his hand.

"Don't you dare lay a finger on me! I can't believe you'd sink so low." She banged on the window again. "Stop the car. Now!"

Phillip calmly leaned over and pushed an intercom button above the window. "Stop the car," he said, then turned back to her. "What is wrong?"

The limo immediately swung over to the curb. Megan fumbled with the handle then crawled out the door, her skirts clutched in her arms.

"Megan, wait," he called, moving across the seat to follow her. "What are you doing?"

"Don't you dare follow me!"

"Megan, I don't understand."

She bent down and snatched her turban and tiara from his hands. "I should have known you had some ulterior motive. To think I almost let myself be seduced by you!"

"Damn it, Megan, what are you talking about? What ulterior—"

Megan didn't hear the rest of his plea. With a muttered oath, she grabbed the limo door and slammed it shut. Then she gathered up her skirts and took off in the general direction of her hotel, determined to put this disastrous evening behind her.

Good Lord, what had gotten into her head? A Villeneuve! She'd nearly made love to a Villeneuve! And even worse, she probably would have enjoyed it.

CHAPTER TWO

IN THE HUSHED ATMOSPHERE of the DeWilde board-room, Megan DeWilde glanced around the large conference table, silently evaluating the mood of each and every member of DeWilde's board of directors. She twisted her pen between her fingers. The quarterly board meetings were always a bit tense, but this one was especially so. Most of the meeting had focused on a discussion of her mother's newest venture—a retail establishment of her own in San Francisco.

The board members had once again voiced their concern over the defection of Grace DeWilde from the family fold. She'd been a vital part of DeWilde's success, and many of the board members believed her departure would negatively affect the future of the corporation.

It was impossible to think of her mother as an outsider, but Grace had given her family no choice. The board discussed her as if she were the enemy now. Yet no matter how hard Megan tried, she couldn't separate her family's business interests from the chaos that her parents' separation had caused in her heart. She couldn't choose sides. She wouldn't.

Megan drew a deep breath and straightened in her chair. Her name appeared next on the agenda and she was anxious to introduce her proposal. She'd prepared a thorough report, which she had forwarded to the board members ten days ago, and was confident she'd win approval for her plan.

When it came to business, Megan's confidence rarely wavered. A passion for retailing was part of her genetic makeup, and she knew the business nearly as well as both her father and her mother did. She was determined to prove herself worthy of the name she'd inherited and her position as merchandising manager of DeWilde's Paris. Someday she hoped to take her father's place as president, CEO and general manager of the DeWilde Corporation.

Though most people, including the entire board of directors, believed Gabe to be the heir-apparent, Megan wanted to be considered right alongside her brother, equal in competence, yet slightly different in temperament. And the project she was about to introduce could make everyone sit up and take notice. They'd finally realize that she could run DeWilde's as well as Gabe when the day came for her father to retire.

Strange how facing down the board of directors caused only a small flutter of nerves, yet a simple social occasion nearly sent her into paroxysms of self-doubt. There were times she wished some of her unwavering confidence in the business world would be translated to her personal life. Her mind flashed back to the costume ball in Monaco and she winced inwardly as every detail came rushing back in unwelcome clarity.

Over the past weeks she'd tried to put the whole mess out of her mind. So what if she'd made a complete and utter fool of herself lusting over some stranger? Being left at the altar by her fiancé had certainly taught her how to handle embarrassing situations. But that stranger wasn't just any stranger, he was a Villeneuve—a sworn enemy of the DeWilde family.

Though the details of the feud between the Villeneuves and the DeWildes had never been very clear, she knew it had to do with her great-aunt Marie-Claire and the patriarch of the Villeneuve clan, Armand Villeneuve. At one time, the Villeneuves had been a rival power in the Paris retailing market. But after the Second World War, the family had moved into clothing manufacturing and export, setting up headquarters in Hong Kong.

The day she'd assumed the post of merchandising manager of the Paris store, Megan had received direct orders from her father never to do business with the Villeneuves. Like a loyal daughter and dutiful employee, she'd respected his wishes without question.

She swallowed convulsively, knowing just how close she had come to doing *business* with the scion of the Villeneuve family. Thank God she hadn't actually delivered on her end of the deal. She squirmed in her chair and nervously fiddled with her pen.

Not that it wouldn't have been wonderful, because it probably would have. After all, Phillip Villeneuve was undeniably gorgeous and obviously skilled in the art of seduction. And though her former fiancé had been attentive in bed, he'd never been particularly adventuresome. She stifled a sigh. If she knew just one thing, it was that an evening in bed with Phillip Villeneuve would definitely have been an adventure.

Megan scolded herself wordlessly. Adventure or not, she was a DeWilde and an enemy of the family was an enemy of hers. Her only regret was that she hadn't managed to effect a halfway decent kick to the groin or maybe a slap on the face, or at the very least she could have slammed his hand in the limo door while making her escape.

She felt Gabe's elbow bump her arm. "You're on, Meg," he whispered.

Megan listened as her father introduced her, then with a self-assured smile, she stood and moved to the head of the table.

"Good afternoon, ladies and gentlemen. As I am last on today's agenda, I will try to be brief so that you may enjoy this rare sunny February day here in London. You've all had a chance to read my proposal, so I'll simply review the salient points before I ask for your comments and questions.

"As you know, DeWilde's has experienced some rather rough weather lately. But we've also had some positive turns in our business. The New York store is back on track, thanks to the efforts of Sloan DeWilde and his new wife, Chloe Durrant. They're both committed to the success of the Fifth Avenue store and to solidifying the DeWilde name in the States."

Though she didn't say the words, her meaning was clear to the board members. Her mother's defection would not affect the success of DeWilde's in the least, not in the States or in any of the store's four other branches worldwide. Megan smiled in Sloan's direction and her handsome cousin nodded in reply. She knew she could count on Sloan for his vote.

"The in-store boutiques have proved to be extremely successful here in our London store, as Gabe will attest. This new concept in designer originals for bridal wear has exceeded all of our expectations. Unfortunately, we have been somewhat restricted in our use of the concept in Paris due to our smaller physical space. The store was considered large when my great-grandparents, Max and Genevieve DeWilde, opened it right after World War I. But today, we need more square footage.

"I have located a wonderful piece of real estate across the street from our rue de la Paix location, and I propose that we purchase this building and take the boutique idea one step further. I envision this location as an extension of our flagship store, a building that would house only our boutiques, with retail areas on each floor dedicated to various designers. I also would like to incorporate the designers' workrooms into the floor plan, with large windows overlooking the workrooms. Our customers will be able to see our designers at work on their one-of-a-kind wedding creations. Galeries DeWilde would be a new and exciting twist on the boutique concept, a perfect complement to our current location and one that I believe will cause great excitement in the Paris couture community."

Several of the board members began to whisper to one another, and Megan waited until she'd regained their complete attention before she continued.

"Within my report you found a floor plan, some architectural schematics, photos of the building, a tentative marketing budget and a financing proposal. Now is not the time for a conservative strategy, ladies and gentlemen. We must be aggressive. We must show the public and our stockholders that DeWilde's will do what it takes to maintain our leading-edge position in the retail marketplace in both Paris and the world. I ask for your support and your vote to proceed with the purchase and development of this property—to make Galeries DeWilde a reality."

Megan glanced her father's way. Though his expression was outwardly cool and detached, she could see the pride in his eyes. She turned her gaze to Gabe and he winked. She slowly released a pent-up breath, certain that she'd done her best. "Are there any questions?"

For the next half hour, Megan fielded inquiries, deflected criticism and defended her plan. In the end the vote was only one short of unanimous, an unqualified victory by DeWilde board standards—and exactly the vote she had predicted. She was given the go-ahead to secure financing for the venture and develop the property. Galeries De-Wilde *would* become a reality.

The board members quickly adjourned and the room cleared until only Gabe and her father remained. Megan leaned back in her leather chair and grinned like a cream-fed cat. "That went exceedingly well, didn't it?"

Gabe stepped behind her chair and grabbed it, nearly tipping her over backward. "Don't get a swelled head, Meg. Wait until you have a tougher sell before you gloat. Even an idiot can recognize a good idea when he sees one."

"Oh, is that why you voted yes?" she teased.

Gabe tugged on a lock of her hair, a gesture of affection left over from their childhood together. "I voted yes because you're my sister and you happen to be a brilliant retailer."

A surge of satisfaction rushed through her at Gabe's words. She'd worked so hard to gain her family's confidence in her business abilities. When it came to the stores, she was the perfect DeWilde. It was only in her personal life that she seemed to cause her family great consternation.

"If anyone can make a success of this venture, you can," Gabe said with a grin. "I'm sure I'd do a better job, but then this is your project."

Jeffrey DeWilde cleared his throat, calling an end to their good-natured but subtly competitive ribbing. "Gabe, why don't you ring Lianne and we'll all go out and have some dinner."

"I'd love to, Dad," Gabe said as he headed to the door, "but Lianne has been a bit under the weather lately. A touch of morning sickness that seems to last all day."

"Waking up to your funny face will do that to a girl," Megan teased.

Gabe gave her a gentle punch on the shoulder. "You've never quite gotten over the fact that I was born first, have you, little sister." With that, he made a quick exit, closing the door behind him before she had a chance to get in the last word.

She turned to her father, glad for a moment alone. "So, what did you think of my presentation?" she asked, anxious for her father's approval.

Jeffrey nodded distractedly. "Fine. You did a fine job, Megan. I was very pleased." He paused. "Your—your mother would have been proud."

A stab of disappointment twisted inside her at his half-hearted attempt at a compliment. Her mother *would* have been proud! But her mother was no longer around. In fact, she was prohibited from telling her mother one word about her plans. "Maybe you and I can have dinner," she said softly. "I was hoping we might have a chance to talk."

Her father moved to stand behind his chair at the head of the table. "Is everything all right?" he asked, his voice filled with proper parental concern. "You aren't still stinging over Edward and the canceled wedding, are you?"

Megan groaned. "Daddy, I'm fine about Edward. It's old news. I'm happy he decided to pass on the wedding. Truly, I am. I would have made him a horrible wife." She stood up and crossed the room. "I'm worried about you. Since you and Mother separated, you've kept us all in the dark. Gabe blames Mother, Kate is mad at you, and I'm stuck in the middle. What is going on between you and Mother? Have you talked to her lately?"

Jeffrey rubbed his forehead with his fingertips and released a tightly held breath. "Megan, I don't want you to concern yourself over my relationship with your mother. I—"

She took his hand. "Don't concern myself? You're my parents. How can I not be concerned? Are we to just stand by and watch as you throw away thirty-three years of a loving marriage? Not to mention one of the most successful business partnerships in the world. And neither of you is doing a damn thing to save it!"

He gave her hand a brief squeeze then turned away from her to study a hunting print on the wall. "This is much more complicated than any of you children realize."

Resolute, Megan moved between her father and the print he seemed so intent on. She looked up into his face but he refused to meet her eyes. Her gaze scanned his features and her heart tightened. He'd always seemed much younger than his fifty-six years. But suddenly, the crow's feet at the corners of his eyes seemed deeper, his hair a bit paler at the temples, his shoulders more stooped. "Can't you work this out?" she begged. "I know you want to and I'm sure Mother does, too."

Jeffrey shook his head. "I don't think that's going to happen, darling." He paused. "In fact, your mother tells me she's contacting her solicitor. I think it's time to consider...divorce."

The word hit her like a punch to the stomach, robbing her of her breath and bringing tears to her eyes. She stepped back and braced her palms against the cool mahogany paneling of the boardroom. "No," she said, her voice choked with emotion. "Daddy, you can't. You have to talk to Mother. You have to work this out."

"That's not going to happen," Jeffrey said, his voice flat and emotionless. "Your mother and I..." He paused, as if trying to put words to an unfathomable situation. "We have irreconcilable differences. We're both to blame. We've both made our mistakes. I'm beginning to think that the only way to correct these mistakes is to end the marriage.''

"But why?" Megan cried, the plea tearing from her throat, burning her lungs. She'd thought she had come to grips with her parents' separation, secure in the knowledge that sooner or later they'd work it all out. But the mention of divorce seemed so final, so irrevocable, as if both her parents had given up. What could have caused such a rift between them? The question had barely entered her mind when an answer came to her.

She swallowed hard. "Is there . . . another woman? I—I mean, are you having an affair?" She couldn't stop now, and she let the rest of her words tumble out. "I told Gabe I thought that might be so, but it was just a cheeky remark, Daddy. You seemed so distracted and Gabe was worried. And when a person lives in Paris, you see it all the time. Men have extramarital affairs, but that doesn't mean they give up on their marriages. Wives even have a name for these women. *Petite amie.* It means little friend. It happens . . . all the time." She bit her lip when she realized she was babbling.

A bitter smile fractured her father's rigid expression. "I'm sure it does," he replied.

"So, is that it?" she asked softly. "I was right?"

"We both had a hand in what happened."

His enigmatic reply did nothing to answer the barrage of questions she still needed to ask. She grabbed his hands again. "Please, Daddy, tell me. I have to understand if you expect me to accept a divorce."

He looked down at her and shrugged. "I simply came to doubt your mother's love for me. And she came to doubt my fidelity to her. We both made mistakes, said and did things we can never take back. Perhaps it's time to move on with our lives. You have to accept that, Megan. The sooner the better."

Megan angrily brushed the tears from her cheeks. "No. I refuse to believe that. I won't. Neither will Gabe or Kate."

"I'm not sure what your mother has told Kate. I haven't told your brother yet about the divorce. I'd appreciate it if you'd keep the news to yourself. Gabe has been thrown for a loop by this whole thing and I'd like to tell him in my own time."

Megan sent him a pleading look, but her father remained impassive, speaking of the divorce as if it were some inconsequential business deal gone bad. Finally, she relented and nodded her assent. "I won't say anything."

Her father smiled, patting her on the shoulder. "Good girl. Now, why don't we get a bite to eat. I'm famished."

She shook her head, trying to keep her emotions in check. "I—I'm really not very hungry. I think I'd like to drive out to Kemberly and spend a few days before I head back to Paris. I suddenly feel the need to go there... to be alone."

"I understand," he said.

Megan bit her lip and met his gaze through tear-clouded eyes. "No," she said, "I don't think you do. I don't think you or Mother really know what a divorce would do to our family."

She turned and walked out of the boardroom without looking back. She'd go to Kemberly, to her childhood home in Hampshire, to the place where they'd all once been a happy family. She'd remember all the wonderful Christmas mornings and the sunny summer holidays. She'd remember her mother and her father, together and in love.

And no matter what happened, she'd never, ever believe that Grace and Jeffrey DeWilde didn't belong together.

FROM HIS VANTAGE POINT thirty-seven stories above Victoria Harbour, Phillip Villeneuve watched as a brilliantly painted Chinese junk bobbed across the busy waterway that separated Hong Kong Island from the mainland. Harbor lighters chugged between the moored commercial vessels and the docks on the waterfront, delivering cargo to the island and the city of Kowloon on the opposite side of the harbour. And in the distance, monolithic buildings stood in stark relief against lush green hills.

Outside the climate-controlled offices of Villeneuve Enterprises, in the streets below, the city ebbed and surged with constant movement, a reminder to all who lived there that the colony of Hong Kong was one of the most densely populated places in the world.

In all regards, Hong Kong was his home, but Phillip Villeneuve felt no more at home here than he did in London or Tokyo or Brussels, or even Paris. He'd been born in the British colony nearly forty years ago but had rarely spent more than two or three consecutive months in Hong Kong. At first, he traveled with both his parents. After his father divorced his mother when Phillip was eleven, he continued his globe-trotting life-style with his father.

Nothing was too good for the son of Armand Villeneuve. The finest tutors, the most exclusive boarding schools and, finally, an Oxford education. When Armand divorced Cecille Smyth-Pemberton, he had purchased exclusive rights to his son. And he wasn't about to take a loss on his investment.

As part of the divorce settlement, Armand had forbidden any contact between Phillip and his mother, in return for a handsome yearly stipend for Cecille. But Phillip refused to abandon his mother and had secretly visited her when he began his first term at Oxford. Twice a year at her country home in Kent, he had a real parent, someone he could feel comfortable talking to—unlike his father, who was more boss than blood relative.

"It's about time you returned."

Phillip slowly turned from the window to face his father. Straight and imperious, Armand Villeneuve stood in the doorway of his own office. He had turned eighty only a few months before, but he looked at least twenty years younger. His hair, still thick and wavy, had been white for as long as Phillip could remember. Though Armand didn't exercise, his tall frame carried not a pound of extra weight. He was as lean as Phillip, though no longer quite as agile.

"Is it done, then?" Armand asked.

"It's not available," Phillip said with a casual shrug. "I called the broker while I was in Tokyo. The owners had a previous offer and they've accepted it. They're just waiting for the final approval on financing. But I found another property, a much better location on—"

"Who?" Armand demanded. "Who made the offer?"

Phillip leaned back against the window ledge. "I don't know. It doesn't matter. The point is, the property isn't available."

His father cursed. "I sent you to Paris to do a job."

"I had exactly two days in Paris to work out this deal and that was nearly two months ago. I've been trying to sew it up over the phone, but you know how that works. I've had other priorities, Father. Much more important priorities, here in Hong Kong."

"I don't care about your other priorities. I want that property and you're going to get it for me."

Phillip's jaw tightened and he held back a sharp retort. He had learned to humor his father's thirst for revenge, but he'd never been directly involved in Armand Villeneuve's private war against the DeWilde family until now.

Pushing away from the window ledge, Phillip began to pace the office. "Why *this* property? There's plenty of good real estate to be had in Paris, especially for the price you're willing to pay. I looked at several outstanding properties, one on boulevard Haussmann and another on avenue Montaigne. Why not buy something else?"

"*Why* is none of your business," Armand snapped as he took his place behind his massive rosewood desk.

Phillip crossed the room and placed his palms on his father's desk, leaning closer as if to keep their words more private. "If you think you can destroy the DeWildes, you're deluding yourself. They've had a retail establishment on rue de la Paix for nearly eighty years. They're an institution in Paris—in the world, for that matter."

"Don't you tell me about the DeWildes," his father replied, meeting his gaze coldly. "I know more about that family than you ever will."

Phillip straightened and raked his hand through his hair. "Why? Just tell me why you can't let this feud die? Maybe if I knew what had caused it all, I'd be able to understand."

For an instant, the stubborn glint in his father's eyes faded, replaced by a vulnerability Phillip had never seen in him. But as quickly as this strange softening occurred, it was replaced by an icy disdain. "Do I need to remind you what happens on the first of July?"

Phillip shook his head wearily. He'd heard this argument before from his father and had made his own views known. But Armand Villeneuve rarely listened to what his son had to say on the subject. Phillip was the optimist and his father the pessimist in the family.

"This entire colony will soon be turned back over to the Chinese government," Armand continued. "We have no idea what the future might hold for our operation here. We will not be in control. The Communists will."

"The agreement allows a great deal of autonomy for Hong Kong," Phillip argued. "Capitalism will continue, as will the life-styles of the inhabitants, at least for another fifty years. The agreement stipulates this."

"And you can guarantee that the Chinese will honor the agreement?" Armand laughed bitterly. "I certainly can't. And I won't. So we've been diversifying for the past thirteen years. This is simply another phase in our diversification."

"This is not a phase, it's a vendetta. You want to open a retail store across the street from DeWilde's," Phillip said, no longer able to keep his irritation in check. "You want to throw good money after bad to reestablish the Villeneuve name in the Paris market. Our family moved out of the retail market after the Second World War, and I personally think that was the best move we ever made."

"I don't need a lecture on the Villeneuves any more than I need one on the DeWildes," he muttered.

Phillip barely heard his father's words before he continued. "The worst of it is, you want me to approve this plan. I can't do that, Father. I won't. This is not good for business."

"You'll do what I tell you to do," Armand replied, his voice even.

"*I* run Villeneuve Enterprises," Phillip countered.

Armand leveled a contemptuous glare at him. "That can easily be changed."

Phillip cursed beneath his breath, knowing that when it came to vindictiveness, his father would stop at nothing—not even firing his only son. "All right, I'll get you this property. But after that, I'm out of it. You're on your own. I'm not going to be part of some ridiculous family feud. It's a waste of money and a waste of time." He turned and walked to the door.

"You'll leave for Paris immediately?" Armand asked.

He stiffened, his hand on the doorknob. "I've got to visit our factory in Yuen Long and I've got a meeting scheduled with some investors in Macau," he said. "I'll try to leave tomorrow night."

"Do whatever it takes," Armand said. "I want that property. Stop at nothing to get it. I'm leaving for our Sydney office on Monday and I expect a full report when you've made the deal."

"Father, I don't think—"

"Just get it done."

Phillip nodded curtly, then walked out the door without looking back. There were no fond goodbyes or personal exchanges between father and son. These days, he and Armand shared a business relationship and not much more. Over the past few years, his father had become almost obsessed with the DeWildes. Perhaps he felt his time was running out, that if he didn't best them soon, he might never get the opportunity.

Phillip found it hard to think of his father as mortal. He'd always seemed so strong and in control, and though they had their differences, Phillip truly admired Armand Villeneuve. And in his own way, he loved him—or tried to.

From the time he was a child, he had known their relationship was different. His schoolmates had fathers who encouraged them. Phillip's father drove him, grooming him to one day take over Villeneuve Enterprises. Desperate for some sign of acceptance, Phillip had done everything he could to gain his father's love and approval. But no matter how hard he worked, his father was never satisfied.

In the end, he had come to accept Armand Villeneuve for the man he was—a man incapable of love. A man filled with bitterness. A man bent on revenge.

There were times when it took all his will to keep his mouth shut regarding the subject of the DeWildes. Overall, his father rarely interfered in the day-to-day running of Villeneuve Enterprises. But when it came to any matter that involved the DeWildes or *that* family's business interests, Armand was adamant. Win at all costs was his motto, and damn the financial consequences.

Phillip returned to his office and snatched his date book from his briefcase before he sank back into his leather chair. If he took a hydrofoil to Macau in the morning, he could be back in time to make it to the factory in the late afternoon. Then he could catch a night flight to Paris. But how long—and how much money—would it take to undo a real estate deal?

He leaned back in his chair and thought about all he had to accomplish. At least he'd be dealing face-to-face with the broker. And seven days in France might not be so bad after all. He'd thought often—too often—over the past two months of the woman he'd met at the Waldheims' masked ball.

He'd wondered who she really was and why she'd run out on him the way she had. Strange how such a capricious creature could fascinate him so. Maybe it was the mystery of her identity. He'd always known the women he planned to seduce. There was an element of excitement and danger in seducing a complete stranger—albeit a stranger who became completely unhinged at the prospect.

But was that all he wanted from her—a night of lust and champagne? Or was there something more?

Phillip banished the thought from his mind as he picked the file folders off the surface of his desk and tossed them into his briefcase. What else could it be? He had little time for a real relationship. Hell, he barely spent more than a week or two in the same country—a schedule that did not endear him to most women. There were a few hardy souls in his life who were satisfied with the occasional evening out followed by a night of feverish sex. But lately, Phillip found little satisfaction in the occasional one-night stand.

So why had he been so determined to seduce Megan Whatever-Her-Name-Was? And why hadn't he been able to put her out of his mind? What was it about this particular woman that made her different from all the rest?

Phillip punched his intercom button. "Lei Lin, please cancel my appointments for next week. Then book me on a flight to Paris tomorrow night. Have the tickets delivered to the condo at Repulse Bay before midnight. Then I'd like you to find out whether the Baron and Baroness Waldheim are still in residence at their villa in Monaco. If not, I'd like you to track them down for me. I need to speak to the baroness." He paused and considered his strategy. "Tell her I'd like to discuss a sizable donation from Villeneuve Enterprises to the Opéra Monaco."

Fifteen minutes and fifty-thousand francs later, Phillip had what he wanted—the name of the woman he'd nearly seduced at the Waldheims' costume ball. He stared at the name he'd scribbled on a slip of paper and chuckled softly. Well, if he wanted to see this woman again, he certainly knew where to find her.

"Megan DeWilde," he murmured, leaning back in his chair and closing his eyes. "Of all the damn luck."

THE FRIDAY MORNING traffic circling the place de l'Opéra had reached its usual fever pitch by the time Megan emerged from the métro station. Most of the management staff at DeWilde's preferred to drive to work, but after five years in Paris, Megan still hadn't worked up the courage to get behind the wheel. Though most Parisians were courteous in traffic, Megan was certain the rest were all frustrated Grand Prix drivers who thrived on speed and outrageous maneuvers. She preferred to leave the transportation to the tube trains.

She skirted the outside of the *place,* but instead of crossing to the main entrance of DeWilde's, she headed down boulevard des Capucines to her favorite *boulangerie.* She ordered a *tarte aux pommes,* a flaky pastry covered with glazed apples sliced paper thin. The *tarte* had become part of her morning routine along with a pot of rich, dark coffee at the Café de la Paix.

The weather in Paris had been unusually warm for early March, so Megan took a small table outside and ordered her coffee, then unfolded a copy of *Women's Wear Daily.* She scanned the paper, always watching for new trends in the bridal and wedding markets.

Since her mother had introduced the designer boutique idea to the merchandising managers nearly a year before, Megan had been determined to make the idea work in the Paris store. She had just about finalized the deal for the new property and planned to start Galeries DeWilde with a boutique for her sister-in-law Lianne's stunning bridal headwear designs.

At the same time, she'd also found a young and talented Parisian couturiere to provide DeWilde's with original designs for wedding dresses. She'd nearly convinced the irrepressible and extremely talented Chantalle Marillon to leave her tiny rue Christine atelier and join the growing family of DeWilde designers.

How she'd wanted to call her mother and share her good news. But Grace DeWilde had severed all ties to the DeWilde stores the moment she'd walked out on Megan's father. Though her father had made it clear he would not try to prohibit communication between mother and daughter, he *had* ordered Megan not to discuss the family business with his soon-to-be ex-wife.

Megan idly stirred a bit more steamed milk into her coffee and sighed. How had things gone so terribly wrong in her parents' marriage? Of all the couples in the world, Grace and Jeffrey DeWilde were made to be together.

An unbidden image flashed in her mind and Megan sucked in a sharp breath. *Nous sommes faits l'un pour l'autre.* She could recall the sound of his voice as he said the words, recall the color of his eyes and the addictive scent of his cologne. How many times over the past two months had this image of Phillip Villeneuve intruded on her thoughts? And how many times had she brushed it aside?

"*Bonjour,* Meg!"

Megan looked up from her table to see her best friend, Lucy Serrault, weaving through the outdoor tables. Lucy ran Bon Voyage, a quaint shop just a short walk from DeWilde's, filled with travel guides and maps. After Megan had spent her fifth or sixth straight lunch hour at Bon Voyage, Lucy had struck up a conversation and they'd become immediate friends. That had been four years ago, and since then, they tried to meet for coffee at least two mornings a week.

"*Bonjour,* Lucy," Megan replied, pulling out the chair beside her. "*Comment ça va?*"

"It's going very great, of course," Lucy said, her French accent making her grammatical errors all the more charming. She plopped down in the chair and sighed dramatically. "Last night, I have a date with Etienne and he tells me he wants to get married."

Megan grabbed Lucy's hand and squeezed it enthusiastically. "That's wonderful! What did you say?"

"I said nothing. I threw my glass of wine in his face." Lucy frowned. "What a waste. It was a very fine *Châteauneuf-du-Pape*, 1989. A very good year."

"But I thought you loved Etienne," Megan said. "Why don't you want to marry him?"

"He does not want to marry *me*," Lucy explained. "He wants to marry someone else." She sighed again, then shrugged. "Oh, well. *C'est la vie*, eh?"

"That's life?" Megan asked. "That's all you have to say?"

Lucy scoffed. "Men. They come and go. What *can* I say? If you cannot bake, do not turn on the oven."

"If you can't stand the heat, stay out of the kitchen," Megan corrected her, remembering the embarrassment she'd felt after her own broken engagement. But Lucy seemed so indifferent about the entire affair, so blasé...so French. How was it Lucy could risk her heart, time after time, and still manage to come away unscathed and eager to jump right back into the fray?

"That is exactly what I meant." Lucy arched a brow. "And when are you going to turn on your oven?"

"Don't start with me," Megan said. "You just sat down and already you're at it."

"You are in Paris, Meg. The city of love. For five years you have been here and you have not found love. If you don't do something soon, they will deport you as a subversive."

"You forget that I was engaged to be married the summer before last."

"So? That was almost two years ago. It is springtime in Paris and you have not had another man for too long a time. And you were the one who had decided to become more Parisian, to take the chances with your life. Didn't you tell me that?"

"Lucy, you're talking to an original stuffy Brit," Megan replied. "Even though I went to university in the States, I chose Princeton, a very proper Ivy League school. I still buy sensible shoes and make my bed every morning. I eat my fiber and prefer white cotton underwear to silk lingerie. And the last time I threw caution to the wind and took a chance, I managed to get myself dumped at the altar."

"If your horse runs away, you must run after him," Lucy said.

Megan frowned as she attempted to fathom her friend's meaning. "I think you mean that after I've been thrown, I should get right back on my horse."

Lucy nodded. "*Exactement.* There are many horses in the sea, Meg. Believe me, I know this for a fact."

Megan shook her head. "From now on, I'm staying away from horses and water and men. I'm just not good at this, Lucy. You know me. I don't accept failure very well. I never have. When I was a kid, my mother was frantic to find something I was good at—ballet lessons, painting classes, riding school, everything you could imagine. I was a blazing failure at all of them."

It had always been a struggle to find her place in the family, and although she was Gabe's twin, she had been relegated to the role of middle child. Gabe was the only boy, and Kate was the baby. Gabe was good at everything he tried and Kate was pretty and clever. But Megan was simply an ordinary girl tossed into the midst of an extraordinary family—a family that excelled at whatever they attempted, a family that did not take failure lightly.

"But the moment I stepped into DeWilde's," Megan continued, "I knew that I would be good at retailing. And I am. I'm the best. So I concentrate on what I'm good at and avoid everything else like the plague."

"And what about men?"

Megan shrugged. "Like I said, I concentrate on my successes. Right now, men rank somewhere between figure skating and field hockey on my list of activities to avoid."

"And this conclusion you have made because of one man?"

"No, not just one. There have been others. Actually, *one* other. A couple of months ago. And it turned out just as badly."

Lucy leaned forward in her chair. "Another man? Ooh-la-la, tell me! Who was he? Was he French?"

"He was French and he was a scoundrel, just like Etienne. And I'd prefer not to talk about him. In fact, I'd rather forget I even met him." Megan picked up her paper and refolded it neatly, then rummaged in her purse for enough money to leave the waiter. "I've got to get to work. The store is about to open and I'm late."

"I am coming with you," Lucy said as she stood. "I must buy Etienne's *maman* a gift. Perfume, *peut-être*. And then you will tell me about this man."

"Why must you buy a present for his mother?" Megan asked.

"A woman who is cursed with such a stupid son has little hope of gaining a proper daughter-in-law, *n'est-ce pas?* At least she will know what she has lost, even if Etienne does not."

Megan and Lucy crossed the busy boulevard des Capucines and headed for the rue de la Paix entrance of De-
Wilde's. The exterior of the store had changed little since
it opened at the end of World War I. Built with nostalgia
for France's belle époque, the store reflected the era with
a lovely art nouveau entrance.

Inside, at the rear of the ground floor, a wide, sweeping
staircase led to the balconied first floor. Leaded glass windows lined the first-floor gallery, which was set off by an
ornate railing of serpentine vines and flowers. The lifts,
still in possession of their original polished mahogany
doors, etched glass windows and uniformed operators,
carried patrons to the bridal departments on the second
through sixth floors.

DeWilde's interior, one of the finest examples of art
nouveau architecture in Paris, had always been popular
with tourists and art students. The highlight of the visit was
a long look at the "Genevieve" jewels. Protected by an
alarm system, a shatterproof glass case and a vigilant security guard, the famous pieces from the DeWilde collection included a necklace, bracelet and earrings in an ornate
Victorian design.

The set had been a gift to Megan's great-grandmother
DeWilde upon the birth of her first child, Dirk, in 1908.
Designed by Megan's great-great-aunt, Marie, the pieces
used perfect pink topazes and flawless diamonds set in
delicate filigree. The jewels had been on display since the
liberation of Paris in the forties, a mute testament to
Genevieve's untimely death with her husband and mother-
in-law, Anne Marie, in the rubble of a German bombing
raid on London.

As she and Lucy strolled to the perfume counter, Megan watched as a number of patrons gazed down from the
gallery onto the busy main sales floor and clustered around

the display of Genevieve's jewels. She loved the hustle and bustle of the store, the excitement that new merchandise created and the deep tradition that DeWilde's represented.

She led Lucy to the perfume counter, then stepped behind it. "What are you looking for? A floral scent? Our signature scent is quite popular." Megan pulled a tester bottle from a silver tray and daubed a bit on Lucy's wrist with the crystal stopper. As Lucy picked through the tester bottles on the tray, Megan distractedly surveyed the sales floor. She'd been toying with a change in the layout of the cosmetics department and now she—

Her gaze was caught by the figure of a tall, handsome man, a man strangely familiar to her. She frowned as she tried to place him. Then he glanced her way and their eyes met. A few long moments passed before her breath froze in her throat. "Oh, hell and damnation!" she whispered hoarsely. "He's here!"

Lucy looked up. "Who's here?"

Megan bent down and tried to hide behind the counter. "Him. The man I told you about. The big French mistake."

Lucy turned and openly searched the sales floor. "What does he look like? Is he a honk?"

"Hunk," Megan corrected her.

"That is what I said," Lucy replied, craning her neck.

"Don't look," Megan cried. "He'll see you looking and then he'll know I saw him!"

"I think he already does," Lucy replied. "He is coming this way." Her friend peered over the counter and tugged at the sleeve of Megan's jacket. "Get up here and speak to him. You cannot hide from such a handsome man, Meg."

"I can't speak to him! I don't want to."

"Megan DeWilde, do not be a fool! Stand up!"

Megan reluctantly straightened, then grabbed Lucy's arm. "Don't call me DeWilde. Pretend I'm a salesclerk. Please," she pleaded. "I'll explain later. He can't know who I am."

"But—"

"Just do it," Megan ordered. The last thing she wanted was for Phillip Villeneuve to know her real identity. She could just imagine him running back to Hong Kong and telling his entire family how he'd nearly seduced a De-Wilde. No doubt all the Villeneuves would be gloating for some time to come. She wasn't about to heap that particular image on top of all her other bad experiences with men.

Megan forced a smile at Lucy and pushed a bottle of DeWilde's signature scent into her hand. "Will there be anything else?" she inquired sweetly.

"An explanation, *s'il vous plaît*," Lucy said.

"You just push the top," Megan muttered through clenched teeth, "and the perfume will spray out, *madame*."

"Megan?"

His voice was exactly as she remembered it, warm and deep and wonderfully sexy, his subtle accent giving her common name an exotic flavor. She kept her eyes fixed on Lucy's perfume. "If you'll just take this over to the register, the salesclerk will be able to take care of you. And thank you for shopping at DeWilde's."

"Megan, is it really you?"

She bit her lower lip, knowing that she couldn't ignore him forever. Unfortunately, Lucy decided to speak first.

"Of course it is her!" she cried. "Megan, look who is here! Your old friend, uh…" Her voice trailed off and she batted her eyes at Phillip and waited for an introduction.

"Phillip," he said, holding out his hand. "Phillip Villeneuve. And whom do I have the pleasure of meeting?"

Lucy smiled. "Lucy Serrault," she cooed before turning to Megan. "Ah, *il est très charmant, non?*"

"*Non,*" Megan said emphatically. "Now, if there is
nothing else I can help you with, *madame,* I have to get
back to work. Run along now."

With an exaggerated pout, Lucy took the hint and
grabbed her perfume. "The help here is terrible, *n'est-ce
pas?*" she said to Phillip, then moved to find another
salesclerk. Megan could sense her watching them surreptitiously, and she knew that as soon as she rid herself of
Phillip's presence, Lucy would be back, demanding a detailed explanation.

"I—I'm surprised to see you," Megan said as she me-
thodically rearranged the tester bottles on the tray.

He raised his brow. "Are you?"

She shifted uneasily. "Of course. You have to admit that
meeting you again is a strange...coincidence."

"I don't believe in coincidence," he said with a disarm-
ing smile. "Everything happens for a reason. What do they
call it? Kismet?"

She brushed a nonexistent smudge from the glass case.
"Is there something I can help you with, *monsieur?*"

"You can tell me why you jumped out of my limo that
night in Monte Carlo," he replied softly, reaching out to
cover her fluttering fingers.

Megan pulled her hand away, clutching it to her chest.
"If there is nothing I can help you with, I think you should
leave. My employer doesn't appreciate socializing on the
job."

"Your employer?" he said. He chuckled softly, then
shook his head. "Well, I'll just have to buy some per-

fume, won't I. To make your *employer* happy." He picked up a bottle. "Tell me about this."

"That is a very fine fragrance," Megan said. "An oriental scent with hints of jasmine."

He took her wrist in one hand, his firm grip branding the soft skin above her palm, his other hand holding the crystal stopper from the perfume bottle. "Would you mind?"

She shook her head, then watched, wide-eyed, as he dabbed a bit of the scent along the underside of her wrist. Slowly he raised her arm to his nose. He closed his eyes and inhaled. "Mmm, that's very nice."

"Then—then you'd like this one? I'll just ring it—"

"No," Phillip said, opening his eyes. "Let me try another. Something a bit more...tantalizing. How about this one?"

"That has a heavier, somewhat spicy scent," Megan said. "I guess you could say it would be more... tantalizing."

He dabbed a bit on her other arm and inhaled, moving her wrist beneath his nose, his warm lips brushing along her skin. "That's nice also. But not exactly what I'm looking for."

Megan felt her irritation rise. His blatant attempt to rattle her composure was all too obvious. "Perhaps, if you tell me something of the woman you're buying it for, I might be able to choose a suitable scent."

"She's very beautiful. Tall and slender, with lovely dark hair. And she has the most amazing eyes. Hazel with brilliant flecks of green. And her skin is like fine porcelain and as smooth as silk." His gaze dropped to her mouth. "And her lips," he murmured. "She's quite incredible, a woman a man would never forget." He paused, his gaze meeting hers. "Tell me, Megan, what is your favorite scent?"

Megan swallowed hard, then fumbled for the bottle of DeWilde's signature scent, a scent she'd worn for as long as she could remember. He took the bottle from her hand and removed the stopper. "This is nice," he said softly. "I remember this from our night in Monaco."

This time he didn't reach for her wrist but drew the crystal stopper from her jawline to the base of her throat. He leaned over the counter and took her chin in his fingers, tipping her head to the side. She could feel his breath, soft and warm against her neck, as he inhaled. "I remember this," he said softly, his words teasing at her ear. "Yes, I remember this quite well."

"Then—then this is the one you want?" she said, her voice wavering. "Please say you'll take it."

"Yes, Megan DeWilde. This is exactly what I want."

CHAPTER THREE

PHILLIP RELUCTANTLY stepped back, away from Megan's tantalizing body and the sweet jumble of scent that surrounded her. He fought an urge to kiss her, right then and there, to pick up where they left off in the limo. But he knew she would resist him. Instead, he met Megan's shocked gaze and grinned.

"What did you call me?" she demanded.

He lazily replaced the stopper in the perfume bottle and returned it to the silver tray. "Don't act surprised. I know who you are, Megan. Would you have me believe the baroness invites common shopgirls to her masked ball?"

"You can believe whatever you want to believe," she shot back, moving out from behind the perfume counter. "Now that you know my name, just leave me alone."

"Why did you try to keep your identity a secret from me?"

"If you know who I am, then you know the answer to that question," she replied in a frigid tone. "Get out of my store and don't ever come back."

Phillip grabbed her arm as she turned to make her escape. His pulse quickened as he touched her and, once again, he fought an overpowering urge to pull her into his arms. His mind flashed back to the kisses they'd shared. The memory of the desire he had felt for her came back in full force. "You don't want me to leave," he said. "Not really."

"Of all the arrogant—" She yanked out of his grasp, her eyes blazing, her face flushed with anger.

"You're attracted to me," he said in a matter-of-fact tone. Though he said the words as fact, he wasn't entirely sure of her feelings. Most of the women he'd known had been up-front about their attraction to him. But Megan wasn't most women. She held herself back, as if desire were not an appropriate outlet for her energies. Normally, he would have called her uptight, but in her case, he found her reticence a rather charming attribute.

"I am not!" she replied.

Though she appeared quite sophisticated on the surface, he could tell that his presence had thoroughly shaken her. Her hands trembled and her voice wavered. Two spots of color rose in her cheeks and her breath came in quick gasps.

Phillip knew he was taking a risk, baiting her in this way. But behind her anger was a magnetic sexual attraction— there *had* to be. If he felt it so strongly, she had to, as well. He just had to get her to admit to it.

"You are," he countered smoothly. "And if it's half as much as I'm attracted to you, then it's pretty overwhelming."

She blinked and gazed at him openmouthed. "You have a very high opinion of yourself, don't you. Is that common to all the Villeneuves, or are you the only one with the inflated ego?"

"Admit it, Megan," he murmured, leaning closer to her, slipping his hand around her waist. Her body drifted against his and he felt his blood warm. "There is definitely a chemistry between us. There has been from the very start. Why deny it?"

She glanced around to see a number of her salesclerks watching them speculatively. Her color heightened and she lowered her voice. "Because you're a Villeneuve!" she whispered, shoving away from him and heading off in the direction of the lifts.

Phillip strode along beside her, taking one long step for every two of hers. "And what possible difference does that make?"

"Don't be ridiculous. The DeWildes and the Villeneuves have been enemies for as long as I can remember. I won't betray my family. Now, stop following me!"

He pulled her to a halt before she reached the lift doors. "Do you know what this feud is about?"

He watched as Megan searched for an answer. She opened her mouth to reply, then snapped it shut. "No," she finally said. "Not really. But I don't have to know the details to know I'm supposed to hate you."

"Did you and I have anything to do with starting this feud?"

She crossed her arms over her breasts, as if that might protect her from both him and his logic. "Of course not," she replied uneasily. "It started years ago. Before I was even born."

Phillip caught her gaze and held it. She didn't turn away; but simply looked up into his eyes with quiet contemplation. He groaned inwardly, needing to feel her mouth beneath his but knowing he couldn't have her. Lord, this woman affected him like no other.

For most men, *la chasse et la conquête* were more important than the woman herself. But Phillip had never had the time or the inclination to chase a woman. And conquests were rather irrelevant when most of the women he associated with were so willing. But Megan DeWilde was different. She was running full-tilt in the opposite direction and he had no choice but to chase. Or risk losing something he had yet to fully understand.

"We made a mistake," Megan said with forced calm. "And I think it would be best if we forgot what happened that night at the costume ball. We got carried away with the romance and the mystery of it all, hiding behind our masks. We weren't living in the real world. In the real world, we are standing on opposite sides of a battlefield."

He ran his finger down her arm, tracing a lazy pattern until he reached her hand. "We don't have to, Megan. We can meet in the middle."

She laughed dryly, snatching her fingers from his. "And get mowed down by the artillery fire from both sides? No, thank you."

"All right, we don't have to put ourselves in the middle, but we have to be able to find some safe ground. It's not *our* feud, Megan. It has nothing to do with us."

"It would be a mistake." This time, Megan turned in the opposite direction and made for the front entrance of the store. "What do you want from me?" she pleaded as he caught up with her. "Please, stop following me!"

"Dinner," he said.

She glanced sideways at him, a suspicious look in her eyes. "Why? What would it prove?"

"Don't you think we owe it to ourselves to find out where we were going that night in Monaco?"

"I know exactly *where* we were going," Megan said. "And I assure you, I don't want to go there. Not that I haven't been there before. I just don't want to go there now. Especially not with you."

"You would have enjoyed the trip there *and* back," he replied. "Believe me."

Megan turned away from him and motioned to the uniformed doorman standing at the front entrance. When he reached Megan's side, she pointed to Phillip. "Would you show this gentleman out, Fredric? I'm afraid he wandered in here by mistake.''

The doorman nodded and moved in Phillip's direction, but Phillip held his hand up to stop him. "I'll leave," he said, taking in Megan's stubborn expression. He had pushed her to the limit and he knew when to beat a retreat. "But I want you to think about what I said. This isn't our fight, Megan."

"We may not have started it," she replied. "But getting involved with each other would only make it worse." She paused, drawing a deep breath. "Please, stay away from me. And DeWilde's."

"Have dinner with me," Phillip said.

"Lambs don't dine with wolves," Megan replied. "And DeWildes don't eat with Villeneuves."

"You're not a helpless little lamb, Megan. I'm staying at the Crillon. When you regain your senses and change your mind, call me there."

"Don't wait by the phone," Megan shot back.

Phillip grinned as he headed toward the door, accompanied by the glowering doorman. "I didn't plan to."

"I'm not going to call."

"Oh, yes, you will." With that, he turned and walked out of DeWilde's. As he crossed rue de la Paix, his mind still carried an image of her. When he reached the other side of the street, he stopped and looked back at the elegant entrance to the store.

Phillip chuckled, shaking his head and raking his fingers through his hair. Why was he so determined to have her? Was it just a common attraction or was it because of who she was? He'd been trying to sway his father from pursuing this feud for years. What better way to bring his point home than to date a DeWilde?

The truth be told, Phillip didn't know what was behind his attraction to Megan. All he knew was that he had exactly seven days in Paris—another seven days to be near her. The sooner he got business out of the way, the sooner he could dedicate all his time to knocking down the walls surrounding Megan DeWilde.

THE WHITE MERCEDES GLIDED to a smooth stop in front of Château du Plessis. Megan stared up at the facade through the tinted window, admiring the stunning fifteenth-century architecture of her great-aunt's home. Unlike the larger châteaux that dotted the landscape of the Loire Valley, Château du Plessis might better be referred to as a manor house. The rose brick and stone house stood on a small rise above the quaint village of Plessis, overlooking a branch of the Indre and a fertile family vineyard.

Oliver opened the car door and helped her out, then fetched Megan's bags from the boot. By the time they headed up to the house, her great-aunt stood in the doorway, a wide smile on her face.

Though nearly eighty years old, Marie-Claire DeWilde DuPlessis was still a stunning beauty. Her hair was white, drawn back into a neat French twist, but her face was smooth and barely touched by the lines of age. Slender and graceful, she maintained an almost girlish figure with a waist so tiny that Megan couldn't help but envy her.

Megan spent the second weekend of every month at Plessis, a habit that had begun a few weeks after her permanent move to Paris. Since Marie-Claire had run the Paris store until Megan's arrival, their early weekends together were spent talking business. But now Megan came for other reasons. Her aunt had become very dear to her and they'd formed a close relationship, so close that Marie-

Claire had named Megan heir to the château and all the property surrounding it, including the vineyards and the winery.

"Megan darling!" her aunt called in heavily accented English. "Come! Hurry! Oliver, bring her bags and put them in her room. Claudette has our tea ready."

Megan linked her arm through Marie-Claire's and they strolled together through the huge entrance hall. The interior of the house was warm and comfortable, though the larger rooms were a bit drafty in the winter. They wandered toward their favorite room, a small solarium off the library that overlooked the gardens and a weathered stone fountain.

"I'm so glad you're here. How was your drive from Paris?" Marie-Claire asked.

"Quite lovely," Megan replied. "Spring is finally on the way and everything is beginning to turn green."

"Ah, springtime in Paris. I remember it well. And how is business?"

Megan smiled. She and her aunt had a regular ritual. First the drive, and then business. And after dinner they would discuss the vineyards and the winery, a venture that Megan would someday be expected to oversee. Sunday was usually spent with the vineyard manager before Megan headed back to Paris. "Business is quite good. Did you read the prospectus for the new property we plan to buy?"

"I did," Marie-Claire said. "And I think it's a wonderfully creative idea, Megan. Just think, Galeries DeWilde. I'm so very proud of you. You've done a fine job with the store and with this project."

"Thank you," Megan said hesitantly, her voice betraying her true emotions.

"Sit," Marie-Claire ordered. "And tell me why you suddenly have such a sad face."

Megan sighed. "I want so much to tell Mother about my plans," she said. "We used to share so much about the business, and now I can't tell her anything. Daddy is positively paranoid about leaking any information to her. I don't know what he thinks Mother's going to do. She already knows all our secrets."

Marie-Claire took Megan's hand and gave it a squeeze. "Perhaps it will all work out for Jeffrey and Grace."

"Daddy told me he's thinking about the possibility of divorce. How can he even consider such a drastic step? They're meant to be together—can't they see that?"

Marie-Claire poured the tea into delicate china cups as she considered the news carefully. "Sometimes," she said, "people have to spend time apart before they realize how much they truly care for each other." A wistful expression crossed her face, and for a moment, Megan's aunt seemed miles away.

"You sound like you're speaking from experience," Megan said, picking up a cube of sugar and dropping it into her cup.

She shrugged. "Experience can be a very cruel teacher."

Megan watched her aunt's expression mirror the catch of regret in her voice. She'd never seen such undisguised emotion in her eyes. Marie-Claire was always so calm and composed. "Tell me," Megan urged.

Marie-Claire shook her head. "It was a long time ago, dear. It's not something I like to think about. I made so many mistakes, lost so much."

"I didn't think you made mistakes," Megan said.

Marie-Claire laughed softly. "Oh, I've made many. Especially where men are concerned. I suppose it's part of life, don't you think? Every now and then we must risk our heart, or life wouldn't be worth living, would it."

Megan frowned at her aunt's statement. She'd always considered Marie-Claire the perfect role model, a woman who had made an astounding success of her professional life while maintaining utter control of her personal life. Someday, Megan hoped to be exactly like her, content with life as it was, able to live without the love of a man. And now, to find that wasn't true was disconcerting.

"Does this have to do with the family feud?" Megan asked. "With the Villeneuves?"

Marie-Claire looked up, startled by Megan's blunt question. "What makes you think my past mistakes have anything to do with the de Villeneuves?"

"The Villeneuves," Megan corrected her. "They haven't used the 'de' in their name for a very long time."

Her aunt frowned. "And how do you know this?"

"That's not important," Megan replied. "I want you to tell me about the feud."

Marie-Claire placed the teacup on the table and folded her hands primly in front of her. "Why has this subject come up?" she asked warily.

Megan winced, then decided to trust her aunt with the truth. "A few months ago, I met Phillip Villeneuve, Armand Villeneuve's son, and—" She grabbed her teacup and stirred the hot brew with a silver spoon as she considered how to phrase what she was about to say. "I found myself—attracted to him. Yesterday, he came into the store. He asked me to have dinner with him, and of course I refused. But I'm still curious. I want to know what's behind this conflict." She paused. "So I know how to proceed."

"Your father would not be pleased by this," Marie-Claire warned. "And neither am I. The Villeneuves are not to be trusted, Megan."

"Why? Phillip and I have had no part in this feud. We didn't start it. In fact, neither one of us knows how it all began."

"Nevertheless, you are a DeWilde and he is a Villeneuve."

"Please, *tante*, tell me why I'm supposed to hate this man. Because for the life of me, I'm having a very hard time hating him. He's very charming."

"I would have expected nothing less from Armand's son." Marie-Claire picked up her teacup and settled herself into the wing chair. "It happened a long, long time ago," she began. "Before you or your father was born. It was right before the war broke out in Europe. I was eighteen and I was in love with Armand de Villeneuve. *Mon Dieu*, he was a handsome boy."

"Go on," Megan encouraged, curling her feet up under her.

A thoughtful expression drifted across Marie-Claire's face. "Armand and I were engaged to be married, and our marriage was to join two retailing dynasties. The de Villeneuves had a large clothing store on boulevard Haussmann. It was a perfect match, both in business and in love. But then, a few months before the wedding, my older brother Dirk told me that Armand had been carrying on an affair with a dancer from the Moulin Rouge. I was devastated. I loved Armand and I thought he loved me, but you know the French attitude about marital fidelity. Dirk and our brother Charles urged me to break the engagement and, finally, I did. Though Armand claimed that he'd been faithful to me, I refused to believe him. You see, I trusted my family rather than my own instincts."

"He wasn't having an affair?"

"At the time, I believed he was. I was heartbroken and confused and I wanted to hurt Armand as much as he had hurt me. So I agreed to a marriage with an older man, a distant relative of my grandmother's family, Jean-Luc DuPlessis. My father wanted me settled before he moved the family to London to open the new store there. I thought Armand would try to stop the marriage, but he didn't. That only seemed to emphasize his guilt in my mind."

"So you married Jean-Luc?"

"I did. And then Germany marched on France and we were caught in the middle of a war."

"You managed the Paris store during that time, didn't you?" Megan asked.

"When the Nazis took Paris, Jean-Luc and I moved here, to the Loire Valley and his family's château. We left a small staff at the store and only went into the city when we had to. It was very dangerous there at first, especially for those who were not sympathetic to the Germans. They trusted no one."

"What happened to Armand?"

Marie-Claire straightened in her chair, her tone cooling. "I never spoke to him again. I heard he'd worked for the French Resistance for a time. And then I heard he'd been captured by the Nazis and sent to a camp. Later, I heard he'd been killed. I tried to put him out of my mind, but I couldn't. You see, I still loved him."

"Did you try to find him?"

"After my husband died in 1946, I went to see Armand's family. But they refused to tell me anything. Two years later, Armand surfaced in New York. He and Dirk had a terrible fight at the Fifth Avenue store and then he disappeared again. A few years after that, things began to happen, odd problems with our vendors, business relationships suddenly gone sour, orders canceled without explanation. It wasn't long before we traced it all to Hong

Kong and Villeneuve Enterprises. Armand had initiated a vendetta against our family and our business. Since then, he's been determined to destroy anything and everything connected with the DeWildes."

"Because you refused to marry him?"

"Why else? All I know is that Armand hates me and our entire family. This feud has continued for so long that I had accepted the fact that it would end only after Armand and I are long gone from this world. Now it doesn't look like that will happen."

"Why?"

"He's sent his son," Marie-Claire said bluntly.

Megan blinked hard. "But—but Phillip is different. He doesn't like this fight any more than I do. He'd love to see it over and done with."

Marie-Claire grabbed Megan's hands and pressed them between hers. "You cannot trust him," she pleaded. "Please, darling, I would die if I knew I was the cause of any pain to you."

"You're not going anywhere for a long time, *chère tante.*"

Marie-Claire shook her head adamantly. "Promise me you'll stay away from him."

Megan leaned back in her chair and stared out the window at the courtyard fountain. Once again, she'd managed to find herself in the middle of a fight. She'd been caught between her parents ever since they'd separated. And now she found herself standing in the midst of a family feud that had begun with Phillip's father and her favorite aunt.

Every instinct told her that Phillip could be trusted. But then her instincts hadn't been operating at full capacity lately. She had never expected to be left at the altar. Nor had she ever imagined that her parents would be living on two separate continents.

"So you'll stay away from him?" Marie-Claire asked.

Megan sighed, unable to disappoint her aunt. "Yes," she acquiesced. "I'll stay away. I wasn't really interested in him in the first place. I was simply curious."

It was the only decision she could make. If she wanted or needed a brief fling with a man, there were plenty to choose from in Paris, and none of them connected with the Villeneuves. Family was much more important to her than a nagging case of lust. And choosing sides in this dispute was not an option. Her side had been chosen the moment she was born.

She was a DeWilde, and in the DeWilde family, loyalty was expected and rewarded.

"THIS WAS DELIVERED for you a few minutes ago."

Megan glanced up from the sales reports spread across her desk. She took the envelope from her secretary and scanned the return address. "Thank you, Arielle."

The envelope held the return address of the broker handling the sale of the rue de la Paix property. The financing package had been delayed, and Megan had requested an extension on her offer, a request so common in these deals that she had no doubt the owner would agree.

"And there's a Mr. Villeneuve waiting in the outer office," Arielle added.

Megan gasped and looked up at her secretary. "Mr. Villeneuve?" she repeated, her voice tight. "Send him away. Call security and—"

"I knew you'd be anxious to see me."

Megan bit back a groan at the sound of his voice. Phillip stood in the doorway of her office, dressed in his usual impeccable manner—Italian suit, perfectly starched shirt and expensive silk tie. His hair, dark and thick, looked casually windblown, and he wore an exquisitely tailored black cashmere overcoat against the chilly spring weather.

"I've made reservations at L'Ambroisie for lunch. Get your coat or we'll be late."

"A cozy little lunch for two?" Megan asked, arching her brow.

"Of course," he replied. "I wouldn't have it any other way."

"Then you won't need me," Megan said. "You and your ego should have a lovely time."

A giggle escaped Arielle's lips and she hastily excused herself, closing the door behind her and leaving them completely alone.

Phillip leaned back against the door and stared directly into her eyes. "What's going on, Meggie? I expected you to call."

"I have work to do, Mr. Villeneuve. If you'll excuse me?" Megan strode to the door, pushed him out of the way and opened it, then waited for him to exit.

"*Mr.* Villeneuve?" Phillip's jaw tightened. He pushed the door shut. "I'm not leaving. Not until we talk."

Megan returned to her desk and stood behind it as she straightened a stack of file folders and placed them in her briefcase. "Well, then I'll leave," she countered. "I've got a meeting."

Phillip slowly crossed the room and circled her desk until he stood in front of her. She watched him warily, backing up until her legs bumped against her chair. She sat back down with a thump. He leaned over and braced his hands on the arms of her chair.

"You want to stay," he said.

"Leave me alone," she warned. "My aunt told me I shouldn't trust you."

He leaned closer, his mouth hovering over hers, his warm breath the only thing touching her lips. "I don't have any intention of wasting a minute more of our time together perpetuating that ridiculous feud, Meggie."

She swallowed hard and tried to avoid his mouth, but her head was already pressed into the back of her chair. "Ridiculous?" Her voice cracked. "I'd hardly call your father's vindictiveness toward our family ridiculous." His gaze was fixed on her lips and she knew he was about to kiss her. She wanted to push him away but her hands felt as if they were nailed to the arms of her chair.

"As far as I'm concerned," he murmured, "this animosity between our families has nothing to do with us, and I think you agree."

He bent lower and her eyes fixed on his mouth, his lips so firm and perfectly sculpted.

"This is all I care about," Phillip said softly. He brushed his mouth across hers. "You and me." He lingered over her lips for a long moment before he drew back. "Why don't we just forget who we are? Forget you're a DeWilde and forget I'm a Villeneuve. It will be easy. We'll just be—"

"Don and Queenie?" Megan suggested sarcastically, trying to lighten a moment that had turned entirely too serious. But even humor wouldn't deter him.

"I'll make you a deal. For the next five days, we won't discuss our families."

"Five days?"

"We have five days before I have to return to Hong Kong," he replied.

Of course, five days. The man lived and worked on another continent. Which meant that after five days, he'd be out of her life for good. Five days and no one, not her aunt or anyone else in her family, would ever know what had happened between them. Any other woman might find the proposition distasteful at best. Five days and he'd be gone, leaving her with nothing but a lot of vivid memories and a curiosity well appeased.

She considered her options for a long moment. If she were smart, she'd toss him out of her office on his ear and get back to work. Or... or what? She could throw caution to the wind and enjoy a very quick and exciting affair. After that, he'd return to his world and she'd return to hers, no strings, no problems and, most importantly, absolutely no way to get hurt.

Megan fought the impulse to accept his invitation. What if her family did find out? Were a few nights with Phillip Villeneuve worth the risk? And just what was he really after? Was he as dangerous as Marie-Claire claimed?

Take a chance. Megan repeated the phrase to herself. She'd been the one who had decided her life had become boring and predictable. She was the one who had made a vow five years ago to take more risks, only to make a complete hash of it all. But how could she make a mistake here? He'd be gone in less than a week.

She could have a wonderfully passionate affair, a torrid five days, and then she'd go on with her life. And what better man to have a fling with than a forbidden man? Besides, surely after five days she'd be able to uncover his true motives for pursuing her. In fact, if she really needed a reason to let herself be carried away with her desire for him, she'd just consider the whole thing an exercise in corporate espionage.

"L'Ambroisie?" she asked, giving him a sideways glance.

He wove his fingers through hers and raised them to his lips. "Where would *you* like to go?" he murmured.

A shiver skittered up her spine. "How about your hotel?" she said, her own words catching her completely off guard. She felt a warm flush suffuse her cheeks. *When in Paris,* she chanted silently, over and over again.

A wicked grin lifted the corners of his mouth. "You surprise me, Meggie."

"Why is that?"

"I'm afraid I may have misjudged you."

He pulled her from her chair and drew her body against his. This time his kiss was more than a simple brush of his lips against hers. He took total possession of her mouth, kissing her as intimately as if they'd been lovers for years. Her head swam with incoherent thoughts, and sensation flooded to the very tips of her fingers and toes. When he pulled away, she felt both exhausted and exhilarated.

"I'm hungry," he said.

"So am I," she murmured.

"Then let's go."

Megan stepped out of his arms and turned back to her desk. Her gaze fell on the manila envelope Arielle had brought in moments before Phillip had arrived. She reached down to pick it up, then, thinking better of it, threw the envelope back on her desk. A moment later, her practical nature pushed the reckless Parisian attitude aside and retrieved the envelope. She suspected they'd be gone for the rest of the afternoon and this business couldn't wait.

"Before we go I have to take care of something," she said.

"Leave it," he urged. "It will wait until after... lunch."

"I can't. It's probably important." Megan tore open the envelope from the *agence immobilière,* the real estate broker handling the negotiations for the new building. The

DeWilde Corporation had made their final offer and financing had nearly been secured, but she had asked for an extension on the deadline to ensure adequate time to put together a favorable financing package. The broker had promised to send over the extension papers immediately.

She quickly read the cover memo as she fumbled for her pen. Her heart dropped and she blinked in disbelief. "This can't be," she murmured, the pen clattering to the surface of her desk.

"What is it?" Phillip said, impatience coloring his voice.

Ignoring his question, Megan picked up the phone and punched in an eight-digit number. *"C'est Megan De-Wilde. Simon Rosier, s'il vous plaît."* She tapped her foot impatiently as she waited for the broker to come on the line. "All right, Simon, what is this? You told me we'd have no problem getting an extension. If they're playing games trying to get more money, it's not going to work. Our final offer stands."

"There has been another offer made on the property," Simon replied over the phone line, his voice apologetic. "It was well above our accepted offer. And their financing is secure. The owner will not approve an extension. Unless you can put your financing together before your offer expires, you will lose the—"

"Who?" she demanded. "Who made the offer?"

"I don't believe that really matters."

It didn't matter? Well it sure as hell mattered to her! The building across the street was the key to the whole Galeries DeWilde concept. It was the perfect property and the perfect location. "If you value your association with DeWilde's, Monsieur Rosier, you'll tell me who wants to ruin our deal."

She should have expected what she heard next, but it still came as a shock, stealing her breath from her lungs and making her pulse pound in her head. Megan slowly replaced the phone in its cradle and fixed her gaze on Phillip. "You," she murmured.

"Me?"

Megan pointed to the door. "Get out! Get out of my office. Get out of my store. And get out of my life."

"Megan, what's wrong?"

"You know exactly what's wrong!" She raked her fingers through her hair and screamed. "God, I can't believe I almost fell for it again. I should have my head examined. How could I have been so gullible?"

"Megan, I don't understand what you're talking about."

"About 25 rue de la Paix," she said contemptuously. "Do you understand now?"

An expression of utter surprise froze on his face. "How do you know about that deal?" he asked suspiciously.

"*That* deal is *my* deal. That building is mine! I won't let you steal it from me."

"Megan, I—"

She stepped out from behind her desk and came toe to toe with him. "I won't let you get away with this," she warned as she punched her finger into his chest for emphasis. "*I'll* have that building if it takes every penny of available cash I've got." He grabbed her hand, but she yanked it away. "Don't you dare touch me."

"Megan—"

"And as far as I'm concerned, the armistice is off. The feud is back on. Get out of my office, now. And if you set foot in this store again, I'll have the security guards shoot you on sight."

"Your guards don't carry guns," he reminded her.

"That can easily be remedied," she shot back.

Phillip frowned. "Megan, I didn't know—"

"Out!" she cried.

Cursing beneath his breath, Phillip stood his ground, raising Megan's anger to a new level. "I'm not going to leave," he said. "I want to explain."

"Would you like me to call security and have them throw you out?"

Phillip cursed out loud. "This is not over yet, Megan."

"You're right about that. It's only just started. I'm going to have that building and no one, not you or any other scheming Villeneuve, is going to stop me."

With that, Megan strode to the door and yanked it open. She waited for Phillip to step through, then slammed it behind him so hard the pictures on the wall rattled. With a soft moan, she leaned back against the door, her knees wobbling and her breath tight in her throat.

"This is definitely not over, Phillip Villeneuve," she vowed, fighting back tears of humiliation and anger. "This has only just begun."

CHAPTER FOUR

PHILLIP STOOD IN the showroom of the tiny shop on rue Christine, ill at ease in this frothy sea of tulle and lace. All around him, tittering brides and their anxious mothers picked through racks stuffed with sample dresses and sent him curious glances.

He'd received orders from his father this morning. His visit to Paris would be extended to a month, and in that time, he was expected to put together a skeleton staff for the imminent opening of the Villeneuve family's Paris retail venture and manage the Hong Kong operation from a distance of six thousand miles.

He'd been ordered to begin with a bridal designer, a talented newcomer who might immediately be used to undermine DeWilde's trademark business. He took in his surroundings. The thought of the Villeneuve family involved in the business of "happily ever afters" was ridiculous.

Retailing was a fickle business at best, dependent on the whims of the economy and the fashion-conscious customer. The real profit was in manufacturing, in maintaining a worldwide market base that didn't turn on the buying habits of one European city or one outlandish fad.

Phillip had already grown tired of this vendetta, and *his* involvement had been minimal. His mind wandered back to his last encounter with Megan DeWilde. She'd been adamant. As far as she was concerned, the two of them were now full-fledged lieutenants in the battle between their families.

But that's not what he wanted with Megan, to stand on opposite sides of a ridiculous dispute. Like a powerful sorceress, Megan DeWilde had captivated his mind and stirred his desire. Even now, after they'd parted ways for good, he still couldn't help but think about her—her striking beauty, her mercurial personality, and her fierce loyalty to those she loved. She'd cast a spell over him, a spell he could neither understand nor deny.

Phillip drew a long breath and marshaled his thoughts. What had happened between him and Megan DeWilde was in the past, a mistake best forgotten, a fire that had burned white-hot for an instant, then died. With his father's plans, the two families had little chance of working out their differences. He and Megan were just two more casualties.

"Bonjour, monsieur. Puis-je vous aider?"

Startled out of his thoughts, Phillip looked down at an oddly dressed salesclerk. The petite woman smiled up at him from beneath the brim of an old velvet top hat. The hat was only the beginning. She wore a body-hugging T-shirt, baggy black pants, tiny hobnail boots and suspenders. Her makeup was as outrageous as her outfit, her eyelids dark with kohl and her lips crimson.

"I'd like to speak to Madame Marillon," Phillip replied in English.

"Ah!" she cried in delight. "I am Chantalle Marillon." Her English was heavily accented but understandable. She gave him a shrewd look. "And who are you, *monsieur,* for you certainly do not look like the blushing bride?"

Phillip held out his hand. "My name is Phillip Villeneuve and I've come to offer you a job."

"Quel dommage! But I already have a job," she said with a playful pout, indicating the showroom and its contents.

"Is there somewhere we might talk?"

The designer indicated a chair in the center of the busy showroom and Phillip reluctantly sat down. He'd much prefer to discuss business in the privacy of an office, but he suspected Chantalle Marillon's office was in as much disarray as her showroom. Still, with what he was about to offer, he was certain the deal would take only a few minutes.

"I understand that you are quite an extraordinary designer," Phillip continued.

"C'est vrai," she chirped in a matter-of-fact tone. "I am the best. But why would I want to work for you when I may work for myself?"

"I'd like to offer you a position with a new retail venture, a store that will be bigger and better than any store in Paris."

Chantalle Marillon laughed, the husky sound causing every patron in the showroom to turn and look. A bell at the door jingled, but she ignored it and fixed her twinkling eyes on him. "You do not even know me. Who are you to come into my shop and make such an offer? And why should I listen to you, *monsieur?"*

"I represent the—"

"Don't listen to him, Chantalle. The poor man is seriously deluded."

Phillip scowled, then turned as he recognized the voice. Megan DeWilde stood in front of him, a haughty expression on her face.

She looked more beautiful than she had a week ago, her hair wind-blown and her cheeks pink. She wore a baggy raincoat that hid her body from his eyes, but his fingers

twitched in remembrance of her soft curves. He fixed his
gaze on her mouth and felt a sudden flood of desire as he
remembered the taste of her lips, the quiet sounds she
made beneath his kisses.

"We meet again," she said in a cold voice, dousing his
rising desire in an instant. "I thought you'd returned to
Hong Kong."

Phillip cleared his throat. "Change of plans."

"What are you doing here?"

"I was just about to make Madame Marillon an offer of
a job," he said. "An exclusive contract to design for
Villeneuve's. What are *you* doing here?"

"Chantalle already has an exclusive contract," Megan
said, a satisfied smile curving her lips. "With DeWilde's.
In fact, she'll be working at our new store at 25 rue de la
Paix."

He'd thought the games between them were over, but
with this new development, they might just be beginning.
Besides going after the same property, they now were vy-
ing for the same designers. He chuckled and shook his
head. "That may be a problem since I'll own that property," he said. "And *madame* will most definitely want to
work for me."

"I still have two weeks to secure my financing. And she
has a contract," Megan said. "With me."

"Ce n'est pas vrai!" Chantalle interrupted. She placed
her hand on Phillip's arm and graced him with a flirtatious grin. "I have not signed anything yet. I believe I must
consider all offers."

Phillip watched irritation suffuse Megan's expression.
But was there something more? For a brief moment, as
Megan watched Chantalle touch him, he thought he might
have seen a flicker of jealousy. Wishful thinking, he

mused. A pity that's all he could do when it came to Megan DeWilde.

"I'll offer twice what DeWilde's is offering," Phillip said evenly.

Chantalle's brow shot up in surprise. She turned to Megan and gave her a speculative look. "*Double.* That is a very generous offer, *n'est-ce pas?*"

"Very generous," Megan replied, "if he had a store. But Monsieur Villeneuve has no store. All he has is a shaky offer on a property—a property I intend to buy. He hasn't the reputation of DeWilde's or the retailing experience. Go ahead. Take his offer, for he is really offering nothing at all. If he has no store, he has no job, and I suspect you will have no contract."

Phillip had to give her credit. She'd managed to make his offer sound like nothing more than a pipe dream. Her expression was cool and contained, her real feelings hidden well below the surface. Chantalle frowned at them both, clearly confused as to the best choice but enjoying the bidding war nonetheless. Megan reached into her bag and withdrew an envelope, holding it out to the designer.

"Sign now," Megan said, "and I'll make your designs famous around the world." She paused. "Sign now or I'll withdraw my offer."

Chantalle turned to Phillip, then to Megan, then back to Phillip again.

"I can have a contract drawn up by this afternoon," he countered. "You will be paid whether you work or not."

"But is this true, you have no store?"

"Not yet, but I—"

"I will sign," Chantalle said, snatching the contract from Megan's outstretched hand. "I must work. And I have already agreed to your terms."

Megan handed her a pen and watched as the designer scribbled her name. With great dramatic flourish, she retrieved the contract, slowly refolded it and slipped it back into the envelope.

"Thank you, Chantalle," she said. "You won't regret your decision."

She turned to Phillip. "If I were you, I'd admit defeat right now and catch the next plane to Hong Kong." With that, Megan turned and headed toward the door. Phillip quickly stood and made his goodbyes to a wide-eyed Madame Marillon, then followed Megan. He made it to the door in time to pull it open for her in mock chivalry.

"Nice try," she muttered as she stepped out onto the narrow sidewalk, "but you didn't stand a chance with Chantalle. And you won't get that property, either."

Megan stalked down the street, Phillip following at her heels. She picked up her pace twice and he matched it in a bizarre race to see who could walk the fastest. This competition between them was beginning to border on the ridiculous. When they reached place St-Michel, the sidewalk widened and he moved to her side. "We are a pair, aren't we," Phillip said ruefully.

Megan stopped and stared at him. "We are not!"

"You have a designer and no place to put her, and I've got a store with no designers. We'd make a great team if we were on the same side."

"Hah!" Megan said before starting across the square. "I've still got two weeks before the deadline. That building will be mine."

She stopped at the massive fountain with its monster spouting water and St. Michel slaying the dragon. He stood back and watched her for a moment as she stared into the water. All around her, students from the Latin Quarter, tourists, street vendors and Paris's riffraff created a colorful scene. A panhandler approached her and Phillip quickly strode to her side, taking her arm and pulling her away from the fountain.

She took off again toward the métro entrance and he automatically matched her step for step. She stopped and cursed beneath her breath. "Stop following me!"

"Or what? You'll turn your security guards on me?" Phillip turned in a complete circle, then raised his brow. "No guards. And I could easily beat you in a footrace. So, you'll have to deal with me on your own this time."

"I don't have to deal with you at all," she snapped.

Phillip grabbed her arm, and when she tried to pull away, he gently placed her hand in the crook of his elbow. "Let's just walk. We don't have to talk."

He wasn't sure of her destination, so he continued to walk with her toward the Seine. They strolled past several artists hardy enough to have opened their stalls on a blustery spring day, then crossed the Pont St-Michel to the Ile de la Cité.

"Where are we going?" he asked

"I'm going to check on the cherry blossoms in the square," she said stubbornly, as if it were as important as checking the price of DeWilde stock on the morning exchange.

"Cherry blossoms," Phillip repeated.

"I don't need your company," she said.

"No, no, I'd like to see the cherry blossoms." In reality, he had no earthly idea what cherry blossoms had to do with anything, but if it gave him a few more minutes with Megan, he'd be more than willing to discuss botany.

The Square Jean XXIII stood between Notre Dame and the Seine. Most tourists missed it, so in awe were they of the giant cathedral. But Megan barely noticed the famous landmark behind her as she peered at the tiny buds on the trees, gently grasping one of the branches to examine it more closely.

"Almost," she murmured. "At least another week, maybe two if the weather stays cool."

"A week?"

She glanced up at him, blinking as if she'd just realized he was still with her.

"Until they're all out. This is the most beautiful place in Paris when all the trees are in bloom. And the fragrance is incredible. Better than all the perfume Paris has to offer."

He knew it could be nothing like the beauty he saw before his eyes, the picture she made framed by the sparse pink buds, with the cathedral's sweeping architecture serving as the perfect backdrop.

"I'll have to come back," she said softly, letting the branch drift out of her fingers. "I came here the first day I moved to Paris," she said as she walked toward the river.

He slipped his hand into hers, surprised that she didn't pull away.

"I was so scared," she said, as if thinking out loud. "I'd worked in the London store, but when my father gave me the job of merchandising manager in Paris, I really wondered if I was ready. I didn't want to disappoint my family. I didn't want to fail."

"The perfect daughter," he said ruefully.

"What's wrong with that?"

"Nothing," he said. "I know exactly how you feel. I've tried to be the perfect son to my father, but I've never quite matched up to his expectations."

"Well, I intend to make my family proud of me—no matter what it takes. And that includes buying the rue de la Paix property."

She leaned over the wall and stared down into the Seine, then tossed a cherry blossom into the breeze and watched it float to the surface of the water. Pensive, she studied it until it disappeared, her mind distracted by thoughts Phillip couldn't begin to fathom.

"You're not planning to jump, are you?" he teased.

She smiled wryly, the first time he'd seen her smile that morning. "That would give you a distinct advantage," she said, "and I'm not about to give you an inch. Though if *you'd* like to take a swim, I wouldn't try to stop you."

After several more silent minutes, she turned around, sitting up on the edge of the wall and looking up at him. "Why can't you just leave me alone? Go back to Hong Kong. Make life easier—for both of us."

"Would that really make you happy, if I just left?"

Conflicting emotions warred in the depths of her eyes. She nodded, then looked away.

He reached out and brushed a windswept strand of hair from her face, allowing his palm to linger on her cheek. "Is there no way we can fix what's wrong between us?" he asked softly, drinking in the sight of her set against the skyline of Paris. "I feel as if we've been caught up in this against our will."

"I don't know how we can change things," Megan replied wearily. "As long as you're determined to destroy my family's business, I have to do everything I can to stop you."

"Do you really think my father can do that?"

"Can't he?"

"You don't have much faith in your own business acumen, Meggie. Or in the strength of your family's presence in this city."

Megan's jaw tightened and she looked away, focusing on an old man fishing off the quay below them.

"Admit it, Megan. The feud is just an excuse. You know as well as I that it has nothing to do with us."

She turned back to him. "How can you say that? It has everything to do with us."

"Why does it have to? We can put it aside. There's something else holding you back. What is it?"

She frowned, then shook her head. "Are we just supposed to ignore the enmity between our families?"

"Business will be business. What will happen will happen, Megan. But what's happening between us is beyond business. It's between the two of us and has nothing to do with our families."

"I can't ignore it," Megan said. "And nothing you do or say will convince me otherwise." Her words might as well have been chiseled in stone, for at that moment, Phillip knew her mind would not be changed.

"What do you suggest we do?" he asked.

"Leave me alone," she said.

"Are you afraid you might lose?"

She glared at him through narrowed eyes. "Who has the contract with Chantalle? Who still has an accepted offer on the property on rue de la Paix? I won't fail." She paused. "I can't," she added.

"Your offer expires in two weeks, and you haven't secured financing," Phillip said. "The battle isn't won yet."

As he expected, she rose to the challenge. "Oh, I can beat you, all right. In a fair fight."

"I'll fight you and I'll do everything I can to win. Two business people, no holds barred. And between us, we'll make a pact."

"A pact?"

"Once the sale of the property is finalized, we'll meet back here under these cherry trees and declare a winner. And no matter who wins, you and I will start again. No matter what our families have to say about it, we'll give each other a chance. We'll forget this damn fight and everything that goes with it and we'll become... friendly competitors. Very friendly."

Megan bit her lower lip as she considered his offer. "I'll win, you know. Will you be able to handle that?"

"I can handle anything you throw my way." Phillip grinned. "And I'm sure you'll do your best."

With that, he drew her against him and covered her mouth with his, kissing her deeply. If he could have, he would have made the kiss last forever. But as she melted against him, he knew his desire would have to wait. Gently, he unwrapped her arms from around his neck and set her away from him.

"*À bientôt*, sweet Meggie," he murmured, caressing her cheek with his fingertips. "And may the best man win."

She touched her lips, an uneasy expression in her eyes. "Best woman," she amended stubbornly.

He smiled, then turned and left her where she stood. With every step he took, he fought the urge to return to her, to pull her into his arms and try to convince her of what they might share together—right now.

But Megan would remain unswayed. No, there was nothing he could do to convince her beyond handing her the property on a silver platter. But he had his own loyalties, to his father and to the family business. He would wait until she was ready, until every battlement had been breached between them and nothing stood in their way.

As he crossed over the Pont de l'Archevêché, he glanced back at the park, his gaze searching for her along the wall. But she was no longer there, the place they once stood now occupied by a tourist with a camera. An odd feeling of emptiness twisted at his core.

He'd never been a patient man when it came to women. But he sensed that waiting for Megan DeWilde would definitely be worthwhile.

THE PLACE DE L'OPÉRA was ablaze with light, the facade of the theatre illuminated for all to admire. As she stepped out of the cab, Megan pulled her wrap more tightly around her to ward off the nighttime chill in the air. Her gaze took in the ornate friezes and winged horses and garlands of gold. Above it all, Apollo reigned, his lyre held high against the black sky.

Usually, she waited inside the Grand Foyer for Marie-Claire, but tonight Megan was on her own. Her aunt had called to say that she'd be unable to attend the evening's performance due to business with the winery. At first, Megan considered staying home. But then she decided that *Aurora's Wedding* was not worth missing due to the lack of a companion. The brand-new production of the third act of the *Sleeping Beauty* ballet was opening tonight with costumes underwritten by DeWilde's. She would go alone and enjoy herself, then stop by the reception after the performance.

Besides, over the past few days she'd been searching for activities to occupy her mind. At work, she'd thrown herself back into negotiations for the property at 25 rue de la Paix, using every resource she had to push the bankers into a final decision. But in the off hours, alone in her office or apartment, she couldn't help but wonder what occupied Phillip's mind.

Did he think of her as many times each day as she thought of him? Was he as impatient as she was for the time to pass and for their rivalry to be settled? Did he toss and turn at night, images of *her* plaguing *his* dreams?

In a way, she was tempted to give in to him now, to slake her desire for him and then go on about her life as if they'd never met. But the property stood squarely between them, like an unbreachable wall, and she wasn't about to give him any advantage at all. She'd maintain a safe distance and review her options once the deal had been made.

She entered the front doors of the theater and wound her way up the sweeping white marble staircase. Light gleamed off gilded plaster. The rich colors of the wall paintings that decorated the foyer were matched by the colors of the women's gowns reflected in the tall mirrors. Excitement seemed to vibrate in the air and she quickly found her seat in the lowest of the five loges.

The DeWilde family had held the same box seats at the theater for nearly fifty years. She and Marie-Claire attended regularly, and most evenings, Marie-Claire would give the other two seats in the box to friends. At times, Megan's parents had joined them. But Megan found the box empty when she arrived and was secretly glad she would not have to make idle chitchat.

She took a chair at the rail, shrugging out of her wrap, and peered down over the orchestra as they tuned their instruments. Heavy red velvet drapes hung from the sides of the box, allowing her a perfect view of the stage in near privacy. Above the main floor, the massive chandelier glowed softly on the Chagall painting that decorated the ceiling.

Megan had never been much for the arts when she was growing up, dozing her way through two years of painting lessons and trying any number of musical pursuits. To appease her mother, she had even tried ballet lessons. But she'd been a gangly and ungraceful twelve-year-old, and after two months of lessons, the teacher had taken Grace aside and given her the bad news.

Left to her own pursuits, Megan preferred to find her fun between the covers of her books, in fairy-tale worlds where she could imagine herself brave and clever and beautiful. It was only later in life, when she was in college, that she discovered her love of the arts. She didn't have to dance to enjoy ballet, nor did she have to play to appreciate good music. She simply had to sit back and enjoy herself, something she found quite easy to do.

She took her opera glasses out of her purse and surreptitiously began to scan the crowd. It was a ritual her aunt loved, nodding to friends, gossiping about fashions, becoming a part of the spectacle that was opening night at the ballet.

Megan's gaze stopped at a box across the way. She admired the beaded gown of an aristocratic blonde and wondered at the identity of the designer. The woman turned slightly to listen to her companion and Megan peered through the glasses at him.

He was dressed in a finely tailored tuxedo and a perfectly starched shirt. Onyx-and-diamond studs glittered against the white pleats. His formal attire provided a striking contrast to most of the men in attendance, who wore business suits. Still, he didn't look at all out of place. The truth be told, he made every other man appear no more than ordinary in comparison.

She allowed her gaze to drift upward, curious to take in more details, then stopped. She swallowed hard and squinted through the glasses, unable to believe what she saw. "Phillip?" she murmured to herself.

As if he heard her, through all the noise and across the entire width of the theater, he turned and looked directly at her. She dropped the glasses to her lap and sank back into the shadows of the drapery until the lights lowered to signal the start of the first piece.

Megan fumbled with her program. "Bourrée Fantastique," she murmured. She read every word of the program twice, straining in the low light, before she worked up the courage to peer back around the draperies. But in the darkened theater, she couldn't see whether it was really him or just a figment of her imagination.

Though she tried to lose herself in the beauty of the dancers on the stage, her mind constantly wandered back to the man who sat in the box across from her—and the woman who had accompanied him that night.

He certainly hadn't wasted any time! And why was she surprised? A man like Phillip Villeneuve was not the type to suffer a lack of female companionship. And they had agreed not to see each other until this whole battle between their families had been settled.

But what if it never was settled? What if it just continued on, generation after generation? Would she be left to wonder what could have been between them? Worse, what if he couldn't accept her victory in the matter? She intended to win at all costs, costs that surely would include pricking his considerable ego.

The first half of the performance seemed to race by, the dancers blurring together on the stage, the music a distant din. As the lights rose, Megan shoved her chair into the shadows of the drapery, knowing that she couldn't face the prospect of his eyes searching for her—or the temptation to sneak another look at him during the *entracte*.

She wasn't sure when she actually sensed his presence behind her. Perhaps it was the familiar scent of his cologne drifting on the air, or the sound of draperies rustling. Slowly she turned to find him standing in the entrance to her box. He stepped inside and pulled the curtains shut behind him.

"Phillip!" she cried, jumping to her feet. "What are you doing here?" Her voice sounded tight, her emotions rising to the surface to color her words. Nervously, she smoothed at the skirt of her simple black gown.

He smiled and she felt her blood warm. "Ah, Meggie. Are you really surprised? You didn't expect me to come?"

"Of—of course not," she lied. "I didn't know you liked ballet." Megan snatched up her purse and her wrap and made to leave. "Have a seat. Enjoy the rest of the program. Unfortunately, I can't stay."

Grabbing her arm, he stopped her before she could sneak around him.

"Let me go," she murmured in a thin voice. "You promised me you—"

"No," he said, bending close to her ear. "I came here to see you."

"What about your date?" Megan demanded. "That blond obligation in the designer gown?"

"She's not my date. She's an old friend of the family."

Megan scoffed. "If that's old, then I'm ready for the retirement home."

"When I saw that DeWilde's was underwriting the costumes, I knew you'd be here, so I accepted her invitation," he said. "I was hoping I might see you."

"Don't lie to me."

He grinned seductively. "I'm not. I'd never lie to you, Meggie."

Slowly, she backed away from him until they both stood in shadows so dark she could barely see him. His hands hovered above her arms and he stood so near she could feel the heat of him. She closed her eyes, wanting him to touch her but knowing she'd be lost if he did.

"I had to see you," he murmured. "It's been so long."

"It's been four days," she said.

"Mmm," he replied, twisting a lock of her hair between his fingers. "Too long. I can't stay away from you, Meggie."

"We shouldn't do this," she said. "What about our pact?"

"To hell with the pact," he breathed.

He moved closer, his mouth above hers yet not touching her lips, his breath soft against her skin, the scent of him like a powerful narcotic. She stared up into his eyes, and the dark seemed to close in on them like a cocoon of soft spun silk.

In a haze, the music began again, and he trailed his fingers along the length of her neck. Like Aurora dancing on stage, Megan slowly felt herself awakening to his touch, the music swirling around them like the spell of the Lilac Fairy. He pulled her against him and her body melded with his until the pulse of the music seemed to match her quickened breathing.

She moaned softly, torn between desire and propriety. "You should really go back to your seat," she murmured, half hoping he'd refuse.

He looked down at her through hooded eyes. "I'd rather stay here," he said.

Hesitantly, Megan stepped away from him and took her seat again, plucking at the skirt of her gown. They'd watch the ballet together and by the end of "Aurora's Wedding," their passion would have cooled.

But Phillip was not to be deterred. He took her hand in his and slowly rubbed his thumb above her wrist. She was certain he could feel her pulse race and her skin tingle.

"This is one of my favorite parts," she murmured. "The Bluebird *pas de deux*." She kept her eyes fixed on the dancers, though all her attention was focused on her hand as he brought it to his lips. He kissed the tip of each finger, his lips exquisitely warm.

"You should really watch this," Megan urged. "It is quite wonderful."

"Mmm" was his only reply. His mouth moved up her arm as Little Red Riding Hood and the wolf danced their vignette. By the time Florimund and Aurora began their *pas de deux,* his lips caressed her shoulder, then traced a line from the skin behind her ear to her nape.

A shiver skimmed down her spine as he reached up and brushed her hair from her neck, turning her slightly and settling her back against his hard chest. Gathering her resolve, she tried to concentrate on the dancers. The music swelled and Aurora began a series of brilliant *pas de poisson,* turning with great speed on pointe. Just as she plummeted headlong toward the floor, the music coming to a thunderous close, Phillip shifted again, leaning Megan back until she lay in his lap.

"Wha—what are you doing?" she whispered.

"I'm going to make love to you," he said. "Right here. Right now."

An instant later, the auditorium erupted in applause and Megan bolted up, her forehead bumping against Phillip's nose.

Phillip swore, his eyes watering, his jaw tight. "Damn it, Meggie, what the hell are you doing?"

Megan glanced around nervously, certain that every eye in the house was focused on loge C, *premier balcon.* The applause was deafening, punctuated by shouts of "bravo." She groaned out loud, the sound buried in the din. What was she doing? She'd been ready to give in to her desires in the middle of a public place with more than two thousand people in attendance.

"I must be crazy," she said breathlessly. "You're *making* me crazy! It's all your fault." She dropped to her knees, searching the floor of the box for her wrap and purse. Crawling between the chairs, she finally found them both where she'd dropped them, along the wall. "I can't do this. I can't."

She struggled to her feet, then tugged clumsily on the strapless bodice of her dress. He watched her from behind his hand, still massaging his bruised nose.

"I have to go now," she said. "And don't even think of following me!" Her exit was accompanied by the lusty music of the dance of the Three Ivans. Megan hurried down the hall to the stairs and then outside.

Drawing in deep breaths of the crisp night air, she tried to clear her mind. What was *wrong* with her? Where in the world had she gotten the crazy idea that she could handle an affair with someone like him? Megan DeWilde had always been such a practical, circumspect person. After all, that's the way that she'd been raised. Desire and passion had its place in her life—in the bedroom with the lights off and the covers up around her chin. Not in a box at the Théâtre de l'Opéra!

She ran to the taxi stand and waited nervously in the queue, glancing over her shoulder every few seconds to see if he had followed her. Only after she'd settled in the back seat of the cab and the driver had turned out into traffic did the temptation to return to the opera box subside.

"So much for that torrid little fling," Megan muttered. "I should have known I'd make a mess of it sooner or later."

MEGAN LOOKED BOTH WAYS before crossing boulevard du Montparnasse from the Vavin métro station, holding a newspaper over her head as she ran. The familiar white facade of her apartment building looked shiny against the slate gray sky and the wet street. Ornate black wrought-iron balconies surrounded tall French doors that over-looked the street, but all were closed to ward off the dampness of a day-long drizzle.

Marie-Claire had called the store just an hour ago, asking to meet at Megan's apartment. The spacious fourth-floor apartment in the fourteenth arrondissement had been Marie-Claire's Paris home from the time she'd married Jean-Luc DuPlessis, yet this was only the third time she'd come to visit since she'd turned it over to Megan five years ago. In fact, other than her trips into the city for the ballet, Marie-Claire preferred her quiet life in the country.

A nervous knot twisted in Megan's stomach as she wondered about the summons. She had a sick feeling that news of her opening night encounter with Phillip had reached her aunt's ears. Could someone have seen them together at the ballet and so quickly reported back to her aunt? Or was she just being paranoid?

Megan's cheeks warmed in embarrassment. Though they'd been hidden in the shadows of the box, maybe someone had stepped in without their knowledge. Or maybe, in the throes of a passionate kiss, she'd cried out his name. Or perhaps their whole encounter had been visible to the ballet patrons seated in the upper loges.

Megan moaned softly. "I'm an idiot," she said. "And this has got to stop."

Gaspar, the building's vigilant doorman, swept the door open in front of her, and she mumbled a quick greeting and raced across the marble floor to the ancient lift. She yanked it open and stepped inside, then punched the button for her floor, tapping her foot nervously.

When she flung open the door to her apartment, she found her aunt comfortably ensconced on the sofa, a strange man sitting across from her in an overstuffed chintz chair, a teacup balanced on his knee.

"Darling!" her aunt cried. "I didn't expect you so soon."

Megan tried to catch her breath, then forced a smile as she took off her damp coat. "I came right over when you called," she said, stepping into the room. "What are you doing here? Is everything all right?" She kissed her aunt's cheek, watching the stranger suspiciously as he unfolded himself from the chair and stood. He was tall and well-built and darkly handsome with a dangerous air about him.

"This is Mr. Santos, Megan. Nicholas Santos. Your father has sent him," Marie-Claire explained.

"Sent him? For what?" Megan asked bluntly, wondering how her father could have already learned of her misguided foray into the Villeneuve nest of vipers. The family grapevine was fast, but not that fast. And why would he send a stranger instead of coming in person?

Santos held out his hand and Megan took it warily. "It's a matter of family business," he said, his accent marking him as an American. "I'm a private investigator."

"He's here about the jewels, dear," Marie-Claire said.

"The jewels?" Megan asked, trying to hide her obvious relief. "What jewels? The DeWilde family has plenty of those to choose from."

"Sit down, darling," Marie-Claire ordered, "and Mr. Santos will explain himself." Her aunt poured her a cup of tea as Megan took a place beside her on the sofa.

"You are aware of the theft of part of the DeWilde family collection, aren't you?" Santos asked.

Megan nodded. "My father told me all about it months ago. He said he'd hired an investigator and he would let me know if any progress had been made." She paused. "Am I to assume you're that investigator?"

"I am," Santos replied.

"Well, what could I possibly tell you? All I know is what my father knows."

Santos watched her for a long moment from his chair, studying her shrewdly. "A piece of the stolen jewelry—a pavé diamond and pearl tiara known as the Empress Eugénie tiara—turned up in New York last year via an American buyer who purchased it in Australia."

"I'm aware of that," Megan said.

"What you may not know is that Mr. Santos traced my brother, your great-uncle Dirk, to Australia, where he lived under the name of Derrick Freeman," Marie-Claire added. "All this time, the family was never sure whether Dirk was alive or dead, or why he chose to leave." She sighed. "Maybe we never will."

Nick Santos cleared his throat and Marie-Claire smiled apologetically through misty eyes. "Another piece of the stolen jewelry, a bracelet, has been linked directly to Dirk," Santos said, "but we've run into a dead end on the tiara. So we've turned the investigation toward another suspect."

"This is all very interesting, Mr. Santos, but I still don't understand what it has to do with me."

"Mr. Santos is investigating the Villeneuves," her aunt replied for him.

The name hit her like a sharp slap on her face. She swallowed hard and tried to still a tremor in her voice. "Is—is there a reason you suspect the Villeneuves?"

Marie-Claire reached out and took Megan's hand in hers. "Shortly before the jewels went missing in 1948, Armand de Villeneuve showed up in New York," she explained. "He and Dirk fought, a terribly violent confrontation that took place at the store. Armand disappeared, and then Dirk did the same. A short time later, six pieces that were on display in New York were found to be paste."

"The last anyone heard from Dirk DeWilde was a letter postmarked from Hong Kong," Santos said.

"Mr. Santos thinks that Armand might have stolen the jewels. When Dirk learned about the theft, he may have gone after him," Marie-Claire added.

Megan could see that her aunt was upset by the possibility. She turned to Santos. "Just because both Dirk and Armand turned up in Hong Kong at the same time doesn't prove Armand Villeneuve is responsible."

Santos straightened in his chair. "Villeneuve was involved in espionage with the French Resistance. He had the skill to steal the jewels. He stole a number of important documents from the Nazis during the war and put them in Allied hands. He also had contacts to provide him with convincing fakes. And finally, he had motive—a vendetta he carries on to this day."

"But the tiara turned up in New York. Armand Villeneuve lives in Hong Kong."

"As I said, we traced the tiara back to Australia," Santos countered.

"But that seems to point to Dirk more than the Villeneuves," Megan said.

"The Villeneuves have had a satellite office in Sydney since the early fifties. Armand still spends several months there every year."

"Why would Armand choose to reveal himself now?" Megan asked. "Isn't it kind of foolish for him to suddenly flood the market with stolen jewelry?"

Santos shrugged. "Maybe he needed some quick cash. Or maybe he decided it was time to get rid of the evidence. Or maybe, with all the turmoil in your family, he sensed a weak spot in your defenses. If news of the theft leaked out now, it might cause some embarrassment for the DeWildes. Stockholders are still on edge because of your mother's departure."

Megan shifted uneasily against the soft cushions of the sofa and twisted her fingers together on her lap as she considered the detective's words. A weak spot? Had Armand Villeneuve initiated some complex scheme to finally bring down the DeWildes? And had Phillip Villeneuve used her to help in his father's objectives? Her mind raced, returning again and again to the property at 25 rue de la Paix. How could he have known she planned to buy it? And why did he always seem to turn up when she least expected?

"Your grandmother told me that you've had contact with Armand's son, Phillip Villeneuve. May I ask the nature of your meetings?"

Megan felt her cheeks warm. "No, you may not!"

"Megan!" Marie-Claire reached out and covered her hand. "Mr. Santos is only trying to help."

"Do you know where Mr. Villeneuve can be reached?" the detective asked.

"No," Megan lied.

"Have you seen him recently?"

"No."

"Miss DeWilde, is there a reason you'd lie to me? Are you trying to hide something?"

Megan pasted a benign smile on her face, hoping to feign indifference. "Mr. Santos, all this talk is upsetting my aunt. She went through a very difficult time when she and Armand broke their engagement. If you have any other questions for her, why don't you ask them. If not, I have nothing more to tell you."

Santos reached into his jacket pocket and withdrew a business card. Reluctantly, Megan took it from his outstretched fingers. "If Villeneuve contacts you, I'd like you to call me at my hotel here in Paris. The number's on the back. This could be very important to your family. I'm sure you'll do everything to help." With that, he stood. "I'll see myself to the door."

Megan listened for the door to close behind him before she let out a tightly held breath. She braced her elbows on her knees and buried her face in her hands.

"Why did you lie to him, Megan?" Her aunt's voice was soft but laced with admonishment.

"I—I don't know," she mumbled through her fingers. "I just can't believe Phillip Villeneuve might be... using me." She sat up and rubbed a knot of tension from her temples.

"You've seen him again?"

"Oh, yes," she said sarcastically. "I can't seem to stay away from the man."

"And you don't believe he could have... ulterior motives?"

"No!" She paused. "Yes." She took a deep breath. "Maybe he could. I don't know. Do you believe Armand stole the jewels?"

"I don't want to, but after I broke our engagement, he became very bitter. I could understand if he took such a drastic step."

"Understand?"

"Darling, he was very hurt. Armand de Villeneuve was a proud man."

"But he had an affair with a dancer. He's the one who hurt you!"

"Did he really?" Marie-Claire said. "I didn't want to believe it at the time, but Dirk was so convincing. I trusted my brothers, but I've always wondered if I was right to do so. What if I was wrong? What if my misplaced loyalty to the family is what has caused this awful feud?"

"But you have to trust family," Megan said. "Your brothers loved you. They'd never lie to you."

Marie-Claire sighed. "You're right," she said. "I don't want to believe Armand capable of stealing those jewels, but who else could have done it? I've always wondered why he disappeared so suddenly, and without a trace. He left everything behind, his family, their retailing business, his entire life. And the tiara had been promised to me upon marriage to Armand. I was to wear it at our wedding. It seems like more than a coincidence, don't you think, that it was the first piece to turn up?"

Megan stood and began to pace the room, her mind spinning in confusion. "I saw him again," she finally said after a long silence. "A few nights ago at the ballet." She groaned. "I just can't seem to... control myself when I'm around him. I know he's the enemy, but he has this way of... getting under my skin."

Marie-Claire shook her head. "I see he takes after his father. I never could resist that man. Even after I broke our engagement, he haunted my thoughts. I still think of him." She smiled sadly. "Does that sound as pitiful to you as it does to me?"

Megan sat down beside her. "No more pitiful than my behavior around Phillip. I have got to learn to resist that man. You're right. He's dangerous." She paused, wondering if she should tell her aunt the whole story. Megan drew a long breath and decided to continue. "He's out to buy the rue de la Paix property. Villeneuve Enterprises has made a contingent offer on the property if my deal falls through. They want to open a retail store in Paris, right across the street from DeWilde's. *Tante,* I think it may be more than coincidence that the tiara turned up when it did. I believe it might be a sign, or perhaps a warning.''

"Why didn't you tell me about this, Megan?"

Megan shrugged dispiritedly. "I thought I could handle it. I will handle it. There's no need for Daddy or Gabe to know. I'll get the property despite the damn Villeneuves. I still have plenty of time. They won't steal another thing from our family, I'll make sure of that."

"Darling, we don't know for certain that the Villeneuves were involved in the theft."

"Well, I'm going to find out," Megan said, icy determination filling her voice. "The family comes first and no one—not even Phillip Villeneuve—can change that. If he's hiding something, I swear I'll find out what it is.''

CHAPTER FIVE

"I CAN SEE IT ALREADY," Megan said excitedly. "The grand opening of Galeries DeWilde. The Paris couture community will be all abuzz. The fashion press will be begging for an exclusive headline. We'll throw a wonderfully glamorous party, champagne will flow, and we'll invite everyone to see the newest DeWilde success."

"Of course, you will invite me," Lucy said. "And I will buy the perfect gown."

Megan smiled. "I wouldn't think of not inviting you. And my father will be there, and so will Gabe and Lianne...and Marie-Claire...and all the board members."

"And you will be at the center of it all," Lucy continued.

"Reveling in the attention," Megan added. "Knowing that *my* concept will leave a lasting impression on the family business—and on the members of the board, of course."

"Of course," Lucy said in mock seriousness.

Megan stared up at the facade of the building at 25 rue de la Paix, imagining it as it would look on that day. The building had been renovated after the war, but she'd been assured that the original facade could be restored to its belle époque beauty. As soon as the sale was finalized, she'd hire architects and contractors to begin the work. Within the year, two DeWilde stores would flank the rue de la Paix, the flagship store with its traditional atmosphere, and Galeries DeWilde, with its innovative boutiques.

A warm breeze ruffled her hair, and Megan pushed an errant strand from her eyes. She was already late for work and was about to turn and make her way back to the store when she noticed the two men standing in front of the building. Megan watched them for a long moment from across the street. Both were well dressed in business suits and Burberry raincoats. One held out what looked like a blueprint as the other pointed at the arch over the doors.

"Who do you suppose they are?" Megan asked distractedly.

Lucy followed her gaze. "Who?"

"Those two gentlemen standing in front of my building."

"I do not know, but we will find out, eh?" Lucy grabbed her hand, then glanced both ways before dragging Megan across the street.

"The owner said nothing about making any changes to the building before the sale," Megan murmured. "Maybe there are problems with the property." An image of leaky roofs and cracked foundations flashed in her mind and she groaned inwardly. She already had balky bankers to deal with; she didn't need hard-nosed building inspectors, as well.

"*Excusez-moi,*" Lucy said, her smile coy, yet flirtatious. "May I ask what you are doing?"

The taller of the two men turned to her, eyebrows arched speculatively. His expression softened and he gave Lucy an appreciative look. "We are designing a new facade for the new owner," he said in a clipped British accent.

Megan frowned and shook her head. "But that's not possible," she replied. "I'm the new owner and I know nothing about a new facade."

"Ah, then you're working with Mr. Villeneuve?" the second architect asked. He held out his hand. "A pleasure to meet you. Miles Covington of the Hong Kong architectural firm of Gilford and Cho. And this is my partner, Rupert Seachrist."

Megan ground her teeth and refused to return his gesture. "Mr. Villeneuve has ordered this work?"

"He's hired us to redesign and renovate this property," Covington explained.

"And where might we find Mr. Villeneuve?" Lucy asked.

Seachrist seemed confused by her question. "Why, he's inside. In his office. Fourth floor, just left off the lift."

Megan cursed beneath her breath. "He has an office in this—" She stopped short. "Thank you," she said calmly. She grabbed the blueprints out of the architect's hands and shoved them under her arm. "I'll just take these," she explained. "I have a few points I'd like to discuss with that slimy, underhanded—" She paused and smiled. "With Mr. Villeneuve."

She shoved the glass door open and stalked inside, Lucy trailing after her. Only two of the tenants remained on the first floor—a luggage shop and a shoe store. She walked the length of the lobby and punched the button for the lift, ignoring the curious stare of the uniformed doorman.

"I can't believe this," Megan muttered. "Of all the nerve."

"Of all the nerves," Lucy repeated in a huff. "What are we going to say to him? Are we going to lash him with our tongues? Or maybe we will just slap his face silly."

Megan held open the lift door after she stepped inside. "*We're* not going to confront Phillip Villeneuve, *I* am. Alone."

Lucy put on a pretty pout. "*Mais, non!* I want to come. I will be of great help, *je promets!*"

"And I promise to tell you all the details," Megan said.

"All?"

"Every last one," Megan assured her. "Now, get out of here. Go shop for that gown for our grand opening. I own this building and no one, not even Phillip Villeneuve, is going to change that fact."

She let the lift door close, and a few seconds later, she emerged on the fourth floor, her temper reaching critical mass. She stepped inside the door marked Villeneuve Enterprises and was shocked to find a fully functioning office with a receptionist and three administrative assistants visible from a luxurious waiting area. Phillip Villeneuve had been in Paris only a few weeks, and already his office space and staff surpassed hers.

She placed the crumpled blueprints on the receptionist's counter and looked down at her. "I'd like to see Mr. Villeneuve," she demanded.

The woman gave her, then the blueprints, a suspicious look. "Mr. Villeneuve doesn't see anyone without an appointment. Are you delivering those plans?"

"Yes," Megan replied. "And I'd like to make an appointment for—" she studied her watch "—one minute from now, to discuss these plans with him...*personally.*" She paused, still studying her watch, then looked up. "Right on time. You can tell Mr. Villeneuve that Megan DeWilde is here for her appointment."

The receptionist immediately recognized her name and popped out of her chair, smiling graciously. "I'll let him know you're here, Miss DeWilde."

Moments later, a petite Oriental woman stepped into the reception area and held out her hand. "Miss DeWilde, I am Lei Lin, Mr. Villeneuve's executive assistant. He is in a meeting now, but he asked that I bring you back to his office to wait."

Megan grabbed the crumpled blueprints and stuffed them back under her arm as Lei Lin led her down an elegant hallway. As she passed office after office, she couldn't believe the size of the staff Phillip had assembled. Surely he couldn't be that confident in his success, could he?

A nervous knot twisted in the pit of her stomach, and for the first time since she'd proposed Galeries DeWilde, she wondered if she could really make it happen. Did she have the business savvy to beat a man like Phillip Villeneuve—and at his own game? And what would she do if she couldn't? She bit her lower lip. Failure was not an option.

Phillip's assistant opened a pair of mahogany doors and ushered her into a beautifully decorated, ultramodern office. She settled Megan in a guest chair in front of Phillip's wide glass-topped desk and smiled. "Would you care for anything to drink?" she asked. "Coffee? Perhaps a cold drink?"

Megan shook her head, surreptitiously taking in her surroundings. The office had a lived-in look, as if Phillip intended to stay for more than just a few weeks. Damn his ego and his overconfidence! Was he so certain that he'd beat her? She tried to regain her composure, not wanting her expression to betray her concern. "No. Nothing," she murmured.

"I will leave you, then," Lei Lin said. "It is a pleasure to finally meet you, Miss DeWilde." She bowed, then walked out, closing the door behind her.

Megan sat primly in her chair, her mind spinning with all the things she wanted to say to him. But when Phillip didn't arrive after five minutes, she began to pace the office, the blueprints still clutched in her hands. On her third pass of his desk, her gaze skimmed the file folders scattered across the smoked glass surface.

She stopped and hesitantly reached out for one, then snatched her hand back. Snooping was snooping and Megan did not consider herself a nosy person. But she was never one to pass up a chance to "educate" herself. She had decided to find out exactly what Phillip Villeneuve was up to, and here was the perfect opportunity. "All's fair in love and war," she muttered.

She had made it halfway through the folders without finding much worth reading besides production schedules from Villeneuve's Hong Kong factories, when she happened upon a folder that looked suspiciously like real estate papers. Her heart skipped a beat. If she had found a copy of his offer, she'd be able to see exactly what means he'd used to try to snatch the property out from under her.

She opened the folder and scanned the first page of the document, holding it closer to the desk lamp to read the fine print. Riffling through the stapled pages, she hurriedly searched for the terms of the offer, translating from the French as she read.

She'd nearly found the information she sought when the sound of the office door opening reverberated through her consciousness. Her gaze frantically shifted to the rest of the folders, now more than an arm's length away. Megan closed her eyes, then calmly stuffed the folder she held into the waistband of her skirt. She buttoned her jacket to hide the bulge and silently cursed her choice of a fitted suit that morning.

"This is an unexpected pleasure," Phillip said in a warm voice.

Megan steeled her nerves and turned to face him as he walked across his office, knowing that any sudden move would result in the folder sliding beneath her skirt and dropping to her feet. She tried not to breathe too deeply when he bent to brush a kiss along her cheek and stared down at her expectantly.

"Is there a reason for this visit?" Phillip asked. "Or have you come because you miss me as much as I miss you?"

She swallowed hard. "No," she said in a small voice, suddenly captivated by his sensuous lips and seductive smile. She remembered how his lips felt on hers, how just one kiss could cause her pulse to race and her mind to spin. "No reason. I—I was just in the neighborhood." Her gaze drifted down to his wide shoulders and broad chest. He had discarded his jacket and wore an impeccably fitted European-cut shirt that hugged his torso and narrow waist. He had loosened his tie and unbuttoned the collar of his shirt and she realized this was the most casually dressed she'd ever seen him.

"My assistant mentioned some blueprints," he prompted.

Megan blinked. "Blueprints?" She drew a sharp breath, her mind clearing with the fresh oxygen intake. "Blueprints!" she repeated. "Of course, the blueprints." She attempted to work up to her previous level of righteous indignation, but trapped in the same room with him, alone, she discovered that any thought of an argument had suddenly dissolved from her mind.

She reached for the crumpled blueprints on his desk and waved them weakly under his nose. "I confiscated these from a couple of architects in front of the building. Don't you think you're jumping the gun?''

He took the plans from her, uncrumpled them and shrugged. ''Are you going to tell me you haven't made plans for the renovation?''

She crossed her arms. ''Of course I have,'' she replied.

''Then why are you surprised I've done the same?''

''*I'm* going to own this building. *You're* not. You're wasting your time and your money.'' She glanced around the office. ''And I sincerely hope you didn't pay your rent in advance.''

Phillip grinned. ''I needed some space to do business. I can't run Villeneuve Enterprises from my hotel room. The owner was willing to rent to me short term and I thought it would save time once I bought the building.''

''Your overconfidence is mind-boggling,'' she said. ''I'm looking forward to the day when I can evict you.''

Phillip shook his head. ''Would it be so bad if I opened a store across the street from you? I'd be around all the time to make your life miserable. You'd be constantly reminded of my superior business talents. And we could have dinner occasionally.''

''You won't open a store across the street from me,'' Megan said. ''I'll get my financing and you'll return to Hong Kong with your tail between your legs.''

The instant she said the words, an unbidden feeling of regret washed over her. He'd return to Hong Kong and she'd never see him again. Every instinct told her that this would be for the best. Yet she couldn't help but wonder what they might have shared given the opportunity—and different bloodlines.

Phillip sighed and locked his gaze on hers. ''Maybe you will,'' he said. He tossed the blueprints aside and slipped his hands around her waist. ''We're wasting time rehashing this. Perhaps we should find something more—" he touched his mouth to hers "—constructive to do with our time."

"Don't kiss me," she said, frustrated by his ability to rattle her resolve.

"All right, I won't kiss you. But now that you're here, what *should* I do?"

She groped for an answer, not at all certain why she couldn't bring herself to walk out. The truth be told, she *had* missed him. And she enjoyed the feel of his hands on her body, the warmth of his mouth on hers and— She stopped short. And the unmistakable presence of his confidential files stuffed down her skirt. "Lunch," she replied quickly.

"You'd like to have lunch with me?" Phillip asked in disbelief.

"Yes," Megan replied. "I—I've decided that we shouldn't really try to fight this attraction we feel for each other. We should get to know each other better. See if we truly are compatible."

Phillip studied her with a shrewd arch to his brow. "What are you up to? What changed your mind?"

"I—I just think it's silly for us to always be fighting. We're two adults. We should be able to be civil to each other."

"I have much more than civility in mind," Phillip said, pulling her closer and kissing her again.

Her body seemed to fit against his as if they'd been designed for each other. Her breasts flattened against his hard chest and her hips pressed against his. At that instant, she couldn't recall why she had tried to keep her distance from him. He was the most exciting, vital, tempting man she'd ever met.

"Mmm," he murmured, sliding his hand to her belly to unbutton the jacket of her suit. She bit back a moan and leaned into his touch. She didn't realize her mistake until his hands stilled on her waist.

He stepped back and stared down at her, an amused expression on his face. "How does that American saying go? Is that my file in your skirt, or are you just happy to see me?"

Cursing under her breath, Megan grudgingly retrieved the folder. "You can't really blame me, can you?" she asked. "Your assistant leaves me here in your office, alone. I'd have to be a fool not to have a quick look around."

Instead of snatching the file folder from her hands, he pushed it back at her. "Keep it," he said.

"But this is your offer for the rue de la Paix property!"

"I know," Phillip said. "There's nothing in there that you don't deserve to know. If you think it will give you an edge, I want you to have it."

Megan watched him, astounded, waiting for the other shoe to fall. "What is this? This isn't your real offer, is it? You're just trying to trick me."

"Would I do that?" he teased.

"Probably," she said.

"Megan, I don't want any secrets between us. I've got none. As far as I'm concerned, you can ask me anything."

Her mind returned to the conversation she had had with her aunt and Nick Santos. Would Phillip really tell her the truth about everything? Would he admit that his father was a thief? Would he tell her his father had fenced the DeWilde jewels to finance an attempt to undermine her family's business? And would he concede that he'd participated in the plan?

Phillip talked as if it were easy to separate himself from his family. But she knew that couldn't be so. Her loyalties to her own family were perfect proof. No matter what choices a person was faced with, family always came first.

"And I suppose you expect me to reveal all my secrets in return?" she asked.

"Sweetheart, I'd much rather discover your secrets one at a time."

Megan rolled her eyes. "I don't know if I should trust you," she said, suspicion evident in her tone. "After all, you are a Villeneuve."

"If I were Phillip Jones, you'd feel better?"

"I'd feel better if you withdrew this offer," she said, waving the folder at him.

Phillip sighed and shook his head. "Megan, there is much more to that offer than you or I should have to deal with. That's my father's offer, not mine. Why don't we start with something small and less controversial? Forget lunch. I have to be back at the office by two for a call from Hong Kong. How about dinner?"

Megan glanced away uneasily. If she really wanted to learn more about Phillip and his father, she'd have to spend time with him, wouldn't she? Her logic sounded more like a rationalization than she cared to admit. "All right," she said, looking back at him. "We'll have dinner. But I can't guarantee we'll avoid controversy."

"Tonight," he said.

"Tonight? So soon?"

"Now that you've decided to call a truce, I don't think I should waste any time. I'll send a car for you tonight at eight. Leave your address with Lei Lin." He glanced at his watch. "Now, I've got to go. I've got to get back to my meeting." Phillip grabbed her and pressed her against the wall, then kissed her in a swift but seductive manner. With a sexy grin, he reluctantly started toward the door. "I'll see you later."

"What? You're just going to leave me here?"

"Just make sure you return any information you decide to borrow," he said. "Lei Lin is very fussy about my filing."

He closed the door behind her a moment before she hurled the folder after him. She didn't need a damn edge! She could beat Phillip Villeneuve using her own wits and business acumen.

"Dinner with a Villeneuve," she muttered as she grabbed her coat. "The things I do for my family."

HE SAW HER STANDING at the top of the stairs that led down to the Square du Vert Galant. Her arms held the huge bouquet of cherry blossoms he'd put in the back seat of the limo. The warm spring breeze teased at her hair and he realized that all the rhapsodizing about springtime in Paris was more than just a cliché. He also realized at that very moment that Megan DeWilde was the most beautiful woman he'd ever laid eyes upon.

She waved at him hesitantly, then started down the stairs toward him. Her dress was a deep midnight blue, the exact color of the Paris sky after sunset, and she wore a wrap that sparkled in the light from the street lamps. He recalled the time they'd stood beneath the cherry trees on the other end of the Ile de la Cité and vowed that they'd stay away from each other until the sale of the store had been completed. He couldn't help but wonder what had changed her mind.

She'd been so determined to keep him at arm's length, yet now, here she stood, forcing him to confront the question of why *he* couldn't seem to stay away from *her*. He stood against the rail and watched her as she approached beneath the budding leaves that rustled in the chestnut trees.

"I wondered if you'd come," he said softly.

"Why wouldn't I?" she countered.

He smiled and shrugged. "I suppose I shouldn't question good fortune. Are you hungry?"

She glanced around, then nodded. "The driver is gone, though. We'll have to walk. Or get a cab."

He tucked her hand in the crook of his arm, allowing his fingers to linger for a moment on hers. "Dinner is this way." He led her to the walkway along the river. A small group of tourists waited to board the Vedettes du Pont Neuf, tourist boats that offered nighttime cruises on the Seine.

"We're not taking a boat ride, are we?" she asked, eyeing the boats with obvious distaste.

"I thought you might show me this city of yours by night," Phillip replied as they passed the boats. "I've been to Paris so many times I can't count, but I've never really appreciated its charms. And I've never had a boat ride on the Seine."

"But your father was born here," Megan said. "Surely you've been back to visit family."

"My father hasn't set foot in France since he left after the war. When he got to Hong Kong, he altered the family name and tried to forget his French heritage and his life in Paris. And to me, Paris was just another stop on an endless business itinerary. Another hotel room, another night in a city filled with strangers. I never really took a good look at this city—until now."

They walked farther along the quay until he stopped beside a small barge. A tiny table covered with linen and china and crystal sat in the center of the deck. Light spilled out of portholes in the large cabin as the long, low boat gently rocked against its moorings. A cry of delight escaped Megan's lips and she turned to Phillip and smiled.

"You're pleased," he said.

"Is this where we're having dinner?"

"We have a gourmet chef waiting to prepare our meal and a musician ready to entertain us."

He stepped onboard, then reached out and helped her, catching her in his arms as she stumbled slightly. He couldn't resist stealing a kiss then and there, but he knew he'd have to take things slowly if he wanted the evening to go as he had planned.

"The barge belongs to a client of ours," he explained, resisting the temptation to taste her lips just once more. "A designer. We manufacture his ready-to-wear line."

"It's lovely." She slowly wandered around the boat, examining it from stem to stern, watching as the captain cast off the lines and maneuvered the boat into the middle of the river. Phillip followed her as she stepped down into the huge saloon. He could tell she was nervous, her hands clutched tightly around the bunch of blossoms, her gaze deliberately avoiding his.

"Would you like something to drink?" he asked.

She turned to look at him and forced a smile. "Yes. That would be . . . lovely."

Phillip crossed the saloon and took the bouquet from her hands. He tossed it on the sofa beside them, then wove her fingers through his. "Nothing will happen here that you're not ready for, Meggie. This is just dinner. And maybe a little dancing. That's all."

She released a tightly held breath and gave him a grateful smile. "I—I'm glad we decided to have dinner. I think we should get to know each other better."

"And what would you like to know?" he asked, taking her by the hand and leading her back out on deck. "My favorite color is blue. My middle name is Germond, after my father's father. I speak fluent French and Italian, as well as Mandarin Chinese and several other dialects. I'm an expert rock climber. And I prefer Verdi's operas to Wagner's.''

She sat down on a cushioned bench, the gracefully lit facade of Notre Dame gliding by behind her. ''Tell me about your family,'' she said.

Phillip grabbed a bottle of champagne from the ice bucket and worked at the cork while he talked. ''There's not much to tell. My father divorced my mother when I was young. She left Hong Kong and returned to England and her own people. It's been just my father and me for most of my life.''

''Your father,'' Megan repeated. ''What's he like?''

Phillip's jaw tightened and he stared past her at the lights along the bank of the Seine. ''My father is . . .'' He paused, at a loss for words. He'd never been asked to describe Armand Villeneuve. ''He's not at all typical of a parent. I didn't realize that until after I'd gone away to university and had a chance to meet my friends' fathers. We've never been close, not in the way a father and a son should be.'' He popped the cork on the champagne and poured them both a glass, hoping that it would put an end to the subject.

''That must have been hard for you,'' she said softly.

He took a long sip of the champagne and considered her comment. ''It was,'' he finally replied. ''I went through plenty of years of anger and rebellion with him. For a while I'd do anything to get his attention, any kind of trouble was worth the punishment if it made him angry. After I left Oxford, I worked in London for a few years and thumbed my nose at the family business. And then my father offered me a job and I went back to Hong Kong.''

"And you became closer?"

"No," Phillip said. "I hoped that might happen, but it didn't. In the end, I came to admire the man. But he's not much more than my boss."

"That's so hard for me to imagine. My family has always been close. I'd do anything for my parents. Gabe and Kate, too. Even though we're spread all over the world, we still watch out for one another."

"It's that DeWilde family loyalty," Phillip said.

"I *am* loyal to my family," she said defensively. "There's nothing wrong with that. They depend on me and I depend on them."

"What would they say if they knew we were having dinner together?"

She shrugged nonchalantly. "I can have dinner with any man I please."

"And do you?" he asked.

"Do I what?"

"Have many dinners with many men. I just assumed you spent every waking hour in your office at De-Wilde's."

"I lead a very interesting and exciting life," she added.

Phillip suspected she was stretching the truth, but suddenly he needed to know for sure. He needed to know that there was no other man in her life, no fawning boyfriend waiting at home, no torches being carried or unrequited love being mourned.

He stopped short then silently chastised himself. What the hell difference did it make if she did? "What do you do for fun?" he asked instead. "And don't tell me you spend your spare time analyzing sales figures and collecting old balance sheets."

"I don't have much spare time," Megan replied. "And I enjoy my work. I'm learning to run my great-aunt Marie-

Claire's winery in Plessis. I spend one weekend there every month. And last fall I took a cooking class at the Cordon Bleu. I can now make a perfect crepe and an omelet any Frenchman would be happy to eat."

He took in her pretty smile, then realized he couldn't avoid asking the question. "Is there a particular Frenchman you cook breakfast for?"

She shifted uneasily, as if the question had cut too deep. "What are you really asking me?"

He leaned closer and studied her intently. "Have you ever been in love, Meggie? Are you in love with someone now?"

She paused and pondered his question in silence, her wide eyes gazing into his. "I've been in love, or at least I think I was. I almost got married the summer before last, but the wedding—well, it didn't happen. The marriage would have been a mistake, anyway. I know that now. What about you?"

"No, I've never been in love," he said, not feeling the need to explain his answer. Hell, he wasn't sure he'd even know love if it fell from the sky and landed at his feet. And considering his father's history, love was not something he ever wanted to experience.

A long silence grew between them as they watched the city pass by in the night. Paris truly was the City of Lights, with every landmark illuminated against the black velvet sky. The barge approached the Eiffel Tower, which glowed from top to bottom like an enormous Christmas tree, golden light filtering through the massive tracery of steel.

"They were going to tear it down after twenty years," Megan said. "I'm glad they didn't."

Their conversation shifted to topics more suited to tourists as the barge chugged smoothly through the water. Phillip poured another glass of champagne for her before they sat down for dinner, prepared by the master chef he'd hired for the evening. A wizened old man in a battered beret played his accordion from the bow of the boat, the delicate music drifting back to the deck on the night air.

Dessert was a perfect *crème brûlée* followed by dark, rich coffee, which Megan refused in lieu of another glass of champagne. She tipped her head and listened to the music for a moment, then began to sing along with "La Vie en Rose." A smile curved her lips and her eyes reflected the flickering candlelight. Phillip drank in the sight of her, a sight more stimulating than his coffee, more heady than the expensive champagne she drank.

He held out his hand across the table. "Dance with me," he said.

She pushed away from the table and stood, then slipped into his arms so easily and perfectly that it seemed as if they'd been dancing together for years. His mind drifted back to that night in Monaco, the night he danced with a mysterious and beautiful stranger.

She was no longer a stranger. He felt as if he'd known Meggie his entire life. She'd walked into his world and made herself a part of it, and though he couldn't have imagined it possible, she had carved out a place in his heart.

"Thank you for tonight," she said, her words muffled against his shoulder.

He looked down at her and brushed his thumb along her lower lip. "Anytime," he replied.

She smiled hesitantly, then snuggled against him.

"Are you cold?" he asked. Phillip didn't wait for her answer. He grabbed a lap blanket from the bench and wrapped it around her shoulders, drawing her close.

She looked up at him and he could see the need in her eyes. He didn't try to fight the temptation this time but instead kissed her long and deep and ever so slowly, tasting the sweet champagne that lingered on her soft lips.

He slipped his hands beneath the blanket and ran his palms along her hips. She moved with his touch, inviting him to take more, and he did, his hands sliding up to cup her breasts. A tiny moan broke from her throat and his kiss became more urgent, his own need rising to the surface.

"Make love to me," she murmured.

Phillip pulled back and looked down into her flushed face and passion-glazed eyes. "What?" They were the last words he expected to come from her lips. The wine was obviously doing her talking for her. "Meggie, I think you've had a little too much to drink."

She laughed and wound her arms around his neck. "I'm not drunk, Phillip. And even if I was, that doesn't change the fact that I want you to make love to me."

He'd had many women, his first at age fifteen, hired by his father to give him the proper perspective on the ways of passion. Women had always been a controlled commodity in his life, enjoyable but only worth the most cursory attention. Had the offer been made by any other woman, he wouldn't have thought twice about taking her. But Megan... Megan was different.

"Don't worry," she teased. "I'm not asking you to marry me. I mean, you're a Villeneuve and I'm a DeWilde. It's just one night. After all, when in Paris..." She laughed lightly, a little too lightly for him to believe she really knew what she wanted. "And we're attracted to each other, Phillip. Perhaps you're right. It's time to see what it's all about."

"One night," he repeated. "That's all?" She couldn't have made it simpler. Yet something stopped him from accepting her offer. He didn't want just one night of wine-induced pleasure from Megan. He wanted more.

But how much more? A week? A month? Or time until they tired of each other's company. He'd always been able to imagine the end, the words he would say to break off a relationship, the apologies for his inability to commit, his work schedule, the travel, his responsibilities. Try as he might, he couldn't imagine saying those words to Megan. He closed his eyes and bit back a sigh. What the hell was she doing to him?

"Phillip?"

He looked down into her expectant gaze. "Meggie, I..." He paused and drew a long breath. "I think it's time for me to take you home."

She frowned in confusion. "But I thought you would want to—"

He placed his finger over her lips and shook his head. "What I want to do right now doesn't matter. I'm sending you home, Meggie, before you make me do something you're really not ready for."

He signaled to the captain to take the barge back to the quay. When he turned around, Megan had stepped away from his side and stood, alone, at the stern of the boat, the blanket tugged tightly around her shoulders like a shield against him.

Slowly, he approached her and placed his hands on her shoulders. She stiffened slightly under his touch.

"Why did you bring me here?" she asked. "What do you want from me?" She drew a ragged breath. "Why can't you just leave me alone?"

Phillip raked his hands through his hair and smiled ruefully. "I wish to hell I knew, Meggie."

The barge bumped up against the quay and they both watched as the captain tied it up. Megan nimbly stepped back onto the quay without waiting for his help, then started for the stairs that led up to the street level. He cursed and went after her, determined to try to explain himself.

"Meggie, wait!" he called.

She spun around and held out her hand to stop him. "I don't know what you're up to, Phillip Villeneuve. But I'm not going to let you get the better of me. *I'm* in control here, not you. I call the shots."

The limo waited at the top of the stairs and Megan yanked the car door open and slid inside, tossing the blanket out behind her. "By the way, you have absolutely no idea what you're missing," she said, leaning across the seat and staring up at him, anger smoldering in her eyes.

He bent into the car and grabbed her chin, forcing her to look directly into his eyes. "Believe me, I know precisely what I'm missing."

He straightened, then closed the door and knocked on the roof of the limo. As the car sped off down the quai de Conti, he tipped his head back and cursed once more. "What I don't know is *why* the hell I'm missing it."

PHILLIP TOSSED HIS briefcase on the sofa of his top-floor suite at the Crillon and slipped off his jacket. The maid had turned on the lights in the elegant parlor in an attempt to make the room seem more welcoming. The message light blinked on his phone but he ignored it, yanking off his tie and unbuttoning his shirt. He slowly crossed the room and stood at the window, staring down at the city, his hands braced on the marble sill.

He'd spent the day in meetings with his architects, discussing plans for the renovation of the rue de la Paix property, his concentration broken only by thoughts of Megan and their dinner together the night before. She had less than a week to secure her financing before her offer expired. He would be ready to move ahead with his plans once she'd been forced to admit defeat.

He couldn't help but feel a bit guilty. Had it not been for his interference, she would have been granted a further extension on her offer, long enough to finalize her financing package and convince her bankers that DeWilde's was still a solid company. But his sources had told him that with the departure of Megan's mother from the family fold, investors had some qualms about the future of DeWilde's. Grace DeWilde had been a valuable asset to the company, an asset that didn't appear on any balance sheet.

In a way, he hoped that she'd win. He wanted nothing more to do with the DeWilde-Villeneuve feud than she did. But now he could do nothing but wait—five days until their personal battle would be over.

He watched the traffic pinwheel around the place de la Concorde in a wild free-for-all of headlights and horns. Beyond that, on the glassy waters of the Seine, a *bateau-mouche* chugged the length of the river. The boat, which was filled with hearty tourists eager to see Paris by night, was lit up as brightly as the floating restaurants in Hong Kong's Aberdeen harbor. And in the distance, the Eiffel Tower reigned over all.

He had never cared much for Paris...until he'd seen the city with Megan. The glass-and-steel business capitals of the world—Hong Kong, Sydney, New York—paled in comparison. He'd always believed Paris was meant for silly romantics, and Phillip Villeneuve did not consider himself a romantic in the least.

Still, there was an undeniable allure to the city, an ambience he was beginning to appreciate. Paris was Megan's city. Though she wasn't a native, he'd already come to associate his surroundings with her. Other cities were characterized by the business to be done there, the deals made, but Paris would forever be linked with silky dark hair and fathomless hazel eyes and a body made for his hands alone.

He drew a deep breath and turned away from the window, forcing the image of her from his mind. How many times had he cursed his luck—and his parentage—since he'd come to Paris? If he'd been born anyone but a Villeneuve, he and Megan might be sitting across from each other in a smoky Paris bistro, sipping coffee and anticipating the night ahead.

Instead he was stuck in a hotel, one of the most elegant in Paris, alone. He had no doubt that he could find female companionship if he wanted to. The city was full of beautiful women. But for the first time in his memory, just *any* woman wouldn't do. There was only one woman in Paris he wanted.

He tipped his head back. If he knew what was good for him, he'd forget Megan DeWilde. If she were like many women in Paris, a brief but passionate affair was probably acceptable. Hell, she'd offered herself up on the boat that night, no strings attached. It was all that he could do to turn her down. But Megan deserved more than to be one of his one-night stands.

He'd never considered commitment. He'd seen what love had done to his father, how it had soured his life, how it had betrayed his mother. A woman was never meant to become a permanent fixture in his life, merely a passing fancy.

Phillip slipped out of his shirt and retrieved the room service menu from the desk. Just as he was about to pick up the phone, a knock sounded at the door. Frowning, he crossed the parlor in a few long steps and pulled the door open.

For an instant, disappointment shot through him. He'd half expected Megan to be standing on the other side. She was the only person he really knew in Paris except for his employees. But it was his father's gaze he met. Phillip bit back a curse. "What are you doing here?"

Armand pushed past his son, wielding his ebony cane like a saber. He glanced at the phone. "When were you planning to retrieve your messages?"

"I just got in," he replied. "If you had let me know you were coming, I would have met you at the airport."

Armand sat down on the sofa. "I've been in Paris for the last three days. I'm staying at the Ritz."

Phillip frowned, then closed the door. "You've been here for three days and you didn't contact me? Why would you come here?"

His father crossed his hands over the head of his cane and studied his son through cold eyes. "I'm here to make sure you don't ruin my plans."

Phillip grabbed the plush Crillon-crested robe and tugged it on, breathing deeply and trying to control his temper. "I'm perfectly capable of handling this deal on my own," he said.

Armand raised his eyebrow. "Are you? Then why was it up to me to step in and secure it?"

Phillip clenched his jaw and shook his head in frustration, this time swearing out loud. "What are you talking about? I've got everything under control."

"Oh, yes," his father continued. "I know all about your problems with the rue de la Paix property. You were ready to let a *DeWilde*—and a woman, at that—snatch it right out of your hands."

He said Megan's last name with such complete and utter contempt that Phillip felt a fierce wave of protectiveness surge through him. If it had been anyone else, Phillip would have had him up against the wall.

"But I arrived in time to minimize the damage your incompetence might have caused," his father went on.

"How? What have you done?"

"Never mind what I've done," Armand said. "Suffice it to say that the property will be ours."

"Damn it, I told you I could handle this!" Phillip snapped. "I don't need your help."

"You don't need my help because I've decided to handle this deal on my own. You can return to Hong Kong."

Phillip laughed dryly. "Not a chance. I know what you're capable of when it comes to the DeWildes, Father. I won't let you put all we've built in jeopardy just to settle an old score. I'm in the middle of this, whether you like it or not."

Armand's expression was intractable, as hard and unreadable as if it had been carved from stone.

Phillip calmed his anger, then sighed. "Why don't you go to see her?" he said. "This is the first time you've been in France since the war. You could end this feud right now."

"I don't know what you're talking about," he barked.

"There's a fine line between love and hate, Father. I know she hurt you, but don't you think it's time to forgive her? It's been sixty years. You're not the same people you were then. Marie-Claire lives—"

"Don't you dare mention her name in my presence! The DeWildes ruined my life and I will make them pay, if it's my last act on this earth."

"They ruined your life? You left France and built one of the most successful business empires in the world. I'd say you owe the DeWildes a great debt."

Armand stood, leaning heavily on his cane. "If you won't help me with this," he said, "go home. I need your loyalty, not your advice."

Phillip watched his father walk to the door. The older man's shoulders were slightly stooped, his step a bit more labored. "Father?" Phillip called.

Armand looked over his shoulder impatiently.

"Are you all right?" Phillip asked.

He waved his hand dismissively before he walked out of the room. Phillip stared at the door for a long time, worry niggling at his mind. Somehow he sensed that this battle would kill his father. He'd never seen so much anger, so much hate in his eyes.

Armand Villeneuve must have loved Marie-Claire DeWilde with his heart and soul to be filled with such strong emotions after all these years. Feelings that deep were incomprehensible to Phillip. He'd never seen a sliver of affection between his parents and so had grown up unaware of the lasting power of love. At fifteen, he'd experienced the physical release of what he thought was love, but just days later learned was nothing more than lust—paid for in full by his father.

And so it began and continued to this day, an inability to trust in such a mercurial and potentially dangerous emotion. He wanted Megan DeWilde, wanted to find release in her arms. But was that all? Was he really just interested in a brief conquest?

He ran his hands through his hair, trying to organize his thoughts. Contemplation of Megan had an unusual effect on his brain. He couldn't seem to keep it all straight with her—lust instead of love, transitory desire over commitment.

Suddenly, the walls of the elegant suite seemed to close in on him. Phillip shrugged out of the robe on his way to

the bedroom. Digging through his closet, he found a pair
of khakis to change into and a heavy cotton sweater. Once
dressed, he grabbed a leather jacket and headed out the
door.

He needed a walk, a long, exhausting hike along the
Seine. His mind was filled with doubts and questions, all
of them revolving around a woman who should have been
his enemy, a woman he should have been able to resist.

What was it about DeWilde women? His father had
suffered at one's hands, and now another had managed to
turn *his* life into a mess.

CHAPTER SIX

MEGAN SQUINTED AT the clock beside her bed, pushing the cozy duvet out of the way and leaning over her pillow.

"Six-thirty," she murmured. She curled back beneath the covers, ready for another two hours of sleep before she had to get up and go to work. Her thoughts drifted back to the delicious dream she'd just had. She closed her eyes again and a hazy image appeared in her mind—dark hair, brilliant blue eyes, sensuous lips.

She moaned softly and pulled the covers up over her chin. She nearly recaptured the dream when a sharp rap sounded at her front door, a sound she suspected had summoned her from sleep in the first place.

Groaning, she threw back the covers and rubbed her eyes. Only one person would show up at dawn and have the nerve to breeze by the doorman. Gabe obviously had popped into town on business and wanted breakfast before doing whatever he'd come to town to do.

She padded barefoot to the door, grabbing her robe on the way. "Gabe, if that's you, I'll kill you, I swear! I was at the office last night until nearly midnight."

But when she opened the door she found Phillip Villeneuve standing in the hallway, a crooked smile on his face. He peered across the security chain at her. A stubbly beard shadowed his jaw and dark circles smudged the skin beneath his eyes. His hair was damp, as if he'd just stepped from the shower, but his clothes reeked of smoke and

Scotch. "Good morning, Meggie," he said, his syllables slurred with exhaustion.

Megan's heart skipped a beat and she felt a flush warm her cheeks. For a moment, she felt as if she were still lost in her dream. Lord, he was gorgeous. Even in casual clothes, he could take her breath away.

She bit her bottom lip, then shook her head, remembering all that had passed between them the last time they'd been together. Steal her breath? Well, he could damn well steal someone else's oxygen from now on! "Go away, Phillip," she said, slamming the door.

There was no need to be reminded of her foolish behavior that night on the barge. She'd made a simple mistake. She'd assumed the attraction between them had been leading somewhere—right into the bedroom, to be specific. Armed with that notion, she'd screwed up her champagne-induced courage and made the first move, certain he'd follow. She'd thrown away every shred of family loyalty she possessed and jumped in head first, only to hit the bottom with a bone-jarring thud.

But then she'd never really been adept at reading the signals, anyway. Her botched wedding was proof of that. And now Phillip's sudden bout of chastity had been even more confusing. What was with men? Had they all signed some pact to make her life as miserable as possible?

Maybe he didn't find her sexually attractive. Or perhaps he preferred to make the first move. Hell and damnation, maybe he got seasick making love on a boat. Megan groaned. Since that night, she'd managed to put him neatly out of her mind, yet one look at him was all it took to remind her that her dreams had been filled with images of him. Suddenly, all her insecurities rushed back in full force.

"Come on, Meggie. I've been standing outside your building for over an hour. I'm wet and I'm tired and I'm cold."

She pulled the door back open as far as the chain would allow. "How did you get in?" she asked.

"I slipped in with a very accommodating housemaid," Phillip replied. "Can I come in?"

"No," she said. "I don't want to talk to you. In fact, I don't want to see you ever again."

Phillip braced his arm against the doorjamb and leaned closer. "Meggie, I want to explain but I can't do that from the hallway. Please, let me in."

Megan pushed the door shut and removed the chain, then ushered him in. "You look like hell," she said. "Did you spend the night sleeping on a park bench or in the métro?"

He pondered her question for a moment, then shrugged. "I spent the night in a jazz club down the street—under the street, actually. It just closed and I thought I'd stop by and see if I could take you to breakfast. It's raining out. Does it ever stop raining here?"

"It's springtime in Paris," Megan explained. "The tourists demand it. I thought you didn't want anything to do with me. You made that quite clear the other night at dinner."

He flopped down on her couch and covered his eyes with his arm. "I don't know what the hell I want," he mumbled.

"Well, it's certainly not me," she muttered.

"That's not true." He turned and looked directly into her gaze. "I've wanted to see you ever since I put you in that car and sent you home. Don't even imagine that's not so."

Megan braced her hands on her hips. "Why, Phillip? Why can't you leave me alone? You're like...like a bad rash. Really—" she scratched her forearms and shuddered "—irritating."

Yawning, Phillip sat up straight and slapped his hands on his knees, then shook his head as if to clear away the exhaustion. "Well, this rash is hungry. Let's go get breakfast."

"DeWildes and Villeneuves shouldn't eat together. I think we proved that the night before last."

"You make it sound like I've got a communicable disease," he said. "It won't kill you to have breakfast with me."

"Eating rat poison might not kill me, either, but I don't make a practice of it," Megan muttered.

"Come on, Meggie," Phillip chided. "We need to talk."

"We have nothing to talk about," she countered. "You made everything quite clear the other night. You and I are like...like oil and water. No—more like petrol and matches. Or dynamite and...and..."

"Like I said, we've got a lot to talk about and I want to do it now."

She paused, then sighed in frustration.

"I'm not going away," he warned. "So you might as well give in now and save us both some time."

"All right," she heard herself saying, "I'll get dressed and meet you downstairs." She opened the door for him and waited for him to stand. "We can walk over to the Buci market and get some fresh-squeezed orange juice. By the time we get there, maybe the *pâtisseries* and cafés will be open."

He grinned, then jumped up from the couch, his arrogance back in full force. "Downstairs," he repeated. She closed the door behind him, but at his knock she pulled it open again.

"This isn't a trick to get rid of me, is it?" he asked. "You're not going to call the doorman and have him toss me out of here, are you?"

Megan shook her head and closed the door again. "Brilliant move," she muttered to herself, pressing her forehead against the door. "If the man were chocolate, you'd already weigh twenty stone."

Megan dressed quickly, all the while wondering at the wisdom of spending more time with him. But what harm could a simple walk do? Maybe he'd explain what had happened between them that night on the Seine. She was certainly curious. Their walk could be considered . . . an educational experience.

Why had he denied the attraction they both felt, an attraction he'd admitted to just moments ago? Phillip wanted her and she wanted him, or so she thought. It should all be so simple—a brief affair, no strings, no expectations, great sex. Megan ran her fingers through her tangled hair and tried to quell a sudden surge of desire. Maybe they did need to talk.

She joined him in the lobby ten minutes later and they walked down boulevard du Montparnasse in the gray light of dawn. The streets were wet and shiny and everything smelled fresh and new. Water bubbled in the gutters and a pair of street cleaners, dressed in their brilliant green uniforms, swept the *trottoirs* along the boulevard.

Megan drew a deep breath of the sweet air. There wasn't a season she didn't love in Paris, but springtime was her favorite. Summer was crowded with tourists, and winter could be mercilessly damp and cold. Fall was lovely, but it signaled the coming of a long gray winter. Spring was filled with a special beauty, an anticipation of something wonderful to come.

She felt that anticipation now, had felt it since Phillip had appeared at DeWilde's perfume counter. But what was it she was waiting for? Certainly not some Prince Charming to sweep her off her feet and marry her. What she wanted—or more precisely, needed—was a lover, an affair that, once sated, could be easily forgotten.

But was she really prepared to accept a man on purely temporary—and sexual—terms? She glanced over at Phillip. Another surge of desire washed over her and she sucked in a sharp breath. He was so incredibly handsome, a man any woman would find irresistible. Yet, she felt something deeper for him, something she hadn't felt for Edward... a connection, a magnetism that seemed to be ever present, drawing them closer against her will.

The observatory fountain gleamed in the gray light of morning, the four bronze maidens holding a hollow globe aloft. Water trickled softly, the sound made louder by the silence that surrounded them. They approached the Luxembourg Gardens and the palace of Maria de' Medici palace on a long avenue flanked by tall plane trees, green with new leaves. On this morning, the end of the avenue and the palace were invisible, shrouded in the morning mist.

Phillip took her hand, and for a moment, she forgot that they were rivals and imagined them as lovers. What if they had made love that night? Would she have been able to forget it, to treat it as just a one-night affair? Or would making love to Phillip Villeneuve have changed her in some way?

She glanced over at him again and tried to imagine what she might feel right now, strolling beside him in the early morning mist, her hand in his, knowing they might go home and make love again. Or what she might have felt lying in bed with him, their limbs twisted together, his lips exploring her body.

"I'm glad you decided to come with me," Phillip said.

"Are you planning something nefarious at breakfast? Murder, perhaps? Knocking off your only competition would make your life a lot easier."

"Why do always believe the worst of me, Megan? Would it surprise you to know that I enjoy your company?"

She paused. "A lot of things surprise me, Phillip. Not the least of which is you."

He tugged on her arm and led her to a park bench overlooking a small, tree-shrouded fountain. She sat down next to him and he took both her hands in his.

"Meggie, I wish I could change things for us," Phillip said. "The more we go on, the more complex this all gets. It's like a runaway train. If we don't stop it, sooner or later we're going to end up in the rubble. I guess I'm just a little—overwhelmed by it all."

"What are you trying to say, Phillip?" she asked, her voice trembling. "This sounds a lot like a brush-off. If it is, I want you to know that *I* was the one who said this wouldn't work. I said it first and if you think you can—"

"Meggie, be quiet and listen to me," Phillip said impatiently.

"What are you trying to say?" she repeated.

"Meggie, I want us to be together. Really together... you know... intimately."

"I don't understand," she gasped. "I thought after the night on the barge you—"

"Forget about that night." He cursed softly. "I was... caught off guard. I know what I want and I want you."

She swallowed hard in an attempt to calm her nerves. "Then—then you want to have an affair?"

"No!" He paused, then frowned. "Well, I wouldn't call it that. An affair sounds so... well, it doesn't sound like what I want. We shouldn't have to keep our feelings for each other a secret. The way I see it, we should be up-front about the whole thing."

"And what will your father say if he finds out?"

"Oh, he'll find out," Phillip said dryly. "He's in Paris."

"He's here?" Megan asked, astounded. "Since when?"

Phillip's expression turned hard. "He arrived a few days ago, but he made his presence known to me just last night."

She gave him a wary look. "What do you really want, Phillip? Why this sudden...need? Are you trying to prove a point to your father?"

"I *want* to know you better. I want to forget everything that's happened between our families and get on with what's happening between *us*."

"Just forget about everything?"

"We can't let this dispute get in the way anymore. I'm willing to defy my father. I'm willing to take this chance if you are. Are you?"

Megan considered his question for a long moment. Why was he making it all so complicated? Why couldn't they just have a discreet affair, a simple sexual relationship, enjoyable until they tired of each other? She was no good at the other kind, the "family dinner—call me later—let's get married" kind. "But what about Hong Kong?" she asked. "You have a job there."

"I can work here in Paris."

"You'd stay? Here?"

He nodded. "Maybe this is what our families need, a reason to call an end to this. What do you think?"

Megan's mind raced with the possibilities. She could have the store on rue de la Paix *and* Phillip Villeneuve's incredibly sexy body? But was she prepared to defy her family for this man, to betray their trust and her own common sense for simple lust?

A relationship. What did that really mean? It didn't *have* to mean commitment and happily ever after. It could just mean . . . great sex. And if she explained the whole thing very carefully to her family, convinced them of the benefits to ending the feud, perhaps they might not be so disappointed in her.

She bit back a curse. Not a chance. The moment her family found out she was involved with a Villeneuve, they'd probably toss her right out on her ear, all their doubts about her ability to handle her personal life finally coming true.

"Well?" Phillip prodded.

Megan took a long breath. "I'll think about it," she said. She rose to her feet and he looked up at her expectantly. "I said I'll think about it." Megan held out her hand. "Come on, let's get breakfast. If we can make it through a meal together without tearing each other apart, I'll consider your proposal."

Phillip grinned and yanked her onto his lap. His mouth came down on hers and he kissed her, deeply and thoroughly, until she felt as if she might never breathe again. When he finally pulled away, she gazed up at him wide-eyed, unable to speak.

"I'm just making a case for my proposal," he said, nuzzling her neck.

Megan closed her eyes and tipped her head back. A soft sigh escaped her lips, and at that moment she realized something very . . . frightening. Family loyalty forgotten, she realized she had absolutely no control over her desire for Phillip Villeneuve.

MEGAN GLANCED AROUND the bank director's office, then looked at her watch. She'd known this moment was coming for weeks, but instead of looking forward to it, she was almost dreading it.

Monsieur Lacroix's assistant had called her this morning to arrange a private meeting for eleven, obviously to put the final signatures on her financing package. Ordinarily she would have been accompanied by her financial staff when dealing with her bankers, but she'd personally been on the phone for the past week, pressing Lacroix for a decision, selling and reselling him on the concept of Galeries DeWilde.

She'd considered bringing in her father as backup, hoping that he might be able to speed up the process, but then she decided against it. Gabe would have handled the deal on his own without outside help, and so could she. It would serve to prove her point that Megan DeWilde was entirely capable of running the corporation when the time came. She was a mere thirteen hours from the April 1 deadline, and she'd done it all on her own.

She breathed a silent sigh of relief. Once Lacroix had given her the good news, she could proceed with all her plans. She'd begin with the building renovations and then start looking for additional designers. But first, she'd ring up her father and tell him that the Galeries DeWilde project was right on schedule, just as she'd promised.

Megan closed her eyes. There was one task that superseded all others, even the telephone call to her father. She'd have to break the news to Phillip. They'd scheduled a lunch date for that afternoon, before she'd even known about Lacroix's decision.

He'd be angry, maybe even furious. But they had decided, that day beneath the cherry blossoms, that no matter who won the competition for the property, they would put the feuding and the fighting behind them for good.

The door to the office opened and Megan stood as Monsieur Lacroix entered the room. "Good morning, Mademoiselle DeWilde. Thank you for coming on such short notice."

She studied his expression, confused by his serious demeanor. "I've been quite anxious to get your commitment on my financing package," she said. "All of us at DeWilde's believe that Galeries DeWilde will be a great success."

The banker cleared his throat, then stepped behind his desk and distractedly straightened a stack of papers. "I'm afraid we can't proceed with your financing package, Mademoiselle DeWilde. We simply couldn't convince enough of our investors to back the project."

Megan felt as if the breath had been torn from her lungs. His words reverberated in her mind, yet she couldn't believe what he was telling her. She slowly sat down, trying to regain her composure, rubbing her suddenly icy hands together and blinking back a flood of emotion.

This couldn't be happening! DeWilde's had never had problems securing financing in the past. She had maintained an excellent relationship with her bank and they'd always been willing to do business with her, no questions asked.

"But the last time we spoke you were certain everything would be approved," she said.

"You must understand, what with your mother no longer involved, we had some concerns about this boutique concept. It was Grace DeWilde who was the driving force behind DeWilde's merchandising success. With the

French economy the way it is now, we just can't ask our investors to take such a risk."

"Why?" she asked. "My financial analysts provided you with all the statistics—demographics, sales projections, economic forecasts, everything. They've been meeting with you nearly every day. And you gave them no indication there were problems."

"It wasn't a matter of paperwork, Mademoiselle DeWilde," he said. "All your information was in order. We'd be happy to review your request in another six months."

"Six months will be too late," she said. "My offer on the property is only good until midnight tonight."

"Certainly you can get an extension on your offer," he said. "These things happen all the time, especially with a project this complex."

"I don't have time," Megan stressed, her voice betraying her desperation. "If you don't approve my financing right now, I'll lose the property."

He seemed quite astonished by her revelation. "Surely you must have a contingency plan, Mademoiselle DeWilde. Perhaps your corporate bankers in London would be able to help you. I hope you understand our position."

"Go to another bank?" she said, her voice rising a few decibels. "But the DeWildes have done their Paris banking here for years. You told me that financing for this project would be approved without a hitch."

"I'm sorry, but there is nothing we can do for you at the moment."

"There's nothing you *want* to do," she snapped. Megan grabbed her purse and briefcase, then nodded curtly at the banker. "Please have your staff prepare a summary of our accounts here, Monsieur Lacroix. I'll be looking for a new bank."

"I'm sorry to hear that. Surely we can work this problem out, given time."

"I don't have time," Megan repeated angrily. She grabbed the door before he could open it for her and stalked out. She didn't stop until she reached the street. Only then did she allow her true emotions to rise to the surface.

"This can't be," she murmured as she sat down on a bench at a bus stop. This was *her* deal, *her* responsibility. Her family was counting on her. She just couldn't fail, not after all the hard work she'd done. How could such a sweet deal have turned so sour? Everything was going so well until...

She pinched her eyes shut and an image flashed in her mind. "Phillip Villeneuve," she muttered.

Megan jumped up from the bench and hurried to the taxi stand. A taxi appeared in front of her within seconds and she got inside. "Rue de la Paix, *numéro 25*" she told the cab driver.

The driver swung the car out into traffic with all the speed-loving mania so characteristic of Parisian drivers. But for once, Megan didn't care how fast they wove through traffic. The sooner she confronted Phillip, the sooner she could put him out of her life once and for all.

The cab screeched to a halt a few minutes later in front of the building that was meant to house Galeries De-Wilde—until Phillip Villeneuve had ruined all her carefully laid plans. Megan paid the driver, then stepped out of the cab.

Why couldn't he have stayed in Hong Kong where he belonged? If he hadn't interfered, she could have had everything she wanted—the property, Galeries DeWilde, a shot at the presidency of the company when the time came.

He'd taken it all away from her and given her nothing in return but a bad case of lust.

The reception area was deserted when she arrived. She walked past the receptionist's desk and headed toward Phillip's office. Not bothering to knock, she flung his office door open.

"I hope you're happy," she snapped, her last word punctuated by the crash of the door against the wall. It was only then she learned exactly where the staff had gone. More than a dozen heads turned to look at her from Phillip's conference table.

He sat at the head of the table, a frown furrowing his brow. "I hope you're happy, too," he said. He stared at her for a long moment as if trying to read her expression, then turned back to his staff. "We'll continue our meeting at another time. It looks like Miss DeWilde has arrived early for our luncheon appointment."

Phillip slowly stood. Taking his cue, his employees efficiently gathered their papers and folders, then filed out the door. Phillip's secretary, Lei Lin, lagged behind. "Is there anything I can get for you, Miss DeWilde?"

"A bottle of arsenic might be nice," Megan replied in an icy tone.

Lei Lin closed the door behind her and Megan turned to Phillip. "I hope you're satisfied," she said, her jaw tight. "What was this, a little victory celebration? Where are the champagne and cigars?"

His frown deepened. "What are you talking about, Meggie?"

"Don't you know? Well, let me be the first to congratulate you. It's all over. The bank won't commit to my financing package. They gave me some ridiculous excuse about my mother and risk and investors. The property is yours."

Phillip blinked in surprise. "Meggie, I—"

She held up her hand to stop him. "I don't want to hear anything you have to say. You've won. This is what you wanted and now you've got it. Congratulations." Her last word was infused with bitterness.

She turned to leave, but he grabbed her hand to stop her. "Megan, this is *not* what I want. I tried to stop him, but he was determined to go through with this."

"Him?"

"The great and powerful Armand Villeneuve," he said with a sarcastic edge. "He took the whole deal out of my hands. He told me he was prepared to do whatever it took to get that property. I didn't think he was serious, and even if he was, I didn't think he'd be able to kill your deal."

Megan gasped in disbelief. "But you promised this would be a fair fight. Is this your idea of fair?"

"No, it's not at all fair. But when it comes to your family, my father doesn't operate with his ethics in gear."

"Don't you dare make excuses for him!"

"I'm not excusing what he's done," he shot back. "What the hell were your bankers thinking? Why didn't they approve your financing? Surely your financial advisers knew what they were doing."

"Don't blame my bankers! Or my staff. It's your fault. You and your father ruined my deal."

"That's not true, Megan," he said.

"Why didn't you do something to stop him?" Megan cried. "I can't lose this deal. It means too much to me— and my family. They're depending on me. This was my project!"

Phillip turned away from her and gripped the back of his chair with white-knuckled hands. Through the fine fabric of his suit jacket she watched the muscles across his back tense. "Damn it, Megan, what do you want me to do? This is my father's battle, not mine. I never wanted to get stuck in the middle of it and you know it.''

"But you are. And so am I.''

He spun around to face her. "Meggie, you have to know that I never intended to hurt you. My father has planned this revenge his entire life, saved for it, invested every penny with the intention of someday coming back here and making your family pay.''

"You could have stopped him . . . if you'd really wanted to.''

Phillip grabbed her arms and gave her a gentle shake. "Don't blame this on me. We made a pact, you and I. After this was all over, we were going to start again, no matter who won. We'd put this feud behind us. You made a promise.''

Megan twisted out of his grasp. "You don't expect me to keep that promise any more than I expected you to keep it if *you* had lost.''

"I expect you to be able to separate your business life from your personal life. I'm not part of this dispute any more than you are, and I think you realize that.''

She shook her head. "You're a Villeneuve. You're as much to blame as your father.''

He cursed beneath his breath. "That's the excuse you're going to use, then?'' He shook his head in disgust. "How convenient. And so logical. I shouldn't be surprised. You've been looking for a way out since the start.''

"What are you talking about?''

"Us,'' he said. "You're afraid—afraid of how you feel, afraid of how I *make* you feel. And most of all, you're afraid of what your family might say if they found out about us. So you use this as an excuse.''

"*I* was the one who wanted to make love on the barge,'' Megan said.

"Make love? You didn't want to make love, you wanted one night of sex, simple lust with no strings. I think you were under the misguided notion that that would be the end of it."

"Well, maybe it would have."

"Not a chance. I want more than that, Meggie. And *you* deserve much more. Until you acknowledge that, we'll never have a future."

Megan laughed bitterly. "A future? That's what you think I want with you? You're a Villeneuve, a sworn enemy of my family. I'd be safer sleeping in a pit of vipers than with you."

"I have nothing against your family and you know that. I care about you, Meggie, more than I've ever cared about a woman before."

A wave of emotion flooded her senses at his simple, heartfelt words, but Megan steeled herself against her reaction. "Don't you dare try to manipulate me. This was all part of your plan. You thought you could use me to bring my family down. Well, you may have won this round, but I won't let you win the next. If you open a retail store on rue de la Paix, I'll do everything in my power to see that it closes within a year."

With that, Megan turned and made for the door, knowing that if she stayed one second longer, she might find herself in his arms. He called her name once, but she ignored him, all the while fighting the temptation to return and make things right between them. It wasn't until she reached the street that the pain in her heart overwhelmed her.

As she walked aimlessly in the direction of DeWilde's, his words of anger and regret ran through her mind over and over again. Slowly, an unbidden realization seeped into her jumbled thoughts, a notion so startling it hit her like a slap to the face.

She forced herself to walk, and with each step recited the words like a mantra, hoping that the thoughts that raged in her mind would somehow dissipate like an ugly black cloud in the springtime breeze. But no matter how hard she tried, she couldn't ignore the emptiness that crept into her heart.

"I'm not," she murmured to herself. "I am not in love with Phillip Villeneuve. I'm not."

The more she said the words, the more she knew they weren't true. She'd fallen in love with Phillip Villeneuve.

She'd fallen in love with the enemy.

PHILLIP STRODE THROUGH the elegant lobby of the Hôtel Ritz, his footsteps echoing in the hushed silence. His mind still replayed the conversation he'd just had with Megan, every accusation like a knife to his heart. What the hell had happened? How could her bankers have backed out on her financing?

A few weeks ago, he would have popped open the champagne and celebrated his success. But all he could think about right now was making this right for Megan. He headed for the house phone and punched in his father's room number, but there was no answer.

The desk manager smiled as he approached the front desk. "May I help you, sir?"

"I'm Phillip Villeneuve," he said. "I'm looking for my father. Has he left a number where he can be reached? It's an emergency."

"Monsieur Villeneuve is having an aperitif in our terrace bar," the manager said. "After that, he has reservations for lunch at our restaurant, L'Espadon. You may find him in either place. Would you like me to announce your arrival?"

Phillip didn't bother to answer or thank the man. He turned and stalked toward the hotel bar, all the while formulating what he'd say to his father. He found Armand on the terrace, a bottle of expensive champagne open and chilling in a silver ice bucket beside him.

"Celebrating, Father?"

Armand looked up, then raised his brow. "I suppose I am. Have you come to join me?"

Phillip yanked out a chair and sat down. "What did you do? And how the hell did you do it?"

His father smiled coldly. "I assume you're talking about the rue de la Paix property?"

"You know exactly what I'm talking about. How did you do it?"

Armand poured champagne into a crystal flute then took a discerning sip. "I simply convinced the Banque de Paris to delay their decision on the DeWilde request for financing."

"You bribed her bankers?"

"Don't be foolish," Armand said. "I didn't bribe them. That would probably be illegal. I simply made it more profitable for them to deal with Villeneuve Enterprises. We'll be moving most of our money out of our Hong Kong banks and into the Banque de Paris as soon as possible. I'll leave the arrangements to you."

Phillip ground his teeth, trying to school his temper. Why couldn't he spend more than five seconds with his father without erupting in a torrent of frustration and rage? "No," he finally replied. "Absolutely not. I won't be a part of this anymore."

"Don't be foolish. You're a Villeneuve, and this is business. *Villeneuve* business."

"This is *not* business," Phillip countered. "This is your sick need for revenge against a woman you once loved. It's nothing more. For God's sake, Father, it's been sixty years. When are you going to give this up?"

"Not until I have satisfaction," Armand replied.

Phillip grabbed the champagne flute from his father's fingers and slammed it down on the table, heedless of the delicate crystal. "You talk about it like it's some eighteenth-century duel. There are no pistols, no seconds. Only people, people you're determined to hurt. People who don't deserve your wrath."

"You've gone soft, boy," his father said in disgust.

Phillip bristled at the word *boy*, a term his father had used to put him in his proper and obedient place since childhood. "Maybe I have. But it's better than being filled so full of hate you can't see yourself for what you are."

"And what am I?" Armand challenged. "Tell me, for I'm sure you have an opinion. You always do."

"You're a bitter old man," Phillip replied, lashing out with words that he knew might do irreparable damage to their already fragile relationship. He didn't care. He had tried to reason with his father, but the situation had gotten out of hand. It was time for the truth. If the truth hurt Armand Villeneuve, then so be it.

His father chuckled, as if immune to Phillip's words, and shook his head. "She did this to you, didn't she," he said.

"What the hell are you talking about?"

"That DeWilde girl. She's turned you into a besotted fool. She's used her wiles to draw you in, to trick you into taking her side. I should never have trusted you with this, should never have sent you to Paris. You've never been able to control your baser impulses with women."

"You don't know a damn thing about Megan DeWilde, or me for that matter, so don't talk like you do."

"Megan? Is that her name? Tell me, has she lured you into her bed yet?"

Phillip clenched his fists and he fought the urge to throw the table aside and take a swing at his father. He wanted to erase the knowing smirk off Armand's face, but he knew he couldn't hit him. The man was eighty years old, yet he still had the ability to egg Phillip on like a playground bully.

"That's all you can expect from DeWilde women, you know," his father continued. "They're fickle and deceitful. They care for no one except their own. They'll turn on you in an instant and make your life hell."

"I won't let you go through with this," Phillip warned.

His father shrugged. "You can't stop me. It's done. We're going to open our store right across the street from DeWilde's. And we're going to run them right out of Paris. After that, who knows? I might want to open a store in London. And after that, Sydney, or possibly New York."

"Then I'm out of it. *I'm* done."

"You'll do what I order you to do," Armand said coldly. "Or I'll—"

"Or what?" Phillip demanded. "You'll fire me? Well, don't trouble yourself, Father. I quit. You can take your job and your empire and this damn feud and stuff it."

His father scoffed and shot him a dubious look. "You can't quit," he said dispassionately. "This business is in your blood as much as it's in mine. You live and breathe Villeneuve Enterprises."

Phillip shoved out of his chair. "Not anymore. You don't need me for this. You've never really needed anyone, not me or my mother or any one of the thousands of people you employ. All you've ever needed was a way to exact your revenge. And now you have it. Enjoy it, Father. While it lasts." He turned on his heel and started for the door.

"Don't you walk out on me!" Armand shouted.

Phillip waved his hand dismissively, ignoring his father's order. As he strode back to the lobby, his temple throbbed with tension. He cursed to himself as he tried to rub it away, knowing he'd been overly harsh and impetuous. But he'd also been right. This had gone far enough. It was time for him to take a stand, and if that meant turning his back on his father, he'd damn well do it.

Megan had been hurt enough by his father's machinations and he wouldn't allow it to go on. He cared about her and he'd defend her against anyone who might try to destroy her happiness—including Armand Villeneuve.

As he walked through the lobby, past the concierge, an idea sprang to life in his mind. He stopped and turned back to the concierge. "Would you have a piece of stationery and an envelope?"

"Of course, Mr. Villeneuve." The concierge reached into his desk and withdrew a sheet of water-marked vellum and an envelope. He handed Phillip an expensive fountain pen, then discreetly turned away as Phillip scribbled a note on the paper.

When he was finished, Phillip folded the note and addressed it in his best imitation of his father's scrawl. "My father would like this delivered immediately. By messenger," he added. "Please charge his account."

"As you wish, sir," the concierge replied.

A smile lifted the corners of his mouth as he stepped outside and strolled through the place Vendôme on his way back to the office. He still had a few tricks left to try. If he couldn't stop Armand Villeneuve, maybe someone else could.

CHAPTER SEVEN

THE AIR WAS WARM and filled with the smells of spring—freshly turned soil, new grass and the tangy scent of burning grapevines. Megan stared across the wide sweep of vineyards from her position at the top of the hill. Below her, beyond the rolling rows of grapevines, the château could be seen, and past that, the river.

"These are the oldest and the best vines in the vineyard," Marie-Claire explained. "*Vieilles vignes* are what they're called. In a good year, we harvest and press the grapes from these Sauvignon vines separately. They make, perhaps, two hundred bottles of our finest Pouilly-Fumé, a lovely bouquet with a nice flinty taste. Jean-Luc's great-great-great grandparents planted these before the French Revolution. When the château was returned to the family in the last century, these vines were nearly dead from neglect. But with love and care, they survived."

Megan stared down at the ancient gnarled vines, then reached out to touch a grape leaf, listening halfheartedly to her aunt's explanation.

She'd come to Plessis to escape, to give herself time to accept her failure. Yet even after several days, it still stung. How would she explain to her family—to her father and Gabe—that she'd lost the deal for Galeries DeWilde? What would she say to the board of directors? She'd invested her future in this deal and she hadn't had the ability to make it happen.

"Megan?"

Her attention snapped back to the present. She smiled apologetically at Marie-Claire. "I'm sorry. I've been a little preoccupied, haven't I. You were telling me about the vines."

An expression of concern suffused her aunt's face. "Megan, what's wrong? What has brought you here? You seem so troubled, not at all yourself."

"Nothing is wrong," she replied, a little too quickly to be believed. "I just wanted to visit you."

Marie-Claire took Megan's hand and tucked it into hers. "If you believe you can fool me, you're wrong. I've come to know you quite well over the past five years. Perhaps I might be able to help."

Megan sighed and gave her hand a squeeze. "Would you like to be the one to tell my father that I lost the rue de la Paix property?" Her aunt's startled expression was nearly as painful as the disappointment Megan saw in her eyes.

"Oh, darling, I'm so sorry! What happened?"

Megan grabbed a strip of fabric from her great-aunt's basket and retied a grapevine to the support. "The bank wouldn't finance the project. They're concerned about how the company will fare without Mother. They consider DeWilde's a bad risk right now."

Marie-Claire handed her another strip and pointed to a vine. "I know how important this was to you. But surely there is a—"

"There's no way to fix it," she interrupted. She stared for a long moment at the sun-bleached fabric attached to the vine, then sighed. "I had a chance to prove myself and I failed. I wasn't up to the task." With clumsy fingers, she ripped off the old fabric, inwardly berating herself as she'd done so many times in the past few days.

"I'm sure Jeffrey will understand. And so will Gabe. You did your best. What more could you do?"

Megan turned back to her aunt. "What more could I do?" she asked, a cynical edge to her voice. "I could have secured the property, that's what I could have done. And you're right. Daddy and Gabe won't care. They've always been very accepting of my failures."

"Megan!" Marie-Claire cried. "What a thing to say!"

"It's true, *tante*. And it's been true since I was a child. Daddy and Gabe, and even Mother, have never had much confidence in my abilities—from piano lessons to Edward Whitney. But I was always good at DeWilde's, better than good. It's been the only place I've been able to prove myself...until now."

"You've proved yourself in so many ways, Megan. This deal will not shake their confidence in you. And don't you think you're the only person to feel the pressure of DeWilde family expectations."

Megan looked at her aunt. "What do you mean?"

"I mean, those same expectations have been around a lot longer than your thirty-some years. Look at me," Marie-Claire said with a smile. "I was always the perfect little sister. My father and brothers never expected me to be anything more than a pretty face at the dinner table. They protected me from anything that might hurt me. They thought I was weak. But I proved them wrong, Megan."

"Didn't you ever just want to run away from all the pressure?"

"Being a DeWilde was sometimes the hardest thing in the world," Marie-Claire replied.

Megan nodded. "Kate was the smart one. From the start, she wanted nothing to do with the family business. There are times I'd give anything not to be a DeWilde."

"There's nothing you can do to change your blood-lines, Megan. But you are more than just a DeWilde. You're a beautiful, brilliant woman with a gentle heart and a compassionate soul. Everyone in the family knows that."

Megan drew a deep breath and forced a smile. "There's more to this than just losing Galeries DeWilde. It gets much worse."

"Worse? How could it possibly get worse?" Marie-Claire teased.

"To add insult to injury, I lost the building to Armand Villeneuve. He was in Paris for little more than a week and he managed to kill my deal just like that."

Marie-Claire stopped, her hand tightening over Me-gan's. "Then it's true." She closed her eyes for a long mo-ment, then shook her head. "When will this end?" she murmured.

"Don't blame yourself, *tante*. It was my fault. I made a mistake in trusting our bankers. I should have written the offer differently. Or maybe gotten an extension earlier. I could have planned more carefully, maybe brought my fa-ther or Gabe into the deal. I just wanted to prove I could handle it all on my own. I guess I was wrong."

"A man filled with hate can be a ruthless enemy," Marie-Claire said softly. "If Armand truly wanted that property, I'm sure nothing you could have done would have stopped him."

They continued their walk through the old vineyard, but Marie-Claire seemed distracted as she instructed Megan on pruning techniques. Megan sensed that her aunt was deeply troubled by her news, and she regretted telling her. But she had always confided in Marie-Claire, especially now that she'd been cut off from her mother's sage coun-sel.

They silently finished the last row of vines, then gathered their tools and sat down on a small lichen-stained bench. Marie-Claire fixed her gaze on the river's lazy flow in the distance. "And what about Phillip?" she asked softly. "You haven't mentioned him."

Megan released a tightly held breath. She wasn't prepared to answer questions about Phillip. She hadn't decided exactly how she felt about him. "There's nothing to say." She studied the worn fingers of her goatskin work gloves. "There was never anything between us in the first place. Perhaps a slight attraction, but that's all. It was probably exacerbated by the fact that we really ought to hate each other. I think we were attracted because we both knew there was no way it could possibly work out."

Marie-Claire frowned in confusion. "I'm not sure I understand."

"I'm not sure I do, either. I thought a lot about this on the drive out here. Neither Phillip nor I was looking for a real relationship. We're both afraid of commitment. The attraction was doomed from the start, but it was more exciting because it was forbidden. But it's over. I want nothing more to do with Phillip Villeneuve."

Marie-Claire studied her shrewdly, her gaze penetrating Megan's nonchalant facade. "Are you sure this is how you feel? Or is this simply the way you are rationalizing the feelings you still have for him?"

"I don't have any feelings for him," Megan lied. "He means nothing to me. No more than Armand means to you."

Marie-Claire shook her head sadly. "You've fallen in love with him, haven't you."

Megan stared at her aunt and frowned. "No...I mean, I was attracted to him, that's all. He's a very charming man." She paused. "All right, maybe I loved him, a little bit."

"And you would throw away these feelings because of the tension between our families?"

Megan rose from the bench and paced restlessly in front of her aunt. "*Tante,* I have a responsibility to my family. I've already let them down once with Edward. I won't disappoint them again. Phillip Villeneuve means nothing to me."

Marie-Claire stood and idly brushed a spot of dirt off her canvas apron. "I once tried to convince myself that I felt that way about Armand. I wanted so much to forget him that I married another man. That didn't make the love I felt disappear. Denying it only made it stronger."

"This is different," Megan said.

"Is it?" she asked. "Don't make the mistake of ignoring what's in your heart for the sake of some misguided notion of family loyalty."

"Misguided? How can you say that? Family makes all the difference."

"And sometimes it should make no difference at all," Marie-Claire replied. She reached into her pocket and withdrew a folded piece of paper. "I received this earlier today. I wasn't sure I should tell you, but perhaps it's best that you know."

Megan unfolded the note, written on elegant, gold-embossed Ritz stationery, and scanned the message, her trepidation growing with each word she read. "Are you going to see him?"

"I hadn't planned to respond. Why would Armand want to see me?"

"Maybe he wants to gloat," Megan said, her words dripping with sarcasm.

"After what you've told me, you may be right. I just never expected him to return to France. I never thought I would see him again."

"Don't go," Megan said. "He's made his intentions quite clear. He's out to ruin our family and make you suffer in the process."

Marie-Claire took the note from Megan's fingers, then studied it intently. "Perhaps if I see him, I can convince him to forget his quest for revenge," she said in a hopeful tone. "I can't help but think that if I'd only reached out to him sooner, none of this would have happened. You wouldn't have been hurt."

Megan knew she should try to stop her aunt, but she'd seen all too well the power of the Villeneuve vendetta. Perhaps Marie-Claire was the only one who could put an end to it. She'd been there when it began. She'd loved Armand Villeneuve and he'd once loved her.

"I'll go with you," Megan offered.

Her aunt shook her head. "I think it would be best if I met with him alone. The invitation is for lunch tomorrow. There will be other patrons in the restaurant so I'm sure I'll be safe."

Megan paused for a long moment. "Do you think he stole the jewels, *tante?*"

Her aunt carefully folded the note, almost caressing the paper with her fingers before she put it back into her apron pocket. "He certainly had a good reason. Being accused by my family and given no chance to defend himself was not something easily forgotten."

"But if he stole them, he has to pay for his crime," Megan said.

"And what good would that do?" Marie-Claire challenged. "Would that change the past? Would it bring back all that we've lost, all the years? We've all been paying the price for this feud. Perhaps it's time we simply refused. Perhaps it's time *I* refused to take any more."

Megan reached out and drew her aunt back to the bench. "You don't have to do this," she said. "I can handle the Villeneuves on my own."

Marie-Claire patted the back of her hand. "When I was younger, I used to dream about Armand. And after he left, those dreams stayed with me. I still find myself looking for his face in a crowd, wondering where he is and how he is. Now I have the chance to find out for myself. I want to see him, Megan. It's time."

Megan smiled. "Then you need to go."

They sat on the bench for a few minutes longer, both of them silently staring down at the river. Megan couldn't help but hope that her aunt would find a way to end the feud between the DeWildes and the Villeneuves.

Deep in her heart, she wanted another chance with Phillip, an opportunity to see what they shared after all the enmity was stripped away. She wanted to know if what she felt for him was really love, for she knew the emotion was much deeper than any she'd ever experienced before.

They needed a chance. They deserved a chance. And maybe, if she hoped hard enough, they'd get just that.

MARIE-CLAIRE CLUTCHED the note in her hand as she stood on the sidewalk in front of the Hôtel Ritz. The unassuming facade did nothing to hint at the luxuries to be found inside, for the Ritz was considered the most exclusive of Paris hotels. Set on the place Vendôme, it was surrounded by shops of equal exclusivity—Boucheron, Cartier, Chaumet and Piaget. She couldn't help but think Armand had chosen this place for what it said about himself.

He was a man of power and great wealth, a man who was not afraid to wield that power against his enemies. But why did he want to see her now, after all these years? Did he simply want to gloat, or was he hoping that she might beg him to spare her family any more trouble?

"Would you like me to accompany you inside?" Oliver asked.

Marie-Claire turned to her driver and smiled weakly. "I would very much like that, Oliver," she said, "but I don't think it will be necessary. Mr. Villeneuve and I are... old friends." She stared for a long moment at the bronze column that marked the center of the place Vendôme. Old friends? Would he greet her with a smile? Or would he be like that monument, rigid and unmoving, rooted in the past?

Her hand fluttered to her hair and she tried to imagine what it would be like to come face-to-face with the man she had loved all those years ago. Would time dissolve between them and would they find that things had not changed? Or would she look upon a man she did not know, a man who was nothing like the wonderful, handsome, dashing Armand she'd wanted to marry?

"It might be best if you wait," Marie-Claire said. "I'm not sure how long I'll be."

She smoothed the skirt of her blue Chanel suit. The shade of blue she wore now had been his favorite, azure, the same shade as the party dress she'd worn the night they'd been introduced. The strains of a Strauss waltz drifted through her mind and she could almost hear the rustle of silk and the smell of the gardenia corsage her father had bought her. She'd been only sixteen that night, but she had known with a woman's certainty that she would spend her life with Armand.

Summoning sixty years of courage, she stepped up to the door and waited as a uniformed doorman pulled it open for her. She had to force her feet to move, one in front of the other, as she slowly walked through the opulent lobby toward the restaurant. The note had requested her presence at lunch at L'Espadon, the hotel's garden restaurant. She glanced at her watch and saw that she was already ten minutes late. She also noticed the tremble in her hand.

Clasping her fingers around her handbag, she approached the maître d'. "Mr. Villeneuve's table," she said, the tremble now evident in her voice. "He is expecting me."

"This way," he said. He led her through the maze of tables until he found the proper one. He pulled out the elegant chair, but she refused to sit down. Instead, she gazed upon the man who had left her all those years ago, the man who had visited her dreams, the man who had taught her to love. If she had met him on the street, she wasn't sure she would have recognized him. The planes and angles of his face were the same as she'd remembered—only harder, less forgiving.

"Hello, Armand," she said.

He glanced up from the menu he studied. At first, she saw no recognition in his eyes, then slowly, confusion was replaced with an icy disdain. "What are you doing here?"

Marie-Claire held out the note as if it were the only proof she had that she was not caught in some bizarre nightmare. He snatched it from her fingers, read it, then tossed it on the linen-covered table. "I didn't send that. It looks like something my son might have done. He can be overly sentimental at times."

She stiffened her spine. "You didn't want me to meet you here?"

"I have nothing to say to you or any DeWilde."

Bristling, Marie-Claire slid into her place at the table and looked directly into his indifferent expression. She snatched her napkin up and neatly arranged it on her lap. "Well, I have something to say to you," she replied stubbornly.

Armand grabbed his own napkin and dropped it on the table, then moved to stand.

"You're a coward, Armand de Villeneuve," Marie-Claire said.

His brow arched imperiously. "You've come all this way to tell me that?"

"I've come all this way hoping that you and I might put an end to this feud once and for all, before anyone else gets hurt."

He slowly sat back down. "What would you know about hurt?" he demanded.

"Do you think I was happy when we broke our engagement?" she countered. "I was devastated."

"Devastated enough to marry a few months later?"

Marie-Claire winced at the bitterness in his voice. "You were gone," she said softly. "I didn't think I'd ever see you again. What was I supposed to do?"

The waiter diplomatically appeared beside their table. She waited while Armand ordered another glass of wine, taking it as a sign that she'd be given a bit more time to plead her case.

A few moments later, he turned his attention back to her. "Was there something else you wanted to say, or will you be leaving now?"

"Are you aware that your son is seeing my grand-niece?"

For an instant, she noticed a crack in his impenetrable expression, but he recovered quickly.

"You didn't know?" she continued.

"Of course I knew. And I warned him against seeing her."

"I don't care what you do to me, Armand. And our family business is strong enough to survive whatever you throw our way. But I will not allow you to hurt my niece."

"Then tell your niece to stay out of my way."

"My niece is a very determined woman," Marie-Claire said. "What will it take to make her happy? Megan wants that property for her new store. I will give you anything I have. I have money, property, jewelry. I could buy the building from you."

"The building belongs to Villeneuve Enterprises. It's not for sale."

"She's in love with your son," Marie-Claire said.

"Many women have loved Phillip," Armand replied. "He has money and charm, both in abundance. He must have had some good reason for seducing your niece."

"Or maybe the reason is yours," she said. "Maybe you have poisoned him against our family and he sees hurting Megan as a way to hurt all the DeWildes."

"You give my son too much credit." He paused and chuckled humorlessly. "Or perhaps I haven't given him enough."

"What do you want from me? Would you like me to apologize? I'm sorry for anything I did to hurt you—real or imagined."

"Imagined? Did I imagine your brothers, Dirk and Charles, appearing at my family's home to accuse me of cheating on you? Did I imagine the embarrassment I felt for my parents when our engagement was called off? Or Dirk's threat to kill me if I ever came near you again? Or Henry trying to beat me up when I came to see you?"

"I—I didn't know."

"You believed them," he said bitterly. "Your letter said it all. You sided with your family and not me. That told me all I needed to know."

"Was I wrong?" she asked softly.

"Does that make a difference?" he countered.

"Yes," she said. "I believe it does. I'd like to hear the truth—from you."

Armand pushed back his chair and stood. "I was faithful to you," he said. "I loved you. Your brothers lied."

With that, he turned and stalked out of the dining room with the same graceful, long-legged stride that she'd seen in her dreams so many times. She closed her eyes, and suddenly, all the years seemed to fade away. She saw the boy she'd once loved. In her heart, she believed that boy was still there, buried deep inside Armand.

But a lifetime of armor, wrought from the strongest of emotions, had created an impenetrable shield around him. And she wasn't sure she had the determination to break it down or the strength to face the man hiding inside. All she knew was that she had to try. Megan and Phillip had a chance to capture what she and Armand had lost so long ago.

They had a chance to find a love that could last a lifetime.

NIGHT HAD DESCENDED on the château at Plessis. Megan stood at the tall diamond-paned window in her second-floor room, watching for her aunt's car to come up the long, winding drive. She shivered against a draft, then pulled her robe more closely around her.

Marie-Claire had left early in the day for her luncheon with Armand. She'd phoned Claudette to say she had decided to stay in Paris and do some shopping, then have dinner with friends before returning to Plessis. It was only eight now, but Megan couldn't help but be anxious. The stores closed early on Saturdays and the drive back to Plessis was only a couple of hours at the most.

Her aunt's phone call had not hinted at the success or failure of her meeting with Phillip's father. Megan could only hope there was no longer a feud, for then there would be no reason for Armand Villeneuve to open a store on rue de la Paix... and no reason for her to stay away from Phillip.

She frowned. But if there weren't a store, would there be a reason for Phillip to stay in Paris? No matter what happened, she seemed to be doomed either way.

She reached out and traced her finger along the lead mullions between the old panes, peering out into the dark through the swirled glass. Why couldn't she put him out of her mind? She'd never had this problem with Edward, this uncontrollable infatuation that shredded her concentration and jangled her nerves and made her long for the time she might touch him again. Phillip's image drifted through her mind and she closed her eyes and lingered over it like a sip of fine wine.

What would happen if there was nothing to stand between them? Would the attraction that flamed like a white-hot fire burn out of control? Or would it suddenly dim? Would they enjoy a brief but satisfying affair, or would they look to the future? She'd tried to imagine a future with him, but she couldn't.

She'd made such a mess of her relationship with Edward. But from that chaos she'd learned one important fact. Megan DeWilde was not meant for marriage. Her career came first, well before a personal life and a relationship with a man.

Besides, introducing Phillip at the next family gathering would cause untold uproar. She could just imagine

Gabe and her father grabbing him by the scruff of the neck and tossing him out the door—and her right after. If Phillip's father really had stolen part of the DeWilde family collection, there would be no forgiveness and acceptance, only accusations and recriminations. Megan made a mental note to call Nick Santos when she returned to Paris. Surely, he must have some news on his investigation.

Turning from the window, she walked over to the fireplace and stared down at the embers. She poked idly at the fire, then returned to her bed. The bed she slept on at Plessis was several centuries old. When she first visited the château as a child, she'd chosen this room because of the bed. She had pretended to be a princess, perched high upon the soft mattresses, surrounded by brocade curtains and thick down pillows. The kingdom had been at her command and she felt as if her life were perfect.

And only a few short years ago she might have thought her dream had come true. But silly childhood dreams weren't meant to last a lifetime. Her engagement had ended in disaster, her family was falling apart before her eyes, and her professional life was at an all-time low. To top it all off, she'd managed to fall in love with the son of her family's worst enemy.

How had all this happened? Megan had made a point of living her life in a very orderly and rational manner. She'd always tried to conduct herself as the rest of her family had, with a keen sense of purpose and an unwavering attention to decorum. Now she couldn't keep her own life from spinning out of control.

Megan crawled into bed and pulled the covers up to her chin. Closing her eyes, she tried to clear her mind of all the worries and stress of the past few days, but a cold draft teased at her face. As she reached up to untie the cords that held the bed curtains to the ornately carved bedposts, a knock sounded at her door.

She sat up and ran her fingers through her hair. "Come in," she called.

Claudette, her aunt's housekeeper, appeared at the door. "You have a visitor, Mademoiselle Megan," she said.

Megan frowned. "Company? Here?" She swung her feet to the floor. "Is it Gabe? Or my father?"

Her aunt's housekeeper shook her head. "Phillip Villeneuve is here. Should I tell him to leave?"

Megan scrambled out of her bed and grabbed her robe, then stopped herself. "Yes," she said emphatically, "tell him to leave."

Claudette quickly turned to do as she was told.

"Wait," Megan cried. She fought back a surge of temptation. She wanted to see him, to touch him, to look into his eyes and be assured that everything would work out between them. But she already knew that it couldn't be so. "No, no, tell him to go."

Claudette stood at the door for a long while, watching Megan inquisitively.

"All right," Megan finally said. "I will see him. I'll tell him to leave myself. Have him wait in the library. I'll be down in a moment."

She raced to her dressing table and ran a brush through her hair, then smoothed the collar of her deep blue silk robe. What was he doing here? And how had he found her?

There was no time for makeup, so Megan finished with a dab of perfume and hurried out of her room. The stone stairs were cold beneath her feet, but she didn't bother to go back for her slippers.

When she walked into the library, he was standing with his back to her, his hand braced on the mantel, his gaze fixed on the cold grate. She silently watched him, taking in his leather jacket and casual attire. He seemed less imposing, more vulnerable in everyday clothes.

He slowly turned around, as if he had sensed her presence. His face was unshaven and he looked as if he hadn't slept in the past twenty-four hours. He ran his fingers through his hair and smiled hesitantly. "I didn't expect you to be here."

"You—you didn't come to see me?" Megan asked.

"You mentioned Plessis that night on the barge. I stopped at the local bistro and asked directions. I really came here to talk to your aunt."

"She's in Paris. She got a note from your father asking to meet him for lunch. I think they may be trying to put an end to this feud. It's a positive sign, your father sending the note, don't you think?"

"I sent the note," Phillip said. "I asked my father to meet me for lunch at his hotel. Then I arranged for your aunt to meet him there instead. I thought if I threw them together they might be able to make amends."

"Marie-Claire hasn't returned from Paris."

"It didn't go well," Phillip said, a grim expression settling on his face. "My father was so angry he stormed into my hotel suite and ordered me back to Hong Kong. From what I understand, he made quite a scene in the restaurant. I hoped I might apologize to your aunt for my mistake."

"Marie-Claire should be back...soon." Megan pointed to the sofa. "Would you like to sit down? You look tired."

Phillip shook his head wearily. "I tried, Megan. I tried to make this trouble between our families go away. But there's not much chance of that happening, according to my father."

She sat instead and folded her hands across her lap. "Are—are you going back to Hong Kong?" she asked, the question echoing in the hollow spaces of her heart.

"I don't know." Phillip sighed. "I guess I don't have to since I no longer have a job waiting there for me."

"What?"

He shrugged. "In a moment of extreme frustration, I tendered my resignation. I no longer work at Villeneuve Enterprises. And after today's disaster, I suspect I've already been legally disowned."

"You quit your job?" Megan asked. "But—but you can't just quit. It's your family. You don't *quit* your family."

"Well, I did," Phillip said.

"What will you do?"

Phillip raked his fingers through his hair again. "I don't feel as if I can leave Paris. Not until things are settled here. Between your aunt and my father." He gazed into her eyes. "And between you and me."

Megan rubbed her arms against the chill in the air and fought the urge to stand and step into his warm embrace. "I've been thinking about what you said yesterday in your office. Things have become very... complicated between us. With all that's going on, it's hard for me to know how I feel. And—and I'm really not ready for a relationship, physical or otherwise."

"I'm sorry for what I said, Meggie. I don't blame you for being confused—or for mistrusting my motives. There was a time, not too long ago, that I wouldn't have thought twice about using any means to achieve a business goal."

"And now?"

"I see what this vendetta has done to my father and I don't like what I see. I won't be a part of it anymore."

"They were in love once," Megan said.

"I have a hard time believing my father capable of loving anyone."

"He loved Marie-Claire. And I'm sure, in his own way, he loves you."

Phillip chuckled mirthlessly. "Why would you think that? Because he spent his life building a business empire to leave to his only son? He built Villeneuve Enterprises in order to finance the demise of DeWilde's."

"You're not your father," Megan said. "And I know you'd never deliberately hurt me."

Phillip sat down beside her, then reached out and stroked her cheek. "I'm my father's son, though. And I've already hurt you. I took the property away from you."

"Your father did that, not you." His thumb traced her lower lip and she felt a shiver of desire skitter down her spine. One night, that's all she wanted with him, just one night together, in each other's arms, far away from the outside world.

"When I met you," Phillip said, "I wanted you more than any other woman I'd ever met. Now all I want is for you to be happy again. From the moment I walked into your life, I've caused you trouble. Perhaps it would be best if I went back to Hong Kong."

Megan covered his hand with hers, pressing her cheek into his warm palm. "It's not going to work out between us," she admitted, trying to steady her tremulous voice. "I've gone over and over it, trying to find a way. But there's too much history between our families. No matter what we do, someone will get hurt."

Phillip pressed his lips together in a tight line and nodded his agreement. "I think I've known that from the start." He leaned closer and kissed her cheek. He stared into her eyes for a long time and she fought back tears of frustration and regret. "Tell your aunt that I'm sorry for any embarrassment or pain that I caused her."

Megan nodded. "I will."

"Goodbye, Meggie," he said softly. "Take care."

"Goodbye, Phillip," she murmured.

He stood and walked to the door, then turned back to look at her once more. With every beat of her heart, she willed him to stay, to tell her they could work it out somehow. But she knew as well as he that they were better off apart.

Claudette appeared in the doorway of the library a few moments later. "Are you all right, Mademoiselle Megan?"

Megan took a deep breath and forced a smile. "I'm fine, Claudette, just fine." She stood and pushed her trembling hands into the pockets of her robe. "I'm just very tired. I—I think I'll go to bed now."

MEGAN GROANED and threw off the bed covers. Somewhere, in the depths of the house, a clock chimed midnight. Since Phillip had left two hours ago, she had tried to sleep. But every time she'd closed her eyes, images of them together had plagued her thoughts.

She sat up in bed and began to punch her pillow. "I'm better off without him," she muttered, emphasizing each word with a blow to the pillow. "It never would have worked. Never in a million years."

Flopping back on the bed, she pinched her eyes closed and willed herself to fall asleep. But a few minutes later, she grabbed her robe and was up again, this time pacing the floor beside the bed.

"Why am I bothered by this?" she asked. "It's over. It never really got started. It's not like we actually said the words." She closed her eyes. "We never said we loved each other."

She walked across the room and pushed the window open, then leaned out. Resting her elbows on the sill, she drew in a deep gulp of the crisp night air. Soft gray clouds scudded across the night sky, playing with the light of the moon on the long lawn in front of the château. She reached out as if she might touch the moon, as if it might somehow fill the empty space in her heart. The breeze billowed the soft, full sleeves of her robe.

"But I could have loved you," she murmured into the wind. "If we'd been born different people, I would have loved you."

"You look beautiful," a voice called.

Startled, Megan straightened, then searched the darkness below her window. A tall, lean figure stepped out of the shadows and looked up at her. Her heart stopped for a moment as she recognized Phillip's face.

"I thought you'd left," she said in a loud whisper.

His gaze locked with hers and he slowly shook his head. "I tried, but I couldn't," he replied. "I've been driving around for the past hour, trying to figure out a way to make this work, and I think I understand it now. I would have been back earlier, but I got lost."

"Phillip, please. Don't make this any more difficult than it is."

"This shouldn't be difficult, Meggie," he shouted. "We want each other. It's that simple."

"Shhh," she warned in a loud whisper. "You'll wake up the servants." She paused. "And you think this is simple? Look at us. It's always going to be this way, this huge distance between us. Every time we try to build a bridge, it just topples under the pressure."

"Then we have to keep trying, Meggie. Maybe we're just going about it the wrong way."

"I can't," she cried. She put her fingers in her ears. "I'm not going to listen to you anymore, Phillip Villeneuve. Now, get out of here. Go back to Paris and mend fences with your father. All this confusion is giving me a headache."

He glanced around, then moved to grasp a copper drainpipe. "I'm coming up," he said. Bracing his feet against the stone wall, he nimbly shinnied up the pipe.

Megan gasped and gripped the windowsill with white-knuckled fingers. "Get down from there! Don't climb on that thing! You'll fall."

"I've climbed rock faces far worse than this," he muttered, finding a toehold on a windowsill below her. She watched uneasily as he climbed higher and higher. When he reached the level of the window, he swung his leg out and caught the edge of the sill. She grabbed his foot and held on for dear life, knowing she was the only thing between him and the hard cobblestone driveway below.

Before she knew it, he was in the room, standing in front of her, so close she could feel the heat of his body on her cool skin. He stared down into her eyes with a gaze so intense a surge of warmth flooded her body. She shivered, but she wasn't cold.

"You made it," she said softly, patting her hand on his chest to prove he was real. His heart thudded beneath her fingers and she hesitantly pulled them away.

He grasped her hand and pressed her palm back against his chest. "Were you worried?"

She shrugged. "Maybe. A little bit."

Phillip grinned in satisfaction. "Then you do care."

"I never said I didn't care about you!" she snapped. "I just didn't want to see you splattered on the drive."

"And I never said I didn't care about you," he countered.

She reached up and placed her hand over his lips. "Stop it," she ordered. "No talking. Every time we talk, things just get worse. Maybe we should be quiet for a while and see how it goes."

"I can do that," he said beneath her hand.

She slowly pulled her fingers away and waited. They stood in front of the window for a long time, staring into each other's eyes. Slowly, Phillip reached down and cupped her face in his hands. His thumbs caressed her lips. "Tell me what you want, Meggie," he whispered. "But don't tell me to leave, because I won't."

She swallowed hard, fighting the impulse to turn and run from the room. But she'd been advancing and retreating for far too long. It was time to stand and fight for what she really wanted. Time to forget family loyalty. "Perhaps you should just—just kiss me," she said in a shaky voice. "If you kiss me, everything will be all right. Everything is always right when you kiss me."

Suddenly, his mouth was on hers, soft and gentle. He deepened the kiss, becoming more urgent and demanding. Megan knew there would be no going back. No matter how much she wanted to deny it, she wanted him. And he wanted her. They'd waited far too long.

All her defenses dropped beneath his touch. His hands drifted down to the sash of her robe and he worked at the knot with his fingers. The robe fell open and he stepped back to gaze down at her. Slowly, he traced a line along her neck to her collarbone, his finger drawing a lazy, tingling path.

"God, you're beautiful," he murmured. "You're the most beautiful thing I've ever laid eyes on."

Megan felt her cheeks flame and she turned away in embarrassment at his words. But he took her chin between his fingers and made her face him again.

"Don't ever doubt what I say, Meggie. I've never lied to you."

"It's just that... you said that to me the night we met."

"Tu es belle," he murmured. "I remember."

"No one had ever said that to me before."

"Then no one has ever looked at you the way I do," he replied.

She took a deep breath. "What do you see, Phillip?"

His gaze lingered for a moment on her body, then he looked up and met her gaze. "I see a passionate, desirable woman. A woman I want to touch. A woman I want to make love to. A woman I can't resist."

He stepped away from her and reached out to close the windows. Then he turned and crossed the room, flipping the lock on the door before turning back to her.

"What are you doing?" she asked.

"I'm shutting out the rest of the world," he said. "We're alone now and I'm not about to let anything—or anyone—come between us. This is the way it should have been from the start, Meggie. Just you and me. No one else."

He returned to her side, then took her hand and led her toward the bed. He sat down on the edge of the mattress and drew her to stand between his legs. Slowly, he reached up and pushed her silk robe over her shoulders. It slid to the floor and pooled around her bare feet. She watched him, waiting for him to make the next move, knowing that if she said or did anything, she might make a total hash of it.

Phillip took her hands in his, then guided her to the buttons of his shirt. "Do you remember that night on the barge, Meggie?"

She nodded nervously, unable to take her eyes off his handsome face, his hooded eyes and sculpted lips.

"You wanted to make love to me that night on the boat," he said. "Do it now, Meggie. Do what you wanted to do that night."

Megan blinked in surprise. "But I—I'd had too much champagne. I—I've really never been—very good at this."

"Then you've never been with a man who appreciates you for who you are," he replied, twisting a lock of her hair around his finger. "Whatever you are is exactly what I want. Make love to me, Megan."

Bolstered by his words, she forced a smile. "All right." She hesitantly reached out and pushed his jacket off his shoulders, then waited.

He brushed his thumb along the length of her arm and she felt a slow shiver follow in the wake of his touch. "Good start," he said with a quiet chuckle.

Megan scowled at him. "Must you torment me all the time?"

He grinned as her nervous fingers worked at the buttons of his shirt. Her fingers brushed against the bare skin of his chest and he moaned softly. She froze and bit her bottom lip at the sound, certain that she'd done something wrong.

"I believe you're the one tormenting me," he said. Phillip leaned back on the bed and Megan's gaze fell on the muscles of his abdomen as they flexed and rippled. He drew the bed curtains shut behind him and then, reaching around her, did the same on her side of the bed. Clasping her hand in his, he guided her up onto the bed, into the soft depths of the thick mattress and the down-filled duvet. She sat back on her heels as darkness enveloped them.

"I can't see," she said softly. "How can I make love to you if I can't see?"

He pressed her hand against his naked chest. "You don't need to see," he replied. "You just need to feel."

She felt his quickened heartbeat beneath her palm. Without sight, her other senses became more attuned to him, her hands absorbing the hard warmth of his skin, the spicy scent of his cologne teasing her nose. He knelt in front of her and brushed the straps of her nightgown down over her shoulders.

Slowly, they undressed each other, each article of clothing disappearing into the darkness right along with her inhibitions. When the last barrier between them had been discarded, he slipped his arm around her waist and pulled her against him, blind to all but the sensation of skin against skin, hot and smooth like warm satin sheets.

Somewhere in the midst of their passion she realized she was no longer the aggressor, they had become equals. She closed her eyes and tipped her head back as Phillip buried his face in the curve of her neck, unable to hold back his own desires any longer. His mouth moved across her skin, branding each inch with a tingling heat until she felt as if she were a slow, smoldering ember, ready to ignite.

And then his mouth found her breast. As he drew her nipple between his lips, she burst into flame. She cried out, the sound catching in her throat. She was on fire, hot and out of control, her hands frantically skimming over the muscle and sinew of his body until she found the core of his desire, warm and hard in her hand.

Slowly, she stroked him, each movement causing him to draw a sharp breath as her hand slipped along the silky length of him. "Make love to me," Phillip urged. "Please, Meggie."

She smiled to herself, suddenly realizing the power she held over him, the power she'd always possessed simply by being a woman. But she'd never wanted to wield that power until now. She'd never wanted a man to love her as much as she did Phillip. Gently she pushed him back into the pillows, then straddled his thighs. She moved above him until his hard shaft brushed her moist entrance. Sinking down over him, she felt a low moan tear from her throat.

And then he was inside her, his erection filling her until she thought she could take no more. He twisted beneath her, trying to move, but she remained resolute. Finally he stilled, and after a few moments, she began to move on him, rocking slowly.

"God, Meggie, you're driving me mad," he whispered, his hands skimming over her breasts.

She bent over him and brushed his hair from his forehead, drawing her tongue along the curve of his eyebrow, kissing his eyelids in turn. And then she found his mouth and he arched up to meet her lips, bracing his hands behind him and drinking her in like a man parched with thirst.

He wrapped her legs around his waist and pulled her beneath him, pressing her into the bed. His control shattered as he shifted his hips against her and began to move, each thrust deeper than the last, more urgent, more perfect. A warm quiver spread through her body then focused at the place where they were intimately joined.

Her desire seemed to grow by degrees with each movement he made, and she felt herself hurtling toward the inevitable. She'd never been more alive, yet closer to dying, and she wanted to experience it all with him, the dizzying heights, the shattering climax and the slow, delicious fall back to reality.

He pressed his hand between them and touched her there and suddenly she was on the edge. "Let go, Meggie," he whispered in her ear. "Don't hold back. Give yourself to me."

The words barely registered through the haze of passion that surrounded her, but she closed her eyes and let her mind focus on the torrent of sensation that rushed through her body. And then she was there, at the precipice. She felt him tense and knew he was near. She shifted beneath him and they both stepped closer.

Suddenly, a thousand stars exploded around her and she cried out his name as she found her release. He joined her, reaching his climax and spiraling down into the night, then collapsed against her, burying his face between her breasts.

They lay perfectly still for a long time, drifting lazily back to reality. When his breathing finally slowed, Megan gently eased away from him and drew the curtain back, letting in a small measure of light. She looked down at him and smiled.

"What?" he asked sleepily.

"Nothing," she said.

"No, tell me."

She shrugged. "It's never been that way for me before."

"Or for me," he murmured, sliding his fingers through the hair at her nape and drawing her near, brushing his lips against hers.

"What do we do now?" she asked. "I mean, I don't want to fall asleep."

He smiled lazily and pulled her against his side. "I think I need to rest for a while, sweetheart."

"I—I meant tomorrow. And the next day, and the next."

He gently kissed her forehead. "That's up to you, Meggie. What do you want?"

"I don't know," she said. "Couldn't we just stay in this bed for the rest of our lives?"

He nuzzled her ear. "That's fine by me."

She nestled into the curve of his arm. "Then that's what we'll do," she said softly.

But in her heart, she knew the morning would come, and with it, all the issues that had yet to be resolved between them. For now, she just wanted to push the world away and enjoy the feel of her body touching his. She would deal with the real world in her own time and in her own way.

CHAPTER EIGHT

PHILLIP STOOD OVER the bed, half dressed, and watched her sleep. Lord, she looked beautiful, her dark hair fanned out on the white pillow, her face so peaceful and content, as if she hadn't a care in the world.

They'd shut out that chaotic world last night when they'd made love. An image of her drifted through his thoughts...Megan below him, above him, around him, her face flushed with passion, her eyes bright with desire.

Their lovemaking had only proved that they were made for each other. She fit so perfectly against his body, responded so ardently to his touch. In the past, he'd only cared about his own needs, but last night, he'd wanted more than anything to please her, to prove the depth of his feelings by the intensity of his actions.

He fought the temptation to crawl back into bed with her, to wake her slowly with his touch, to kiss the sleep from her eyes and make love to her again. To retreat into the safe world they'd created for themselves in the dark of night.

If only it were that easy, to pull the bed curtains and shut out all that stood between them. But with the light of day came the cold reality that their problems could not be so easily brushed aside.

He listened to a car pull up the drive and knew at that instant that the world could not be kept at bay. With soft steps, he walked to the window and watched as Megan's aunt emerged from her car, aided by her driver. Then he returned to the bed and took a long last look at Megan. "Sleep, Meggie," he murmured. "And dream of how it was between us, how it was when we shut the world out. Maybe it will be that way again . . . soon."

He quickly finished buttoning his shirt, then tugged on his shoes. When he had retrieved his jacket, he bent over her once more and kissed the tips of his fingers before pressing them to her soft lips. She stirred for a moment at his touch, then drifted back into her deep sleep.

"*A bientôt,* sweetheart," he whispered. "I'll count the minutes until I see you again."

He moved to the window and pushed it open. The car still sat in the drive where it had been parked, but no one was about. He swung his leg over the windowsill, then easily caught hold of the drainpipe and shinnied down. When his feet hit the ground, he quickly turned away from the house and headed for the road, where he'd left his car. But a voice stopped him and he froze for a moment.

"You look very much like him," the woman said in a quiet voice.

He slowly turned and met the curious gaze of Megan's aunt, Marie-Claire, watching from the open doorway. They stood that way for a long moment, not speaking, Marie-Claire staring at him as if she'd come upon a ghost.

Phillip glanced up at Megan's window, then back at Marie-Claire, knowing that she'd most likely seen everything. What was he supposed to do in this situation? An apology seemed entirely inappropriate. Acting as if nothing had happened seemed hypocritical. "I—I actually came here to see you," he finally said, figuring honesty was the best choice.

She arched her brow. "Did you?"

"I wanted to apologize for setting you up with my father. I had hoped that you two might work out your differences, but I'm afraid I made a mistake."

Marie-Claire watched him warily, then glanced up at Megan's window. "Do you love her?" she asked.

Her blunt question startled Phillip, and for a moment he wasn't sure how to answer. Did he love Megan? He knew he felt something for her that he'd never felt in his life. When they'd been wrapped in each other's arms, the words had been on his lips. But was it love? Or was it merely passion. "I'm not sure," he said, knowing she'd be able to sense a lie. "I think I might. But love has never been a part of my life, thanks to my father. I'm not sure I'd recognize it."

Marie-Claire smiled regretfully. "I am sorry you never had the chance to know the Armand that I knew. He was a warm and wonderful and very brave man, capable of much love." She held out her hand. "Come. I was about to have Claudette prepare breakfast. I'd like you to join me."

She slipped her arm through his and they walked toward the front door as if he were a welcomed guest rather than a sworn enemy. He looked up at Megan's window once more, wondering what her aunt actually thought of his climbing out her bedroom window. She certainly couldn't approve, but then she didn't seem particularly upset, either.

Marie-Claire led him through the house to a small breakfast room at the rear. The table had already been set and the housekeeper who had answered the door the previous night now fussed over a vase of fresh flowers. She turned to welcome Marie-Claire, then stopped short when she saw Phillip.

"Monsieur Villeneuve is going to join me for breakfast," Marie-Claire said. "Would you set another place for him, Claudette?"

Claudette regarded him with a suspicious look, then nodded curtly. "Would you like me to wake Mademoiselle Megan?" she asked.

"No," Marie-Claire replied. "I believe we should let her sleep, don't you think?" She turned to Phillip inquisitively, a smile quirking the corners of her lips.

Unnerved by her knowing gaze, Phillip cleared his throat. "I think that would be best," he murmured.

He pulled out her chair and she sat down, then indicated a spot next to her at the table, all the while watching him. "You'll forgive me if I stare. It's just that you bear such a striking resemblance to your father as a young man."

"It's hard to imagine my father as a younger man," Phillip said.

She poured him a cup of coffee and passed him a pitcher of steamed milk. "Your father and I fell in love at a very difficult time," she began. "Talk of war seemed to be on everyone's lips."

"You were young," Phillip said.

She took a sip of coffee and nodded thoughtfully. "We were sixteen when we first met. Two years later, we were deeply in love. I was frightened that he might have to fight, but he was ready. He would have given his life for France. Every night we pored over the newspapers, wondering how the war would affect our future together. We decided that we wanted to marry immediately, and at first, both our families approved."

"What happened?" Phillip asked, curious about the man who had raised him.

"Has he never told you?" she asked, surprised.

Phillip shook his head. "My father has told me nothing about his life before he moved to Hong Kong. My mother didn't even know of his past, only that he came from a very wealthy and well-respected Parisian family. Whenever the subject came up, he'd become cold and unresponsive, almost angry."

Marie-Claire sighed. "I never realized until now how much pain I must have caused him. You see, my brothers came to me shortly before we were to be married and told me that Armand was...involved...with a dancer from the Moulin Rouge. They had proof, a letter they intercepted from this woman to Armand. I was young and naive and I believed them. I broke our engagement."

"Were your brothers telling the truth?"

Marie-Claire shook her head. "Yesterday your father told me that he'd been faithful to me, and I believe him."

"My father is not a man who lies," Phillip said.

"I think I've known that all along. But I was just a girl with very little experience in these matters. I had to trust my family. I believed that they had my best interests at heart."

"Then this whole feud between our families began with a lie?" Phillip asked. "A lie perpetuated by your brothers?"

A rueful smile curled her lips. "It seems rather silly now, doesn't it? And I can't imagine why Dirk and Charles would deliberately set out to destroy our relationship. Why would they want to hurt me like that?"

"I don't know," Phillip replied. "And perhaps we'll never know. But they hurt my father just as badly."

"Whatever their reasons, I don't think my brothers ever expected Armand to react as his did, with such vehemence. I don't think they understood the depth of his love for me. But your father was a very passionate man. He still is. He sees everything in terms of right and wrong, good and evil. I suppose that's why he was so valuable to the Resistance."

Phillip frowned. "The Resistance?"

She nodded, then plucked a warm croissant from the basket that Claudette offered. "Your father worked for the French Resistance during the war," Marie-Claire explained.

Phillip leaned back in his chair, astonished by her statement. "I never knew," he said.

"At first, he joined the French army, but our soldiers were sadly outnumbered. Near the end of June in 1940, German planes and tanks had rendered our troops nearly ineffective. I remember how we all denied the inevitable. The city was nearly surrounded by Germans, the sky lit up with artillery fire, and we still dined at the Ritz, drinking champagne and eating fine food. Nothing had changed, yet everything was about to change. France fell and the Vichy government took over as puppets of the Reich. And I heard from friends that your father had gone underground."

"Then you still kept in contact with him? Even after you broke your engagement?"

"Oh, no. What I learned, I learned secondhand. I was married by then. My husband and I left the city and retired to this place, to Plessis. Most of the Germans stayed northwest of Tours, so we weren't much bothered by them. In Paris, there were soldiers everywhere. Most of them behaved well, and after a while, we ignored them and tried to go on about our lives. But there were many Frenchmen who secretly continued to work against the Germans. I learned that your father was one of them. Every time I visited Paris, I would look for him on the street. But the life of a resistance worker was short. They usually worked little more than a month before the Germans would find them and arrest them. I knew his chances were not good, but then I believed your father wanted to tempt fate. Perhaps he took such risks because he had nothing to live for."

"Was he arrested?"

"I wasn't sure," she said. "There were rumors that he'd been captured and shot. Then I heard that he'd been sent to a camp. But no one could say for certain. The war went on and on and I secretly prayed that he was safe, for I was still in love with him. But I was a married woman and I couldn't speak of that love."

For a moment, Phillip saw tears glisten in her eyes, but then she regained control of her emotions and forced an embarrassed smile. "What did you do?" he asked.

"I did what everyone else did. I waited for the war to end. I was in Paris tending to business at the store and there was much news of the Allied invasion. Jean-Luc, my husband, wanted me to return to Plessis, but I didn't want to. I wanted to remain in Paris. I remember the day as if it were yesterday."

She stared out the window and a distant expression suffused her face. It wasn't hard to see how his father had fallen so deeply in love with this woman. Even at eighty, she was a woman to be reckoned with, a steely will hidden beneath great beauty and aristocratic poise.

"The sun had just risen over the city," she continued, "and there was great noise on the streets outside my apartment on the boulevard du Montparnasse. I went outside and learned that the Allies were in Antony, south of the city. There were crowds along the roads, cheering and throwing flowers and shouting their thanks to the soldiers. *Merci, merci, merci* was all we heard. I made my way through the crowds to the store. Then we heard de Gaulle was marching through Paris. It was like a dream come true, and all I thought about was your father, that if he were still alive, he'd be safe now."

"It must have been quite a sight," Phillip said, wanting her to continue.

She reached out and patted his hand, smiling. "Oh, it was. All of us who worked at the store ran down rue de la Paix and through the place Vendôme to rue Rivoli. And there he was, Charles de Gaulle. And through all the excitement, I looked for Armand's face, for his dark hair and his tall form, for I knew if he were still alive, he would be there, watching as Paris was returned to its people."

"Did you find him?"

She shook her head. "In the following weeks, I continued to look. I spoke with many of those who worked with the Resistance, but no one could tell me for certain what had happened to him. Only that he had been in Paris toward the end, that he had managed to elude the Germans for a very long time."

Phillip slowly shook his head. "I never knew," he said. "It's an amazing story."

"Your father was an amazing man," Marie-Claire replied.

"Do you ever wonder what might have been, had you married him?"

She toyed with her coffee cup, lost in her thoughts. "There is no changing the past," she finally said. "Had things not happened as they did, you might never have been born. Or perhaps you would have been my son...and Megan's cousin, instead of her lover."

"You disapprove?" Phillip asked.

Marie-Claire stiffened slightly, then folded her hands on her lap. "Experience has taught me that families should not interfere in affairs of the heart. I am concerned for Megan, but she knows her own mind."

"I would never do anything to deliberately hurt her," Phillip said.

"Deliberate or not, there is much hatred between our families, forces at work that you cannot control. You may not be able to prevent her from getting hurt."

Phillip nodded, then stood. "I should probably leave before Megan wakes."

"That would be best," Marie-Claire said. She stood and held out her hand. Phillip wrapped his fingers around hers. "If you truly love Megan, then don't let anything stand in your way. But if your motives are not so pure, then please, leave her alone. She doesn't deserve to be hurt by the mistakes I made."

Phillip nodded his understanding, then bent over and kissed her gently on her cheek. "Thank you," he said. "For telling me about my father and for trusting me with Meggie's feelings. I won't betray that trust, I promise."

"I'M NOT GOING IN THERE," Megan said, crossing her arms over her chest in an intractable posture. Phillip grinned, an irresistibly seductive smile that sent a prickling warmth down her spine.

He looked nothing at all like the smooth, sophisticated businessman she'd come to know. The chiseled angles of his jaw were now covered with a dark stubble of beard. His hair, usually combed neatly, now looked shaggy and slightly disreputable. He'd been officially unemployed for just over a week, but already he was enjoying his freedom immensely.

He reached out for her hand. "Come on, Meggie. Don't you want to see what it's like?"

"Not particularly," she said. She stared up at the inscription over the door. *"Stop,"* she read. *"Beyond here is the empire of death."*

"Spooky," Phillip teased, wiggling his fingers in front of her face. "Don't be frightened. I'll protect you."

"If I'd known you wanted to tour the catacombs, I would have stayed home. Why couldn't you have picked something nice and sensible to see, like the Eiffel Tower or the Rodin museum? All that's down there is a bunch of old skeletons."

"This was the headquarters for the French Resistance during the war. They knew the Germans wouldn't set foot inside, so they set up their radios and a whole telephone switching network underground."

"It's also where they dumped the few million poor souls they dug up from the Innocents Cemetery when they moved it two hundred years ago."

"This is where my father worked during the occupation. Your aunt told me all about him."

"My aunt?" Megan frowned. "When did you talk to my aunt?"

Phillip winced, then forced a sheepish smile. "She caught me climbing out your bedroom window at Plessis."

Groaning, Megan covered her face, the heat from her cheeks warming her fingers. "Why didn't you tell me? I thought she was acting strangely at lunch. She kept watching me, as if she were waiting for me to say something. And all the time she knew we'd slept together."

He pried her hands from her eyes. "Your aunt and I had a very lovely breakfast together," Phillip said. "We talked about my father when he was a young man. She told me he fought with the French Resistance. I've been doing some research and I read about this place."

"So you just had to come here and see it for yourself?"

"I thought maybe it would help me understand him better," Phillip said softly as he turned to stare at the entrance. "I've known him all my life, yet I really don't know him at all. Does that make sense?"

She reached up and placed her hand on his shoulder. "Have you spoken to him yet?" Megan asked.

Phillip shook his head. "He's a stubborn old man. As long as he's determined to stay on this course, I've got nothing to say to him."

"He *is* your father," Megan said.

"That doesn't automatically make him right." Phillip stepped closer and placed his arms on her shoulders. "Do you agree with your father all the time?" When she didn't answer, he leaned down and pressed his forehead against hers. "I've made my choice," he said, "and I chose you."

Megan pushed back a flood of guilt. Why did he have to put it that way, as if she'd been the sole reason he'd quit his job and abandoned his father? It was a notion she couldn't begin to fathom. Would she be able to make the same choice? Could she give up her family so easily? Over the past week she'd thought about the possibility, but even after concentrated consideration, she knew it would be almost impossible.

A woman who truly loved a man should be able to give up anything for him—even her own family. But would she ever love a man enough to make that sacrifice? Perhaps she really didn't love him, after all.

Yet she felt more for him than she'd ever felt for Edward. They seemed perfect for each other. He asked nothing more from her than what she was prepared to give. He was happy just spending time together. After Phillip's unconventional childhood, she suspected he had no idea what he wanted from a—

What? A lover? Or a wife? Megan scolded herself inwardly. How had she managed to make the jump from a brief affair to marriage in less than a week? Perhaps it had been all the time they'd spent together, nearly constant outside of the shortened days she'd been spending at work.

"I don't want to be the cause of this rift between you two," she murmured. "He's your family. You can't ignore that fact."

He kissed her quickly, then grabbed her hand. "I know what I'm doing, Meggie. I gave my father a choice. It's up to him now to decide what's important. Come on, let's go."

Megan tugged her hand out of his and slapped at him impatiently. "No! You go. I'll wait for you. I'll be right here when you come out. And we're going to continue this discussion."

He smiled and brushed the back of his hand along her jawline. "You promise you'll wait?"

"Just be careful," she warned. "The guidebook says that in 1793 some poor fool took a wrong turn from his wine cellar and ended up lost in the tunnels down there. He wasn't found until nine years later."

"His girlfriend probably wouldn't go with him, either," Phillip teased.

"Very funny," Megan replied. "Just remember, I'm not coming down there to get you."

"Yes, you would," he said. "Because you can't live without me."

Megan gave him a gentle push. "Go see your tunnels. And after that we'll get some lunch."

Megan found a place to sit in the tiny square across the street, near a small fountain. The sun was warm on her face. She closed her eyes and tipped her face up, sighing softly.

On one very basic level, life was nearly perfect. Since returning from Plessis, she and Phillip had been spending all their free time together. By day, they'd lunched at cozy bistros and quaint sidewalk cafés. And by night, they'd made love, tumbling into bed and falling asleep only after their hunger for each other had been sated.

She couldn't remember a time when she'd been happier—or more uncertain. There were moments when she forgot all about the feud and their families, moments when they were just lovers with nothing but passion standing between them. But every so often, reality would creep in and she'd remember just how complicated their relationship really was.

She'd stopped herself from even thinking about a future with Phillip. The odds were stacked so strongly against them. Yet the more they came to know each other, the more she believed that there might just be hope, a chance for their feelings for each other to rise above the acrimony.

If only she knew how Phillip felt about her—really felt, deep down inside. He said very little, only that he cared about her and didn't want her hurt. The word *love* had never touched his lips, even at the heights of desire. To him, the future meant the next week or, at the most, the next month, and had nothing at all to do with a lifelong commitment.

Why that bothered her she couldn't say. She had convinced herself months ago that she'd never be a candidate for wife of the year. She'd never even qualify. She had her work and her family and that was what counted ... wasn't it? Suddenly the answer wasn't so clear anymore.

Megan glanced around uneasily, only to see Phillip stride across the street. She sighed inwardly as she watched him move, a now familiar surge of desire welling up within her. He waved at her, then dodged through the traffic until he stood in front of her.

"Was it interesting?" she said.

"I can see why the German soldiers stayed away," he replied. "I also can't believe my father spent time in a place like that. It's really grim down there."

Megan slipped her hand into his. "You should go see him."

"I thought we weren't going to talk about it anymore."

"I've been thinking about what you said . . . about your conversation with Marie-Claire. Now that she knows, maybe it is time to tell my family about us."

"You haven't told your family about losing the rue de la Paix property yet," Phillip said. "Maybe you should start with that."

Megan ran her fingers through her hair in a frustrated gesture. "This is all too complicated. I can't even bear to think about it. First I'm going to have to tell my father. And then I'll have to face Gabe. After that, the whole board of directors. I got them all enthused about my plans and now I've got to tell them that they're not going to happen. I'm going to look like a real idiot. I can forget any hopes I have of being considered CEO material."

He put his arm around her shoulders and pulled her close. "You're not going to look like an idiot. Business deals fall through all the time."

"Not at DeWilde's," she countered. "Failure is not in our corporate vocabulary. And if I tell them I lost the property to your father, they're going to go right over the edge when I tell them about us."

"Meggie, sweetheart, they're not going to be happy about me, anyway. Just tell them everything. There's no way to soften the blow."

She tipped her chin up defiantly. "I'll just tell them that I don't care what they have to say. You and I are having a—a relationship, and there's nothing they can do to break it up. If they don't like it, they can just stuff it."

"But you do care. You care a lot about your family. And they care about you, Meggie. I only hope someday you'll feel as strongly for me."

She smiled up at him. "What makes you think I don't?" she teased.

He kissed her on the forehead before they started back to her apartment just a few blocks away.

"I think we should go away," Phillip said, staring down the avenue.

"Go away?"

"Take a holiday. Get out of Paris, away from my father and all this trouble. I want to spend some time alone with you."

"We spend a lot of time alone," Megan said.

"I own a piece of property in Provence, near Roussillon, and I thought we might drive down there and see it."

"You own property that you've never seen?"

"It was left to me. Actually, it was given to me. My father's mother was born there."

"Another journey into your father's past?"

Phillip shrugged. "I don't know what it is," he said. "I've always felt that family wasn't important. But now, with all that's happened between me and my father, and my father and your family, I've realized that perhaps I've missed out on something. You've shown me that, Meggie."

She smiled to herself, warming at his heartfelt words. "We could go next weekend," she suggested.

"Let's go now," he said. "Let's just take off. You can call in sick."

Megan opened her mouth to refuse, then snapped it shut. Why not? She'd been working awfully hard lately and she hadn't had a vacation in years. Besides, it was about time she did something spontaneous and irresponsible.

As she considered his invitation, she realized that she hadn't been acting much like the old Megan DeWilde, at least not since she'd first set eyes on Phillip Villeneuve. He'd changed her life in such strange and unexpected ways that she barely felt like the same person anymore.

"All right," she said. "I think I'd like to take a holiday with you. And after we get back, maybe I'll just call my father and brother and we'll have a nice civilized lunch together."

Phillip grinned. "That's why I like you, Megan De-Wilde. You're such an unabashed optimist."

THE MARKETPLACE IN Gordes was awash with color and alive with activity. Megan fingered a bolt of fabric, designed in a traditional blue-and-yellow Provençal pattern, as she watched Phillip and a small child pet a goat. The little goat advertised its master's special goat's milk cheese, and from the moment Phillip had spied him, he'd been enamored of the creature.

They'd spent the previous night in a lovely hotel perched on the edge of a cliff—much as the entire village was. Every building in the medieval town was made of hand-hewn stone and topped by a red clay tile roof. An eleventh-century castle dominated the center of the town, and around it, narrow streets wound up impossibly steep grades. A short walk in any direction to the edge of the village would yield an astounding view of the surrounding valleys of the Coulon.

Earlier that morning, they'd driven the narrow curving roads of the valley to the tiny town of Roussillon, another hillside village. Below the village, they found Phillip's property, a small farm with a crumbling ochre-plastered house and overgrown vineyard. They ate the pastries they'd purchased for breakfast as they sat on the rickety porch.

Phillip had been oddly silent, preoccupied with thoughts of his own. She was tempted to question him, but her questions would have brought up the sensitive subject of his father. Their trip had been perfect so far and she was loath to spoil it with talk of what awaited them both when they returned to Paris.

Instead, she had commented on the lovely wildflowers that surrounded the house and the pretty view of Roussillon and its red cliffs. And after breakfast, they had walked the boundaries of the property before heading back to Gordes. His mood gradually changed, and by the time they walked through the Saturday morning market, he'd regained his good humor.

Gordes was the most picturesque and romantic spot she'd ever seen, though she suspected her opinion had been colored by her handsome companion. From the moment they left Paris, Phillip had relaxed, teasing and joking with her. The trip took nearly nine hours, yet seemed to pass by in a blur as they sped through the gray spring weather in the north into the sunshine of Provence.

There were times when they had talked for miles on end, and times when they silently watched the scenery rush by. Yet even in silence, Megan felt at ease, as if she didn't have to entertain him. There were no games or pretenses between them, they simply enjoyed being together as if they'd been friends—and lovers—for years.

"What are you smiling for?"

Megan turned to find Phillip standing behind her, his breath soft on her neck. "I'm just happy," she replied.

"And what are you happy about, *mon amour?*"

My love, Megan silently translated. She tried to still the sudden drumbeat of her pulse, wondering at his easy use of the endearment. "I'm happy you didn't buy that goat," she teased. "I'm not sure I'd want to share the car with him."

"The goat's not for sale. But I did buy some *fromage de chèvre* from the man." He handed her a paper-wrapped package and she tucked it into her already full shopping basket. Then he grabbed her hand and they continued their stroll through the market.

"Are you having a good time?" he asked.

"I'm having a wonderful time," Megan replied. "The sun is shining, the weather is warm, and this is a perfect place to get away from everything."

"I was thinking the same thing. I'd like to come back. Perhaps hire someone to fix the house. We could take our holidays here. What do you think?"

Megan's heart fluttered at his simple suggestion. How often had he done the same in the past week, speaking of them as if they had a future together? She'd tried to fight the temptation to revel in his words, and in his simple endearment, not wanting to allow herself to believe that he might love her. Even so, she couldn't help but feel that something had changed between them, that they'd turned a corner and left the past behind.

"I can almost forget that we were once enemies," she said softly.

Phillip turned and brushed a strand of hair from her cheek, his expression somber. "Sooner or later, we're going to have to face what's waiting for us back in Paris," he said.

Megan groaned. "Don't spoil this, Phillip. Let's just forget about our families and have a good time. Please?"

"Meggie, my father knows about us. Don't you think it's about time we told your family?"

"So they can react like he did and boot me out of the family business?"

Phillip's jaw tightened. "Do you have any intention of telling them?"

Megan reached up and grabbed his hand as it stilled on her cheek. "Of course I do!" She paused. "I—I'm just waiting for the right time and place."

"There will never be a right time or place," he said.

"Yes, there will," she countered.

"All right, when?"

"What? You expect me to tell you now?"

He nodded stubbornly.

Megan sighed. "All right. When we get back to Paris I'll call my father first off. I'll ask him to come to Paris for lunch. I'll even invite Gabe. Are you satisfied now?"

He smiled grudgingly, then kissed her. "Not completely, but if we go back to the hotel, I'm sure you'll find a way of finishing the job."

Megan laughed and shoved her shopping basket at him. When he took it from her, she wrapped her arms around his neck and gave him a playful hug. But as she stared at the bustling market over his shoulder, her gaze caught sight of a tall, dark gentleman watching them both from behind a potter's stall.

The man didn't try to hide his presence from her, and it took her a few moments before she connected a name with the striking face. Nick Santos! The private investigator her father had hired to track down the thief of the DeWilde family jewels was here in Gordes. And taking quite an interest in both her and her companion.

Megan gently drew away from Phillip. "Why don't you take the basket and get a table at that little café near the fountain? A table outside. And order a bottle of wine."

"Where are you going?" Phillip asked.

"There's a bolt of fabric I want to buy," she replied. "It will just take a minute."

Satisfied by her explanation, Phillip hefted the basket into his arms and headed for the café. She watched until he was out of sight before she searched the crowded marketplace for Santos. She spied him standing a short distance from her. Cursing beneath her breath, she stalked toward him.

"What are you doing here?" she demanded.

Santos crossed his arms over his chest. "I'm investigating a case," he replied, as if his intent should have been quite clear.

"By following me around? How long have you been watching me?"

"Miss DeWilde, your companion and his father may hold the key to the theft of DeWilde property. I'm following my leads and you just happen to be spending a lot of time with one of them."

"How long have you been following me?" she repeated.

"As I said, I haven't been following *you*, I've been investigating Phillip Villeneuve." He smiled. "I can't help it if you happen to be with him"

"Go back to Paris, Mr. Santos. I can assure you that you'll find nothing here."

His dark, penetrating gaze locked on hers. "Does your father know about your relationship with Phillip Villeneuve?"

Megan met his gaze defiantly. "My personal life is none of your business! Now, leave us alone."

"Be careful, Miss DeWilde. You don't know who Phillip Villeneuve is. Or what he might be capable of."

"And I suppose you do?" she shot back.

"I intend to find out," Santos said. "With or without your help."

With that, he turned and walked away, leaving her standing on the fringes of the marketplace.

Megan cursed beneath her breath. How dare he invade her privacy! Never mind that he'd been hired by her father, he had no right to interfere in her life. She knew that Phillip had nothing to do with the theft of the DeWilde family jewels. Santos should have discovered that for himself by now.

Still, his words echoed in her mind. *You don't know who Phillip Villeneuve is.* But she did know him! She knew he was a sweet and considerate man, a man who made her feel special, treasured. A man who stirred her passion and slaked her desire.

Even though they'd only known each other a short time, she'd come to trust him. He possessed a strong sense of honor, so strong that he'd abandoned his father over what he considered a breach of business ethics. A man like that could not stand by and watch his father fence stolen jewels, could he? Perhaps she should just ask him.

"So, Phillip," she murmured to herself, "does your father have any DeWilde family jewels in his pockets?"

Hell and damnation! Just how did one broach the subject in a delicate way? How could she accuse her lover's father of such a crime, especially when she had absolutely no proof of Armand Villeneuve's guilt? No, it would be best to keep the theft to herself.

Megan buried her uncertainty as she started toward the café. Whatever his father had done fifty years ago had nothing to do with Phillip. And what they shared would not be tainted by it.

She found him at a small table beneath the shade of an ancient plane tree. The fountain softly gurgled beside the table, providing a soothing balm to her jangled nerves.

He stood and pulled out her chair for her, then handed her a glass of red wine. "Where is the fabric?"

She looked up at him, confused by his question. "What?" she asked distractedly.

"The fabric. I thought you went back to buy it."

She blinked, then forced a smile. "Oh, I—" She shook her head. "It wasn't there. Someone had—bought it," she lied.

He reached out and took her hand, an expression of concern on his face. "Are you all right, Meggie?"

"Yes," she said brightly. "Of course. I guess I was just thinking how nice it would be to stay here a little longer."

He reached out and covered her fingers with his. "You can't be frightened of what waits for us in Paris," he said. "If we face it together, we'll be fine."

Megan stared into his clear blue eyes, trying to find courage in his words. She said a silent prayer, then reached out and touched his lips with her finger.

If only she could believe him. If only he had the power to make everything right. But deep in her heart, she knew he didn't. She knew that at any meeting between her father and Phillip Villeneuve, she'd be standing squarely in the middle. And in the heat of battle, she wasn't sure she'd be able to choose sides.

CHAPTER NINE

PHILLIP STOOD AT the window, staring down into the darkness that had settled over the Coulon Valley. The moon hung low in the sky and a gentle breeze teased at his naked body. He drew a long breath of the sweet night air. Tiny lights twinkled from a village in the distance and the sound of a car echoed against the cliffs and disappeared into the night. Behind him, he could hear the even rhythm of Megan's breathing as she slept, her delicate limbs tangled in the bed linens, her dark hair tousled around her face.

He'd lain for a long time beside her after they'd made love, his eyes closed while unbidden thoughts nagged at his brain, keeping him from sleep. A vision of her had drifted through his mind, over and over again, each time bringing home thoughts that he should have wanted to forget.

They'd spent such a perfect day together. After their lunch that afternoon, they had driven to an abbey nestled in a pretty valley just a few kilometers from the village. They had strolled along an ancient lane lined by stone fences and watched as the monks tended fields of lavender. They stood in the simple and spare surroundings of the chapel and stared up at the striking stained glass window above the altar. And then they sat in the courtyard and held hands, neither one wanting to break the feeling of utter peace and contentment that had settled around them.

He closed his eyes and remembered a moment when the sun's rays had streamed down and bathed her in an unearthly light. The birds sang on the breeze and the scent of spring flowers hung in the air. She had turned then and had smiled at him, a simple smile filled with breathtaking beauty. And at that moment, the world seemed to stand still and he knew he was lost.

He loved Megan DeWilde. He loved her more than he had known he was capable of loving, a notion so powerful and so disconcerting that he wasn't sure what to do about it. He'd always considered himself immune to such emotions, but now he found himself in the midst of something he neither expected nor understood.

Phillip scrubbed at his tired eyes with his hands. Now that he'd acknowledged his feelings for her, what was he supposed to do? Their lives were in such turmoil right now that he wasn't sure what would be best. Megan still hadn't told her family about them and he wasn't convinced that she ever would. And his rift with his father showed no signs of ending any time soon.

More important, he still wasn't sure how she felt about him. She acted like a woman in love, yet she seemed to be holding something in reserve. He sensed that she was no more certain about their future than he was, and even more reluctant to put her own feelings into words.

He'd always been able to read women, to sense their most intimate thoughts. But Megan was full of contradictions. There was the woman who had tried to seduce him on the barge that night, and the sweet, naive creature whom he'd made love to at Plessis. There was the steely, implacable businesswoman and the witty and sometimes silly traveling companion.

Who was the real Megan DeWilde? How many times had he watched her over the past few days and wondered?

He felt as if he'd known her forever, yet really didn't know her at all. But he did know one thing for certain—he wanted to explore every subtlety in her soul and every corner of her heart.

He heard her stir behind him and listened distractedly as she murmured something in her sleep. No matter what happened with their families, he knew he could never let her go. He'd fight anyone, including her father, to keep her beside him. Megan was his, and no one would take her away.

"Phillip?"

Her soft call drew him from his thoughts. He turned to find her sitting up in bed, the moonlight streaming through the windows and gilding her naked body. A surge of desire pulsed through him and he fought the temptation to crawl back into bed and lose himself in her body.

"Go back to sleep, Meggie. Everything's all right." He turned back to stare out the window.

The bedclothes rustled and he thought she'd fallen back into slumber, but moments later her arms slipped around his waist, silken and sinuous. She pressed her warm body against his back and ran her palms up his stomach to his chest. A lazy shiver ran through him, and he turned in her arms and looked down at her.

"What is it?" she asked in a sleep-roughened voice.

"Nothing. I just couldn't sleep." He reached down and stroked her cheek with the back of his hand, then pulled her against him, inhaling the scent of her hair and her sleepy body. He felt himself grow hard against her stomach.

Lord, how could he want a woman so much? He felt as if a lifetime together wouldn't be nearly enough time with Megan. He gently kissed the soft curve of her neck.

"I don't want to go back," she said, her words muffled against his chest.

"I know," he replied. "I know."

She looked up at him, her eyes wide. "Can't we stay just a few days longer? I really don't need to get back to Paris. Maybe we could drive down to the Mediterranean. I'd love to visit Eze. Or St-Paul-de-Vence. We could even go back to Monte Carlo and visit the place where we met."

He drew her close and pressed his lips against her forehead. "It's hard to believe that was only a few months ago," he said. "It seems like I've known you my whole life." Slowly he lowered his head and brushed his mouth against hers. Then, pulling back, he stared into the depths of her eyes. "Marry me, Meggie."

For a moment, he thought he'd imagined the words, that they had flashed silently in his mind, then disappeared into the still night. But when he met her shocked expression, he knew he'd made the declaration out loud.

"What did you say?" she asked in disbelief.

He didn't want to deny the words, for now that they'd come out, he knew he meant what he said. He loved her. And he wanted her with him, forever. "I think you heard me," he replied evenly.

"I heard you, but I thought you said—" She smiled in embarrassment and buried her face against his chest. "Never mind. I guess I'm still half asleep."

"I asked you to marry me," he repeated.

She looked up at him and released a tightly held breath. "That's what I thought you said."

Phillip smiled hesitantly. "Well, now that we agree on what I said, perhaps we could agree on an answer?"

Megan stirred in his arms. "Phillip, this comes as a bit of a surprise. I—I mean, we haven't even discussed—well, you know." She nervously crossed the room and flipped on a bedside light. As if looking for something else to do, she pulled a sheet from the bed and wrapped it around her, putting a subtle barrier between them.

"You can say the word, Meggie. *Marriage.* I asked you to marry me."

"I—I know. It's not the word. It's just the concept that rattles me." She sat down on the end of the bed and rearranged the sheet over her legs, plucking at the fabric with shaky fingers.

He sat down beside her and took her hands in his. "Don't you see, it's the perfect solution."

She hesitantly pulled her fingers from his, then wove them together on her lap. The silence grew between them, and he realized that she didn't know what to say to him. He'd never felt so far away from her as he did now, and with each second of silence, she seemed to withdraw even further.

"It *is* the perfect solution," he repeated. "If we get married, it will force our families to face up to this feud and put an end to it once and for all."

"But you have to admit, this is a pretty drastic way to go about it."

"Meggie, I know how I feel about you. We'd make a great pair, you and I. What do you say?"

She forced a smile. "This isn't a decision I can make in a split second, Phillip. I did that once before and it turned out to be a disaster. I need to think about this."

Anger rose inside him, born of impatience and frustration. "What's there to think about? We can't let our families rule our lives. We have to take a stand for what we believe in. And I believe in us. You and me. If we're together, we can withstand anything they throw at us."

Megan stood and walked to the window, leaving him alone on the bed. Her shoulders were tense as he watched her stare out into the night, unmoving, unresponsive.

"I know how I feel about you, Megan," he said.

"But I'm not sure how I feel about you," she murmured, her voice and her posture filled with indifference.

Phillip laughed curtly. "What the hell does that mean?"

She spun around and faced him. "I'm not sure, that's what it means. Not sure enough to talk about marriage, at least. Marriage is for life, Phillip. Rushing into something like this would be foolhardy."

Phillip raked his fingers through his hair and cursed softly. "Well, this is a hell of a mess. The first and only time I ask a woman to marry me and she turns me down."

"I'm not turning you down. I'm just asking for more time."

"What do you need time for? To give your family the chance to talk you out of this? To give the past time to spoil our future? The longer we wait, the more difficult it will be."

She shook her head adamantly. "I will not be bullied into this any more than I'll be bullied by my family."

Phillip shot up from the bed and snatched his trousers from the floor. "Is that what I'm doing? Well, do forgive me for making such a pest of myself." He yanked his pants on, then stood and waited for her to respond. "Well?"

Her expression softened a bit. "Why are you getting so angry?"

"I think I have a right, don't you?"

"It's been such a perfect time here. Don't spoil it by arguing with me."

Phillip sighed. "We've got to be able to disagree, Meggie. There will be times when we'll fight. But that doesn't mean we have to go our separate ways. It doesn't mean I care less about you."

She knotted the sheet between her fingers and twisted it nervously. "Can—can we just wait and talk about this later?" she pleaded.

He raised his hands in frustration. "You need time? I'll give you time." He grabbed his shoes and tugged them on.

"Where are you going?"

"Out for some air," he muttered.

"Don't leave," she said. "Please."

Her voice sounded so small and vulnerable, it stopped him at the door. He felt the anger drain out of him, as he realized that he was doing exactly what he'd accused her of doing—running from their problems.

He drew a deep breath. He could handle this. Hell, if she didn't love him now, he'd just have to make her love him. He slowly turned to face her, then leaned back against the door. "I'm sorry. I shouldn't have gotten angry."

She smiled winsomely, then crossed the room with hesitant steps and wrapped her arms around his waist. Pressing her cheek against his chest, she sighed. "This has all happened so fast. A few weeks ago we were at each other's throats, and now we're lovers. I just need some time to understand it all."

"All right," Phillip acquiesced. "If you need time, then that's what you'll have."

She gazed up at him and smoothed the tension from his face with her fingers. "Make love to me, Phillip."

Phillip groaned inwardly as she pulled him toward the bed. He tugged the sheet off her body and they tumbled onto the mattress. In one smooth movement, he rolled on top of her, capturing her hands above her head and pressing his hard desire against her thighs.

As he entered her, he wanted to say the words out loud, to tell her he loved her. But after her reaction to his proposal, he was afraid of her response. He'd never said the words before, never in his life. And he couldn't face the prospect of his declaration being met by an edgy silence and a stiffening of her pliant body.

So he didn't say anything. Instead, he showed her how he felt in every caress and every thrust, in soft, whispered urgings and fervent sighs. And when she curled against him, sated and sleepy, he closed his eyes and swore to God that he would never give her up.

"I'M AN ADULT. I'M PERFECTLY able to decide these things for myself!"

Megan watched her brother's jaw tighten as he tried to school his anger. There were times when just the tiniest bit of their mother's fiery temper got the better of the cool and implacable Gabe.

He paced back and forth in front of her desk, his fists clenched. Megan sat in her chair, trying to convey a picture of calm while her twin's expression hardened even further. "Then why are you acting like an idiot?" he countered. "He's a de Villeneuve, for God's sake."

"I'm well aware of his parentage," she muttered, idly rearranging the pens in a perfect line on her desk. "And it's just 'Villeneuve' these days," she informed him. This was not the way she'd intended to break the news to her family, but now that the subject had been broached, she was almost relieved.

Phillip had been pressing her to tell her family about them for days, but since his unexpected proposal of marriage, he'd seemed even more determined to face the feud head-on. Her mind flashed back to that night in Gordes.

He'd caught her completely off guard and she knew she'd handled it badly. With a bruised ego, Phillip had the capacity to be completely irrational. She did care about him, and she was actually getting used to the fact that she probably loved him. But she certainly wasn't ready for marriage, not to a man she'd really only known for two months! She'd known Edward for two years, and look where that had gotten her.

"Dad has a file five inches thick on the family," Gabe said, interrupting her thoughts. "They've been out to destroy us for years, and now you're dating—hell, for all I know you're sleeping with him! It's got to stop, Megan."

Megan slammed her hands down on her desk and rose from her chair. "Did you ever think that this might be good for the family? Maybe it's about time someone did something to end this silly feud."

"And you have to be the one?" Gabe asked sarcastically. "Did it occur to you that the Villeneuves might have no intention of giving up? That this son of a—" he cursed beneath his breath "—son of a Villeneuve has ulterior motives where you're concerned?"

"He cares about me," Megan said. "I believe that's the only ulterior motive he has." Her brother remained unmoved. She groaned and shook her head. She shouldn't have to defend the man she loved—or probably loved. "Why do you find that so hard to believe?" she asked softly.

Gabe ran his fingers through his light brown hair and cursed. "I'm sorry if my words hurt you, Meg, but you cannot see him again. I forbid it."

She stiffened at his uncompromising order. "Who are you to be doing any forbidding?"

"I'm here on Dad's orders. He would have come himself, but he's got meetings right up until the time we catch our flight to Australia for Ryder's wedding next week. Nevertheless, he feels the same way I do."

"You can't stop me!" she cried. "I'm an adult and I can do what I like."

"Listen to yourself! Dad's got enough on his mind without worrying about you and Villeneuve getting cozy. Just when were you planning to tell us all?"

"Soon," she replied. "Marie-Claire knows all about it— and she approves. I was planning to invite you and Daddy for lunch, to give you a chance to get to know Phillip. I was going to call today. I forgot all about Ryder's wedding."

"We had to find out about this from Nick Santos, of all people. We had to read about it in his damn report."

Megan felt the color rise in her cheeks as she wondered how detailed Santos's report actually was. "Well, if you hadn't had him following me all over the countryside, you wouldn't have had to read it in a report. I could have told you myself."

"He was following Villeneuve. You just happened to be with the man. And more than just a few evenings a week, I might add."

Megan hesitated before asking the next question, knowing that the answer might not be what she wanted to hear. "What else did the report say? Did Armand Villeneuve steal the jewels or not?"

Her brother bristled. "That has no bearing on this conversation."

"It does to me," Megan snapped. "Now, tell me!"

Gabe pressed his lips into a tight line, then shook his head. "Santos didn't find any evidence that the Villeneuves were involved," he admitted reluctantly. "He's left France to follow up on another lead."

Megan breathed a deep sigh of relief. "I could have told you the Villeneuves weren't involved. Marie-Claire believed Armand was innocent. And I knew Phillip had nothing to do with fencing those jewels. He's a good man."

Her brother scoffed. "A good man? For God's sake, Meg, haven't you been listening to anything I've been saying? He's a damn Villeneuve!" Gabe closed his eyes and sighed. "I'm just trying to keep you from making a mistake. Listen, Meg, I know how hurt you were when Edward stood you up at the wedding."

"I wasn't hurt," she said defensively. "I was—surprised."

"And we know you've been...vulnerable when it comes to matters of the heart," Gabe continued. "You've always been too trusting for your own good. Now, I don't know what brought this reckless streak out. Perhaps it's been all the upheaval in the family, Mother leaving, your broken engagement, Dad's strange moods, all the stress of running the Paris store. It doesn't really matter."

"This is so typical. You're treating me like I'm some feebleminded child. You and Daddy, and even Mother, are guilty of it! From the time I was a child, you've always been so concerned about my feelings, you've never let me make my own mistakes."

"That's not—"

"It *is* true. Well, maybe I didn't succeed at everything I tried. Maybe I wasn't as athletic as you or as clever as Kate, but acting as if my failures didn't make a difference hurt me nonetheless. I can live *my* life without *your* interference. I can make my own mistakes and deal with them. And as for the matter of Phillip Villeneuve, what he and I share is none of your business."

"It is my business if it involves the family business. Stop seeing him, Meg, or Dad will have to take this into his own hands."

"And what does that mean?" she demanded.

"Your job," Gabe said coldly.

Megan cursed vividly, eliciting a startled expression from her brother. "Can't you see how ridiculous this is? Sooner or later we've got to put an end to this animosity between the families. It's not good for either one of us."

"What's not good for *us* is a Villeneuve store opening up right across the street from DeWilde's," Gabe said in an icy voice.

Megan winced, this time cursing silently. "I was planning to tell you about that, as well."

"I'd love to hear your explanation for this one, little sister," Gabe said. "The man you trust stole that property right out from under you. And you're still defending him."

"That may be how it looks, but that's not how it happened. It was his father who made the deal. And it was *my* fault we lost that property. I'm willing to take full responsibility with the board. I should have brought you and Daddy in on the negotiations, but I wanted to prove, once and for all, that I could handle things on my own." Megan paused, then met Gabe's gaze. "I made a misjudgment when I drafted the offer. And I'm sorry for that, but—"

Gabe shook his head and grabbed her shoulders. "Meg, I don't care about the bloody property and I'm certain Dad doesn't, either. I'm only concerned about you."

"Stop it!" Megan cried. "Don't you see what you're doing? You're treating me the same way you always have. You can't protect me from failure, and I don't want you to. I messed up and that's all there is to it!"

She yanked out of his grasp at the same moment that the door to her office flew open. Gabe turned at the commotion and Megan's heart froze as Phillip appeared in the door, her secretary hard on his heels.

He looked at Gabe suspiciously, then turned to her. "Megan, what's going on? Your secretary said you didn't want to see me."

"She *doesn't* want to see you," Gabe said.

Phillip gave Gabe a cursory glance. "I'd assume you're Gabe?"

"You'd assume right," Gabe replied, his voice filled with icy disdain. "I don't have to ask who you are. I'm well familiar with you and your family. Now, get out of here. You've interrupted a discussion of family business."

"Since I suspect I'm the major topic of this meeting, I thought I might sit in," Phillip replied as he sauntered in.

"Like hell you will," Gabe said. "I'll call security and have you thrown out of here."

Phillip grinned as he glanced at Megan, quirking his brow as if they shared some inside joke. "Meggie's tried that more than once," he said. "And I just keep coming back."

His smile sent a warm flood of sensation through her body. She wanted to close her eyes and lose herself in his arms, shutting out the rest of the world as they had the first night they made love. But instead, she stood stiffly beside her desk, staring straight ahead and feeling as if she were caught in a bad dream.

What had ever possessed her to believe that she and Phillip could end this feud? Perhaps she didn't realize the depth of her own family's feelings regarding the Villeneuves. Or the lengths to which they'd go to protect her from a man they considered dangerous.

"Gabe, I think it would be best if we continued this conversation at another time," Megan said. "We're not going to get anywhere shouting at each other."

Phillip slipped his arm around her shoulders and pulled her closer. "I think that would be best," he said.

Gabe stiffened the instant Phillip touched her, and Megan could see the anger flare in his hazel eyes, as if he were preparing to step in and protect her. "You and your thief of a father can stay away from my family," he said, his words thick with rage.

Phillip tensed beside her, his muscles flexing and stretching almost imperceptibly, and she wondered if he'd go so far as to take a swing at Gabe. Right now, Gabe deserved nothing less than a swift punch in the nose.

"My father is not a thief," Phillip said in a deceptively even voice. "What he did to get the store was perfectly legal. Not particularly ethical, but legal."

"I'm not talking about the store," Gabe replied. "I'm talking about the theft of DeWilde family property."

Megan took a step forward and held out her hand. "Gabe, don't. Mr. Santos said that Phillip's father had nothing to do with the theft."

"He said there was no definite proof. Villeneuve probably covered his tracks well."

"What are you talking about?" Phillip demanded. He turned to Megan questioningly, then back to Gabe.

Gabe sent them both a self-satisfied smile. "I'm talking about the jewels that were stolen from our family in 1948. Six of the most valuable pieces in the DeWilde collection. Your father is a suspect, and we've had an investigator looking into his past. And into your activities, as well."

Phillip turned to Megan and stared down at her in surprise. "Megan, is this true?"

Her gaze darted back and forth between Gabe and Phillip. "Well, yes. In fact, that's how Gabe found out we were...seeing each other. But the investigator said that—"

"Why didn't you tell me about this?" Phillip demanded.

"I—I didn't think it was important, Phillip. Besides, I didn't—"

"You believe my father is a jewel thief and you don't think that's important?"

"No!" Megan cried. "I mean, I—I don't know. It doesn't make a difference, does it?"

Phillip stared into her eyes, plumbing the depths of her gaze as if he might somehow find the truth there. "Is *this* why you won't marry me?"

Megan looked up at him, her brow furrowed. At the same time, Gabe gasped. "Marriage? Is that what he said?" he shouted. "You're thinking of marrying him?"

"Yes," Phillip said, stepping away from her to stand in front of Gabe. "I asked Meggie to marry me."

She reached out and took his arm, drawing him back. "Phillip, this really isn't the right time to—"

"It's a perfect time," Phillip said. He took her trembling hand in his, then turned to Gabe. "I plan to marry her, with or without your family's blessing."

"The hell you will," Gabe said, stepping forward to grab Megan's other arm. As her brother tried to pull her away, Phillip held fast. She looked back and forth at them both, then yanked her arms away.

"Stop it!" she cried. "Please!"

"Meggie, tell him," Phillip said softly. "Tell him how you feel. Tell him what you want."

Gabe held out his hand to stop her reply. "Don't bother, Megan. I'll make it easy for you. It's either Villeneuve or your family. Are you willing to give up your position at DeWilde's for this man?"

Megan stared at her brother in disbelief. "You can't do this, Gabe. You don't have the power."

"Dad gave me the power. It's either your job or him. You make the choice."

Megan frowned, her gaze shifting between the brother she'd always loved and the man she wanted so desperately to love. She knew in her heart that Phillip Villeneuve was a good and honorable man, a man that didn't deserve the wrath that her family had heaped upon him.

"Go ahead, Megan," Gabe taunted. "Choose. It's him or your family. Are you going to betray the family like Mother did?"

She bit her bottom lip and tried to stem a flood of tears. "Don't do this, Gabe. Please, don't make me choose. I can't."

"As long as you associate with a Villeneuve, you cannot be a part of DeWilde's."

"Stop saying that!" she cried. "I'm not going to choose. I'm not." The tears flowed freely now and there was nothing she could do to stop them. She stood between Phillip and Gabe, rent in two by emotions that welled up from deep inside her. A sob tore from her throat and she covered her face with her hands.

She felt Phillip's hands on her shoulders. "She won't have to choose," he said softly.

"She will," Gabe countered.

Megan looked up at Phillip through tear-clouded eyes. He smiled and shook his head, never taking his eyes from her. "See, that's the difference between us, DeWilde. I love your sister and I'd never do anything to hurt her. I'd never ask her to give up the family, or the job, she loves. So I'll make the choice for her."

He reached out and cupped her cheek in his palm. His simple caress sent a frisson of joy through her and his words rang in her mind like cathedral bells on Christmas morning. He loved her! He had just said the words she wasn't sure she wanted to hear. And now that he'd said them, her own feelings came rushing forth. He loved her...and she loved him.

"You were right, Meggie," he said softly.

"Right?"

"We can't ignore the past. No matter how hard we try to bury it, it will always be there. And nothing I do can change that." He bent over her and brushed his mouth against hers. "Goodbye, Meggie."

With that, he turned and walked toward the door. He stopped in front of Gabe and gave him a sideways glance. "Take care of her," he murmured. He continued out of her office, closing the door behind him with a finality that felt like a dagger to her heart. She didn't even have time to call his name, to tell him what she knew to be true—she loved him with all her heart and she'd choose him over her family.

She took a few steps, wanting to go after him. But Gabe grabbed her hand and held it tight. "This is for the best, Meg. Believe me. It never would have worked."

She yanked her hand out of his and crossed her arms beneath her breasts, trying to still the shivers that suddenly rocked her body. "You don't know that," she said. "And thanks to you, I never will, either."

"HE'S HERE, *MADAME*."

Marie-Claire glanced up from the volume of poetry she'd been trying to read, then nodded calmly at Claudette. "Thank you. Send him in."

She stared down at the leather-bound volume for a long moment, running her fingers over the well-worn pages. She flipped to the flyleaf and traced the shape of Armand's casual scrawl as she read the inscription. He'd given her the book of French love poems on the night they'd announced their engagement. She'd always kept it with her, reading the poems over and over again, hoping they might somehow preserve her memories of what they had shared.

She closed the book and carefully returned it to its place in her writing desk. There was no need for memories anymore. Armand had come back into her life and she was determined to set things right between them. She smoothed her skirt, then tucked a strand of hair behind her ear.

That he'd answered her summons came as a bit of a surprise, but then she really didn't know Armand Villeneuve at all anymore. She didn't know whether his heart had turned to stone, or whether he still might harbor some sliver of compassion. And she didn't know whether he'd listen to her today.

"At least he's come," she murmured to herself, trying to calm her nerves. "That's a first step."

A few moments later, Armand strode into the room, imperious and impatient. "I've come, Claire. What is it you want?"

Her heart skipped a beat at his use of her second name, a name she'd refused to answer to until she'd met him. She pressed her palm to her chest then nervously indicated the sofa. "Please, sit down. Claudette, bring us tea."

He tapped his elegant cane on the polished floor. "I don't have time for tea."

"Tea, Claudette," she said stubbornly. She turned back to Armand. "And you may stop scowling at me and sit down."

He studied her for a long moment, then did as he was told. He folded his hands over the head of his cane. As she took a seat on an embroidered chair, she stared at the intricate carving and frowned.

"I was shot during the war," he explained in a gruff voice. "It aches in the dampness."

"I didn't know." She smiled sadly. "Such a long time ago. So much time has passed. There are days I look in the mirror and find myself staring at a stranger. I still feel so young inside, as if my sixteenth birthday were just a few years ago. Unfortunately, my body doesn't seem to share that notion."

"You said in your note that you wished to discuss my son. Say what you have to say. I'm a busy man."

Marie-Claire met his unyielding expression. "They're in love," she said in a quiet voice.

He shook his head, then laughed bitterly. "You expect me to believe this?"

"It's true," she said. "I've seen them together. They look at each other like..." She paused, then tipped her chin up. "Like we used to look at each other."

For an instant, his expression softened, but then the barriers rose again. He cleared his throat. "My son has seen the error of his ways and returned to Hong Kong. He has no plans to return to Paris. Perhaps you misread the situation."

"He is there because of us. We did this to them. The two of us and this cursed vendetta. We destroyed something good and pure between them."

"If it were that good, they wouldn't be living on separate continents. True love is indestructible, or so I've heard."

There was no doubt in her mind that his last words had nothing at all to do with Phillip and Megan. "You're right," she said. "True love does last forever. I can speak of this with great confidence."

He glanced around the room, taking in his elegant surroundings. "Plessis," he said as if the name caused a foul taste in his mouth. "It's not hard to see why you made the choices you did."

"I cared for my husband, that much is true," she told him. "But I didn't love him the way he deserved to be loved. You see, I'd already given my heart to someone else. A young man I'd met on my sixteenth birthday." She stopped to still the tremor in her voice. "I still love that charming boy. I never stopped loving him."

"I'm not that boy," Armand said bluntly. "I haven't been that boy since the day you turned your back on me. And all because of a lie, a scheme your brothers perpetrated."

"A scheme? What are you talking about?" Marie-Claire asked. "My brothers were only trying to protect me."

"There *was* a dancer from the Moulin Rouge," Armand replied. "But she wasn't my mistress. She was my father's. And she was also Dirk's mistress. And in a moment of well-paid passion, she let it slip to your brother that our family had designs on the DeWilde store. My father felt our marriage would be the best way to get what he wanted."

"How do you know this?"

"During the war, she came to me. She'd been working for the underground, providing the Resistance with information she'd gathered from her German companions. She wanted money in return for a story she knew I would want to hear. She told me how Dirk paid her to write the note, to lie about our relationship. She said Dirk was determined to stop the Villeneuves from making a play for DeWilde's—at any cost."

"And that cost was us," Marie-Claire murmured as she slowly stood. She walked to the window and pulled the lace curtain back to stare out at the garden fountain. "I'm sorry I didn't believe you."

"That was a long time ago. I'm no longer some besotted young boy."

"But isn't there some shred of that boy left?" she asked. "Some bit of warmth and compassion?" She turned back to look at him.

He shrugged. "For what? For a silly affair between my son and your grandniece?"

"It's not a silly affair," she said, clutching the lace in her hand. "It's as if we have a second chance through them. The love we lost can live on in them. Please, Armand," she pleaded, her voice barely a whisper, "don't let what happened between us destroy their lives the way it destroyed ours."

Armand slowly got to his feet, leaning heavily on his cane. "What are you trying to say, Claire?" He took a step toward her.

"When you disappeared, I nearly died. I looked for you in every crowd, hoping against hope that I'd find you again." She smiled and forced back a tear. "And now, here we are. So much time, so much has changed. And yet nothing has really changed at all."

Slowly, they moved across the room until they stood close enough to touch. Trembling, Marie-Claire raised her hand. He stared down at her fingers, then hesitantly took her hand in his.

"Would you stay for lunch?" she asked. "We could eat on the terrace. The flowers are in bloom and the air is sweet with their fragrance."

"I believe I will stay," he said. "I would like to have lunch with you, Claire."

CHAPTER TEN

"I NEED A HOLIDAY. I need to get away from Paris." Megan ran her finger along a row of travel guides that lined the walls of Bon Voyage, Lucy's rue Daunou shop. "How about this? Tahiti sounds like a nice destination."

Tahiti was exactly what she needed. Beautiful beaches, warm ocean breezes and time alone—time away from a city that only reminded her of Phillip. She had tried to forget, to put what happened between them behind her. But around every corner, on every street, was some reminder of the days and nights they'd spent together.

She couldn't look at the Seine without thinking of their dinner on the barge. A rainy day reminded her of their walk in the Luxembourg Gardens. And every time she slept in her bed at Plessis, she went back to the night they'd first made love. France had become home to her. And now Paris, with all its beauty and splendor, stood as a mute reminder of some of the worst times in her life.

She had expected he would be easy to forget... as Edward had been. But Phillip wasn't Edward, and what she felt for him was far deeper than anything she'd believed possible. In her need to remain loyal to her family, she had betrayed the only man she'd ever loved.

That's what it had been—a betrayal, nothing less. Her thoughts drifted back to that day in her office, the day she'd been forced to make a choice. And even in her refusal to choose, her decision had been evident. She should have sided with him, should have given up everything to be with the man she loved. But she couldn't bring herself to turn her back on her family; she hadn't the courage or the belief in her love for Phillip. With that choice, she'd killed any hope that she and Phillip might have had for a future together.

"Here," Lucy said, handing her another guide. "I understand Hong Kong is lovely this time of year."

Megan pushed the book back at her. "I don't need any reminders from you. I can't even count the number of times I've been tempted to get on a plane and go to him. I made such a mess of everything. I'd just like a chance to explain."

"Then, why don't you?" Lucy asked, as if the notion were so simple to act on.

Megan sighed. "Why? Because nothing has changed. Everything that stood in our way is still there. My family has been through so much lately. If I went to Phillip, if I gave up everything, my father and Gabe would consider it an act of treason, no less detestable than my mother's desertion."

"But you must follow your heart, Meg," Lucy said.

"I made my choice, Lucy. Even if I wanted Phillip back, I don't think he would take me. You didn't see the look on his face that day in my office. He and Gabe were pulling at me, almost tearing me in two. And when I couldn't choose, it was like I'd driven a dagger right through his heart. He was hurt, and nothing I can do will ever erase that." She paused and drew a deep breath. "He made a choice for me, Lucy. He gave up his family for me, and I couldn't do the same."

"Do you believe he loved you?"

Megan nodded. "I think he did. For a while, at least. But after the way I handled things, I didn't love myself a whole lot. I can't see how he could, either."

"A man in love is a difficult thing to understand," Lucy said. "And I don't think you do, Meg. Before you had Phillip, I don't think you ever had a man who truly loved you."

"Edward did," she replied defensively. "Or at least he said he did. And look what happened there. His love wasn't even strong enough to make it through our wedding. Love doesn't always last forever."

"Edward didn't love you," Lucy said softly. "He loved himself. And he loved the idea of you as his wife. You were like a prize to him, but when you didn't act in the way he wanted, he didn't want you anymore. But he never loved you the way Phillip did, in a deep and constant way."

"I can learn to live without Phillip," Megan said. "The same way I learned to live without Edward. But I could never live with hurting my father. Not now. Not after what he's been through."

Lucy threw up her hands in exasperation. "So you are just going to spend the rest of your life mourning this man you cannot have?"

Megan shook her head. "No! I'll forget him. I just need to make a determined effort, that's all."

"A man you love is not like a—a bad tooth," Lucy countered. "You cannot just pull him out of your life and be done with it. You will always feel the loss."

"You're comparing Phillip to bad teeth?" Megan chuckled ruefully.

Lucy shrugged. "So I am not a poet. But you understand my meaning. There is a part of your heart that you left with him. It is in Hong Kong now."

"And you think I should go get it back?"

"I think you should go there and give him the rest of your heart. You love him. This is what lovers do, *n'est-ce pas?* It is not always logical, but it is always right."

"No, not *n'est-ce pas.* I know what I'm doing, Lucy, and this is for the best." She grabbed another book from the shelf, putting an end to their conversation. "Maybe I should go to Switzerland. Or Tuscany. Tuscany would be beautiful this time of year."

Lucy rolled her eyes. "No matter where you go, you will not be able to forget him. This I know. And that's all I have to say on the matter."

Megan knew her friend was probably right. But she wasn't willing to admit that this one man had affected her so deeply that she might never be able to get over him. She was a sensible, practical woman. But then, so was Marie-Claire, and she had carried a torch for Armand Villeneuve for sixty years.

Megan tried to picture herself at her aunt's age, living out her later years at Plessis, gardening, running the winery, spending the odd weekend with a favorite grandniece. Though Marie-Claire seemed happy, the picture brought a twist of apprehension to Megan's heart.

The years ahead loomed long and lonely without the prospect of Phillip in her life. Or any man for that matter, for she knew that no other man would be able to take his place.

"Can we discuss my vacation now?" Megan asked. "You're supposed to be an expert in this area and you're not giving me much help."

"All right, what is it you'd like to do on your vacation?" Lucy asked.

Megan frowned. "I don't know. What do people usually do? That's what I'd like to do."

"How long has it been since you've had a vacation?"

She considered the question for a long moment. "I suppose not since I was a schoolgirl. While I was at university, I spent summers working at the New York and London stores. When I graduated, I went right to work. And then I took the job here in Paris."

As she spoke to Lucy, Megan realized how empty her life seemed. Lucy filled her days with excitement, living every moment as if it were her last, falling in and out of love with reckless abandon. But Megan had spent her time working hard and trying to prove something to her family, something that suddenly didn't seem very important at all.

She gnawed at her bottom lip and turned to stare at the titles on the bookshelf. Was this all that her life was about—her job, her family, regular weekends with her aunt? Was there nothing else? She closed her eyes and fought back the swell of emotion within her. When she'd been with Phillip, her life had been so much more. She'd felt alive, looked forward to every moment of every day, with or without him.

Megan felt Lucy's hand on her arm. She pushed back her feelings and turned, forcing a bright smile for her friend.

"Why don't we go shopping," Lucy suggested. "Then we'll have lunch and talk about your vacation."

Megan shook her head. "I really should get back to work," she said.

"And your vacation?" Lucy asked.

"Not today. Maybe tomorrow. I've just got so much to do. I don't know where I'd find the time for a holiday, anyway." With that, Megan grabbed her purse from the counter and hurried to the door. "We'll have coffee next week," she called over her shoulder.

She walked down rue Daunou with no particular destination in mind. The day was bright and sunny, a perfect

May day in Paris, the kind of day she loved. The kind of day she wished she could share with—

"Stop it," she said, picking up her pace. "You lived without him before. You don't need him now. You wouldn't have even thought of him if Lucy hadn't brought him up." If she truly wanted to be a real Parisian, she'd simply go on with life. *C'est la vie.* Women had love affairs all the time and got over them.

She walked aimlessly, through St-Honoré and then into the Marais, until she found herself in a quiet oasis at the heart of Paris—place des Vosges. The square had always been a favorite spot of hers, the oldest and the most beautiful square in the city. Surrounded by matching red-and-gold brick pavilions with steeply pitched slate roofs, the buildings served as an architectural fortress against the traffic and noise of Paris.

She found a spot inside the wrought-iron gates of the square and sat down on a park bench beneath two perfect rows of chestnut trees. Along the arcade, a tenor sang Baroque arias with a recorded accompaniment. His voice echoed against the vaulted ceilings and drifted on the warm breeze into the park. The smell of fresh-baked baguettes hung in the air. A group of children shouted as they tossed a ball, and near the corner of the square, a student worked on a watercolor of the fountain.

Gazing at her surroundings, she tried to put Phillip out of her mind. She watched an older couple who sat on the park bench next to her, the man in a jaunty black beret and the woman clutching a small paper bag. They tossed out bread crumbs for the pigeons, and every now and then the man would look at his wife and smile to himself. They would speak in hushed tones and laugh a bit, then gaze at the fountain together.

She watched them for a long time as they shared the simple moments of their lives. After the bread crumbs had run out and the pigeons had gone elsewhere, the man took his wife's hand and gently kissed it. She placed her palm on his ruddy cheek and looked into his eyes, sharing a moment so sweet it brought tears to Megan's eyes.

She'd never have that, a love to last a lifetime. She'd never spend her days sitting on park benches and feeding pigeons and looking into the face of the man she loved. She pressed her palm to her chest, trying to stop the pain in her heart. A lump of emotion filled her throat and the tears tracked down her cheeks.

She didn't try to stop them. For the first time since Phillip had left, she didn't want to control her emotions. She wanted to feel the pain of losing him, the frustration of never knowing what the future might have held. It would be just punishment for the way she'd acted. She let the tears go, staring straight ahead at the fountain, closed tight in her own little world.

She cried until the tears wouldn't come anymore, and until the pain was just a dull ache somewhere near her heart. Drawing a shaky breath, she wiped her eyes with her sleeve and stood and smoothed her skirt.

She *could* get over this. She *could* put her life back together and forget him. For whether she loved him or not, she really had no other choice.

PHILLIP STARED OUT the window of the limousine as the traffic came to a standstill on the Périphérique. The sun hung low over the Paris skyline, bathing the city in golden light that had glinted off the landmarks as his plane had landed at Charles de Gaulle. He tapped his fingers impatiently on his knee as he recalled the words of his father's cable.

Gravely ill. Come to Paris immediately. Not much time left.

He closed his eyes and leaned his head back against the seat. He'd hoped the next time he traveled to Paris, he'd be coming at Megan's request. But nothing had changed over the past month. He had made peace with his father and thrown himself back into his work, trying to catch up on all that he'd missed during his brief sojourn in Paris.

He'd even made an attempt to forget Megan with another woman. But he'd failed woefully and sent her home from the Repulse Bay condo immediately after dessert, unable to think of touching anyone else. No matter how hard he tried, he couldn't forget her. Megan haunted his mind, night and day, asleep and awake. She was with him always.

He knew he'd done the right thing, leaving her as he had. Her family would never have accepted him and he couldn't bear to make her choose between them. If he knew anything about Megan, he knew she loved her family unconditionally. He had hoped he might get a taste of that kind of love one day. But it wasn't to be.

Still, he couldn't help but wonder what might have been had they met at a different place or time, had they been born to different families, had she loved him enough to defy her family.

Just being in the same city as Megan gave him a certain satisfaction, and a glimmer of hope. Perhaps he would walk past her store and meet her by chance. Or maybe he would catch sight of her across a busy bistro. The idea that he might see her again warmed his soul.

He glanced at his watch, and as he adjusted it to Paris time, he wondered what she was doing. No doubt she was still at the office. Or perhaps she was having an early dinner. Was she alone, or had she found another man to keep her company? He fought a wave of jealousy and tried to put the notion out of his mind.

How long would it be before she found another man, a man more acceptable to her family? Megan was a beautiful, brilliant woman, and any man with half a brain would be able to see that. He'd seen it the moment he met her that night in Monaco, and he'd seen it every time he had looked at her since.

She was the kind of woman he could spend a lifetime getting to know. He had imagined them together, with nothing but the rest of their lives stretching out in front of them, and he felt complete. But now, when he looked to the future, he saw only emptiness, dry and uninteresting like a desert landscape.

He glanced out the window of the car, surprised to see that they'd just pulled into the place Vendôme. The driver circled the square and parked in front of the Hôtel Ritz. He hopped out of the car and ran to open Phillip's door, but Phillip was already striding up to the entrance.

"Take care of my bag," he said to the doorman. "I'll be checking in for the evening."

He walked through the lobby to the front desk. "I received a cable from my father, Armand Villeneuve," he said to the clerk. "Do you know where I might find him? Has he been taken to hospital?"

The clerk seemed surprised by his question. *"Mais non!"* he said. "As far as I know, Monsieur Villeneuve is in his suite. He came in a short time ago, with his companion."

"He came in?" Phillip asked.

"Why, yes," the clerk said. "With a woman. He seemed fine to me."

Phillip cursed softly, then crossed the lobby to the elevators and ordered the operator to his father's floor. Moments later, he stood in front of the door of Armand's suite, mentally bracing himself for the worst.

Drawing a deep breath, he rapped his knuckles on the gilded wood. But Armand Villeneuve didn't open the door. Instead, Phillip found himself looking down into Marie-Claire's surprised expression.

"Phillip!" she cried. "What are you doing here?" She smiled and held out her hand. "Come in. It's so nice to see you again."

He stepped inside the suite and closed the door, a frown creasing his brow. "I came right from the airport. How is he? If he's ill, he should be in the hospital. Has the doctor been to see him today?"

With a reaction mirroring the desk clerk's, Marie-Claire seemed taken by surprise. Why was everyone acting so strangely?

"Doctor?" she asked. "What doctor?"

Phillip groaned and leaned back against the door. "He hasn't called a doctor yet?"

She shook her head haltingly. "I can't imagine why. Unless his leg is bothering him again. But he isn't even limping. He hasn't used his cane in days."

Phillip stared at her, scowling. "Are you saying there's nothing wrong with my father?"

She gave him an odd look, as if he were speaking to her in Chinese. "I suppose I am," she replied. "Unless there's something he hasn't told me. Has he told *you* something I should know? Armand was always so stubborn about his health, never trusting the doctors."

"He's not on his deathbed? And you're not here to say your final goodbyes?"

Marie-Claire chuckled. "No, dear. Your father and I have a dinner engagement. But first, we're off to a reception at the opera theater. He's just changing. We spent the day doing some gardening at Plessis."

Phillip wandered into the parlor and slowly sat down on a chair. "If my father isn't dying, then why am I here?" he asked. He shook his head to clear the confusion. "And what were you two doing gardening at Plessis?"

Marie-Claire sat down beside him and patted him on the arm. "Perhaps you should ask Armand," she suggested. "Why don't I just hurry him along." She walked to the bedroom door and poked her head inside. "Armand, darling, will you come out here?"

A few moments later, his father appeared at the bedroom door, dressed in a pleated shirt and fumbling with his bow tie. "Claire," he grumbled. "Come and help me with this damn tie. I've never been able to—" He stopped short as he saw Phillip. He straightened, then nodded. "Ah, you're here, then. It's about time. Wasn't sure you'd come."

Phillip stood and took a step toward him. "Of course I'm here. I got a cable from you saying that you were ill. Seriously ill. You seem to have made an astounding recovery."

Armand cleared his throat and two spots of color rose in his cheeks. Looking closely at him, Phillip realized that he'd never seen his father looking healthier. Or happier. The man was actually smiling!

"Have you lied to your son to get him here?" Marie-Claire asked.

Armand looked down at her and patted her hand affectionately. "Well, what was I supposed to do, Claire? It's about time to put an end to this, don't you think?"

She reached up and touched his cheek. "I think that's a fine idea. But couldn't you have just told him the truth?"

Phillip stared at them wordlessly. They were touching each other like young lovers, their eyes alight, their smiles knowing. "What does this mean?" he asked. "Why did you bring me here?"

His father turned his gaze away from Marie-Claire and looked at Phillip. "I thought it was time to set things right between us." He drew a long breath. "I'm sorry. This feud between the Villeneuves and the DeWildes has gone on long enough. It is now officially over. As far as I'm concerned *and* as far as Marie-Claire is concerned. We've made our peace with each other, and now we expect you and the rest of the DeWildes to do the same."

Phillip shook his head in disbelief. "Just like that? Sixty years and all it takes is a snap of your fingers?"

Marie-Claire wrapped her arms around Armand's waist and hugged him close. "Yes," she said. "I suppose you could put it that way. Just like that. It's over now."

"It was over the moment Claire agreed to marry me," Armand said, circling her shoulder with his arm. "It's been a sixty-year engagement, but I think we're ready to take the plunge now."

Marie-Claire laughed and grabbed Phillip's hand. "I do hope you'll be happy for us," she said.

"I'm a little too shocked to know exactly how I feel," Phillip replied. His mind spun with all that they'd told him. But one thought kept returning. It was over. All the fighting and bitterness were gone. And there was nothing left standing between him and the woman he loved.

"I can guess what you're thinking," his father said. "And all I can say is, I'm sorry. I'm sorry I put you and Megan through so much heartache. And I hope you'll both find it in your heart someday to forgive a foolish old man." Armand retrieved his jacket from a chair and pulled an envelope from the breast pocket. He held it out to Phillip. "Perhaps this will help."

"What is this?" Phillip asked.

"Open it," his father said.

Phillip removed an invitation from the envelope. "I don't understand."

Marie-Claire smiled in understanding. "It's for the reception at the opera theater," she said. "For tonight. You're right, Armand. It's been a long day and we really should turn in early." She caught Phillip's confused gaze. "Megan and I *always* attend these receptions together. It's very important for business, you know. She wouldn't think of missing it." She gave Phillip a meaningful look.

"And there's something else," Armand added. He strode to his desk and returned with a packet of papers. He held them out to Phillip. "It's the title to the property at 25 rue de la Paix," he explained. "It's yours. Do with it what you will. I don't have the time to develop that property right now."

Phillip stared down at the packet. "You're giving it to me?"

"You might want to use it as a peace offering. Or perhaps you could consider it an early wedding present," Armand said. "That is, if you're clever enough to get the girl to marry you." He clasped Marie-Claire's hand in his. "You shouldn't have to wait sixty years for the woman you love."

Phillip looked at Marie-Claire. "What about Gabe? And her father?"

"Leave them to me," Marie-Claire said. "It's about time I learned to put my foot down with overprotective family members. After learning about his father's complicity in all this, I'm sure Jeffrey will be willing to make amends. And if Jeffrey makes amends, so will Gabe."

A smile slowly curved the corners of his mouth as Phillip realized what this all meant. He'd come to Paris merely hoping to catch sight of Megan, and suddenly there was a chance he could have so much more. He could have Megan, forever.

"Go to her," Marie-Claire said. "You've spent too much time apart already."

Phillip closed his eyes then opened them again, afraid that the whole scene might disappear and he might find himself in the midst of a dream—or a very hurtful nightmare. But everything was as it had been, his father watching him speculatively, Marie-Claire smiling up at him.

"I—I guess I'd better get going," he said.

Armand stepped in front of him and clapped him on the shoulders. "We will talk more later. I have a lot to apologize for, Phillip. I've not been a very good father. But I will make things right between us if you give me a chance."

Phillip nodded, then turned toward the door. As he pulled it open, he couldn't help but smile, knowing that he was opening another door to a whole new life—a life that he'd spend with the woman he loved.

THE RECEPTION WAS HELD in the Grand Foyer at the Théâtre de l'Opéra, a long elegant hall flanked by ornate columns and brightly lit chandeliers. From just below the vaulted ceilings decorated with lush paintings, a chorus of gilded cherubs looked down on the party guests. An orchestra played at the far end of the hall and a few guests danced. The rest milled about in quiet conversation. Megan had never quite gotten used to the sedate nature of Parisian social events.

The invitation list included all the most important patrons of the Ballet Paris and the Théâtre de l'Opéra. Megan had mingled for a short time, accepting congratulations on the contribution that DeWilde's had made to the previous season's productions. But she was exhausted and her feet hurt and the two glasses of champagne she'd sipped had gone right to her head. She glanced over at the large clock that decorated the mantel above the fireplace.

The reception had started at eight. It was just past nine. Less than an hour and she could sneak away to the peace and quiet of her office. To leave any earlier would be considered quite rude by French standards, though there was no doubt there would be plenty of guests left to dance the night away.

She slowly wove her way through the crowd until she reached the edge of the dance floor. She found a seat near the wall, in the shadow of a tall column, and settled in to wait another hour, sipping at her last glass of champagne.

The band played a waltz, a tune that seemed strangely familiar. She tried to remember where she'd heard it before, but couldn't. Closing her eyes, she listened carefully to the tune, then realized it was the waltz that she'd first danced with Phillip at the masked ball.

"I always make it a point to dance with the most beautiful woman at the party."

She froze at the sound of the deep male voice. It sounded so real, so close. With a trembling hand, she reached up and rubbed her temple. She'd simply had too much champagne. Or perhaps she'd overheard someone else's conversation. Or maybe she'd imagined the words.

But when she felt a gentle hand on her shoulder, she knew the invitation was not merely a figment of her imagination. She said a silent prayer, hoping that she would turn to see a face she recognized.

Slowly, she stood and raised her gaze. In one beautiful, blinding moment, all her prayers were answered. She stared up into his brilliant blue eyes, unable to believe he was standing in front of her. "It *is* you," she murmured. "I—I thought I'd imagined your voice."

Phillip smiled. "Who did you expect? Don Juan?"

She glanced around nervously. "What are you doing here?" she asked.

He pulled an invitation from his pocket. "I was invited, so to speak."

"I mean, in Paris. You should be in Hong Kong."

"But I'm not." Phillip took her hand. "It's a very long story, Meggie, and right now, I think we should dance. I have an overwhelming need to hold you in my arms again."

He led her out to the dance floor, but she was barely aware of putting one foot in front of the other. She felt as if she were in a haze, a wonderful, dreamy state where everything seemed to vibrate with color and beauty. The chandeliers looked as if they were made of diamonds and the marble floor gleamed like glass. And as he held her hand, a sweet warmth crept up her arm, flooding her body with a wave of delicious sensation.

Phillip pulled her into his arms and moved along with the strains of the waltz. She closed her eyes and swayed with the music. "If this is a dream," she murmured, "I don't ever want to wake up. Please let me sleep forever."

He pressed his lips, warm and firm, to her forehead. "This isn't a dream, Meggie."

She leaned into him and buried her face in his shoulder. The familiar scent of his cologne touched her nose and she rubbed her cheek against the fine fabric of his suit jacket. She opened her eyes and noticed that, unlike the rest of the male guests, he wasn't wearing a tuxedo.

If this really were a dream, he'd be wearing a tuxedo, she mused. And she probably wouldn't be smelling his cologne. And her hand wouldn't be sweating, either. She looked up into his handsome face. "You really are here," she said.

He pulled her closer, molding her body against his long, lean form. "And I'm not going anywhere as long as you keep dancing." His hand drifted to the nape of her neck and he wove his fingers through her hair. "Do you remember the first night we danced together?"

She nodded. "It was just like this. Just like a dream."

"But it was real. And you took my breath away," he said. "I don't think I've been quite the same since then. And I don't think I'm breathing right now."

Megan smiled haltingly. "I—I've missed you. I almost came to Hong Kong. I wanted so much to see you, but I was afraid."

"Of what?" he asked, brushing his finger along her temple and tucking a stray strand of hair behind her ear.

She smoothed her palm over his shoulder. "I was afraid you wouldn't want me anymore. That you had stopped loving me. I was such a coward that day in my office, Phillip, and I'm so sorry."

"What are you trying to tell me?"

She sighed. "I thought I was doing the right thing, but after you left, I knew I'd made a big mistake. I—I guess I'm saying that . . . if I had to do it again, I would have chosen you."

"And what about now?" he asked. "Would you still choose me?"

She met his gaze and blinked in surprise. "If you still want me—if you still love me, I'd choose you. I don't care about my family or my job. All I care about is you. I love you, Phillip." He gazed down into her eyes and she knew he saw the truth in her words. "Do you still love me?" she asked, her voice small and hesitant.

He didn't answer. Instead, he grabbed her hand and pulled her along with him, off the dance floor and out the tall doors of the Grand Foyer. She followed after him, taking two steps for each of his long strides.

"Where are we going?" she asked.

"Someplace private," he replied. He drew her into the first alcove they came to, one of the boxes in the first balcony, and pulled the curtains shut behind them. A sliver of light filtered in from the hall and she stared up at him expectantly, her eyes feasting on the perfect angles of his face.

In one smooth movement, he pulled her into his arms and brought his mouth down on hers. He kissed her, long and deep and with all the passion she remembered sharing with him. As his hands cupped her face and he deepened his kiss, she felt her knees go weak and she clutched at his shoulders.

He pulled back and looked down into her eyes. "I still love you, Meggie. I'll always love you. We've faced more problems than any two people in love deserve, but it's only strengthened my feelings for you."

He bent down and kissed her again, this time sweet and soft and lingering. "Marry me," he murmured against her mouth in an almost desperate plea. "Tonight. Tomorrow if we have to wait. Marry me, Meggie."

Megan nervously drew back and averted her gaze. "Are you sure that's what you want? I have nothing. My family will disown me. I won't have a job. And I don't think either of our families will end this feud just because we say 'I do.'"

"All I care about is you. All I need is your love. Nothing else matters. Say yes," he urged.

Megan smiled, then laughed. "All right. Yes!" she cried. "I will marry you. I will, I will, I will." She threw her arms around his neck and hugged him. "I love you, Phillip Villeneuve, and I will marry you. And I don't care what my family says or thinks or does. Between the two of us, we'll face whatever they throw at us."

"Good," he said. "Now I can give you your wedding present."

She frowned. "But wedding presents aren't supposed to come until after the wedding."

He withdrew a packet of papers from his jacket pocket and held them out to her. She reached for them and he snatched them back. "Tell me you love me again," he said. "Let me hear you say it once more."

"I love you, Phillip," she said. She brushed her lips against his. Satisfied, he handed her the papers and she unfolded them. She held them closer to the light from the hallway. "I can't read this," she said. "It's too dark."

He looped his arms around her waist. "Then let me tell you what they say, Mrs. Soon-To-Be Villeneuve. These papers are the title to 25 rue de la Paix and they're yours. Along with the property, of course."

Megan gasped and her gaze snapped up to his. She searched his face for a clue to what he said. "You're giving me the property? But it's not yours to give. It belongs to your father."

"Not anymore," Phillip replied. "He gave it to me and I'm giving it to you. You can build Galeries DeWilde. And maybe, if you're very, *very* good, I'll help you."

"But—but why? Why would Armand give this up after he fought so hard to get it?"

Phillip considered her question for a long moment. "Maybe it's because he has better things to occupy his life. He's been spending quite a bit of time with your aunt."

"Marie-Claire? Your father and my Marie-Claire?"

Phillip nodded. "From what I understand, my father and your aunt plan to get married. As far as they're concerned, the feud is over and they're getting on with their lives together."

"But she never said anything! I know I've been a bit distracted but... Why didn't you say something sooner? Why did you let me believe our families were still at odds?"

Phillip cupped her face in his hands and met her gaze. "I guess I wanted to know if you had to make a choice, you would choose me over everything else. I needed to know that, Meggie."

She reached up and skimmed her fingertips over his forehead, tracing the shape of his dark brows. "I choose you, Phillip Villeneuve. For now and forever. For better and for worse."

"And I choose you, Meggie DeWilde. For as long as we live, and beyond."

He kissed her then, pulling her down on his lap as he tumbled into a velvet-covered chair. His hands skimmed her body, bringing back all the memories of their lovemaking.

Megan twisted in his arms and looked up at him. "Don't you want a real wedding?"

"I want you, that's all." He nuzzled her neck. "No one else."

She bit her bottom lip and frowned. "So we'll run away and get married. My family will still probably kill me, but I don't care."

A look of genuine concern crossed his face. "But the feud is over now. The Villeneuves and the DeWildes have officially called a truce. They'll have to accept me, won't they?"

"Oh, I'm sure they'll accept you. But they'll be angry about our wedding. It seems that for a family who has built a business around weddings, this branch of the DeWildes can't seem to make one happen for themselves. Gabe and Lianne eloped. And now, you and I. We'll just have to hope that Kate makes up for it with a big, splashy affair."

Phillip hugged her hard. "I can't believe we're finally going to be together."

"If my aunt marries your father, doesn't that make us related? Wouldn't you be..."

"I'd be the man who wants to spend the rest of my life with you. And the man who will do anything to make you happy."

"I can handle that," Megan said as she grabbed his tie and tugged him closer. "And if you want to know what will make me happy, then you'll kiss me right now."

He rolled her onto the soft floor of the opera box and, at her cry of delight, pinned her hands above her head and kissed her neck. "Are you happy now, sweetheart?"

"Deliriously," she teased, before closing her eyes and losing herself to his touch.

continues with

FAMILY SECRETS

by Margaret St. George

In an attempt to shed the past and get on with her future, Grace DeWilde has left her new store and her new life in San Francisco to return to England. Her trip results in a devastating discovery about the DeWilde family that has shocking implications for her children, for Ian Stanley, whose unrequited love for Grace has been years in the making, and for Jeffrey DeWilde, the estranged husband Grace can never stop loving.

Available in December

Here's a preview!

FAMILY SECRETS

IAN STANLEY STRETCHED an arm along the back of the banquette, letting his fingertips rest lightly on her shoulder. "You know, I kept waiting for you to phone me after you left London for the States."

A flush brightened Grace's cheeks. "I decided to make my home in San Francisco for many reasons, Ian. I grew up there..." She let her voice trail. "One of the reasons was the hope that if I left England, I wouldn't force our friends to choose sides. I've always hated that." She glanced at him. "I told myself that I wasn't going to lose touch with Caroline, Marla and Diane—I liked all of your ex-wives—but eventually, of course, I stopped inviting them to parties rather than cause any awkwardness for you."

"So you hoped to spare me the painful task of choosing between you and Jeffrey?"

"I'd like to think our friends can continue to accept us both without feeling they have to choose sides."

"I knew which side I was on the minute I saw Jeffrey head-to-head with a woman young enough to be his daughter," Ian said sharply.

Distress darkened Grace's eyes. "You and Jeffrey have been good friends for forty years. He couldn't be fonder of you if you were his brother. Please, Ian. Don't judge too harshly. You of all people must know that it takes two people to make a marriage successful, and it takes two people to destroy a marriage."

Ian might have been better able to understand if Grace could have explained her role in the drama that had led Jeffrey to betray their vows. But some things were too private to share, even with the best of friends. If Jeffrey wished to confide the insecurity that Grace had triggered, that was his choice. A lifetime of loyalty prevented her from doing so.

"Grace." Ian gently stroked his fingertips along the curve of her jawline. "Occasionally even longtime friends do something that cannot be forgiven. I can't forgive Jeffrey for hurting you. He and I will never again be close."

Grace stared at him. "Oh, Ian. I'm sorry. That will be a great loss for Jeffrey. For both of you."

Suddenly it occurred to her that it would surprise and possibly wound Jeffrey if he knew that Ian was here with her now. He and Ian had attended school together, and university. Ian and Jeffrey had been close long before Grace met either of them.

Ian must have read something of what she was thinking when he looked into her eyes.

"Years ago I told myself that if Grace Powell DeWilde was ever single again, I would move the earth to make her mine." His gaze traveled over her wide-eyed expression. "Grace... don't you know that I've been in love with you for thirty-three years?"

She hadn't known. She hadn't had even a suspicion. When he mentioned his affection, she had believed he was teasing her, heaping on compliments as a form of gallantry and friendship.

"I love you, Grace. I always have. I always will."

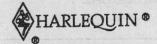

Take 4 bestselling love stories FREE

Plus get a FREE surprise gift!

Special Limited-time Offer

Mail to Harlequin Reader Service®

3010 Walden Avenue
P.O. Box 1867
Buffalo, N.Y. 14240-1867

YES! Please send me 4 free Harlequin Temptation® novels and my free surprise gift. Then send me 4 brand-new novels every month, which I will receive before they appear in bookstores. Bill me at the low price of $2.90 each plus 25¢ delivery and applicable sales tax, if any.* That's the complete price and a savings of over 10% off the cover prices—quite a bargain! I understand that accepting the books and gift places me under no obligation ever to buy any books. I can always return a shipment and cancel at any time. Even if I never buy another book from Harlequin, the 4 free books and the surprise gift are mine to keep forever.

142 BPA A3UP

Name _____ (PLEASE PRINT)

Address _____ Apt. No. _____

City _____ State _____ Zip _____

This offer is limited to one order per household and not valid to present Harlequin Temptation® subscribers. *Terms and prices are subject to change without notice. Sales tax applicable in N.Y.

UTEMP-696   ©1990 Harlequin Enterprises Limited

1997
Reader's Engagement Book
A calendar of important dates
and anniversaries for readers to use!

Informative and entertaining—with notable
dates and trivia highlighted throughout the year.

Handy, convenient, pocketbook size to help you
keep track of your own personal important dates.

Added bonus—contains $5.00 worth of coupons
for upcoming Harlequin and Silhouette books.
This calendar more than pays for itself!

 Available beginning in November at
your favorite retail outlet.

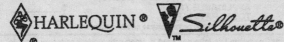

Now's your chance to get the complete

HERE COME THE

GROOMS™

series!
Order any or all 12 of these great titles:

#30116-2	A Practical Marriage by Dallas Schulze	$3.99 U.S./$4.50 CAN. ☐
#30136-7	Marry Sunshine by Anne McAllister	$3.99 U.S./$4.50 CAN. ☐
#30110-3	The Cowboy and the Chauffeur by Elizabeth August	$3.99 U.S./$4.50 CAN. ☐
#30115-4	McConnell's Bride by Naomi Horton	$3.99 U.S./$4.50 CAN. ☐
#30127-8	Married?! by Annette Broadrick	$3.99 U.S./$4.50 CAN. ☐
#30103-0	Designs on Love by Gina Wilkins	$3.99 U.S./$4.50 CAN. ☐
#30126-X	It Happened One Night by Marie Ferrarella	$3.99 U.S./$4.50 CAN. ☐
#30101-4	Lazarus Rising by Anne Stuart	$3.99 U.S./$4.50 CAN. ☐
#30107-3	The Bridal Price by Barbara Boswell	$3.99 U.S./$4.50 CAN. ☐
#30131-8	Annie in the Morning by Curtiss Ann Matlock	$3.99 U.S./$4.50 CAN. ☐
#30112-X	September Morning by Diana Palmer	$3.99 U.S./$4.50 CAN. ☐
#30129-4	Outback Nights by Emilie Richards	$3.99 U.S./$4.50 CAN. ☐

ADDED BONUS! In every edition of *Here Come the Grooms*
you'll find **$5.00** worth of coupons good for Harlequin and
Silhouette products.

AMOUNT	$
POSTAGE & HANDLING	$
($1.00 for one book, 50¢ for each additional)	
APPLICABLE TAXES*	$
TOTAL PAYABLE	$
(check or money order—please do not send cash)	

To order, complete this form and send it, along with a check or money order for the
total above, payable to Harlequin Books, to: **In the U.S.:** 3010 Walden Avenue,
P.O. Box 9047, Buffalo, NY 14269-9047; **In Canada:** P.O. Box 613, Fort Erie, Ontario,
L2A 5X3.

Name: _____

Address: _____ City: _____

State/Prov.: _____ Zip/Postal Code: _____

*New York residents remit applicable sales taxes.
 Canadian residents remit applicable GST and provincial taxes.   HCTG1196

Look us up on-line at: http://www.romance.net

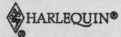 **HARLEQUIN®**   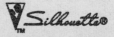 *Silhouette*®

The collection of the year!
NEW YORK TIMES BESTSELLING AUTHORS

Linda Lael Miller
Wild About Harry

Janet Dailey
Sweet Promise

Elizabeth Lowell
Reckless Love

Penny Jordan
Love's Choices

and featuring
Nora Roberts
The Calhoun Women

This special trade-size edition features four of the wildly
popular titles in the Calhoun miniseries together in
one volume—a true collector's item!

Pick up these great authors and a chance to win
a weekend for two in New York City at the
Marriott Marquis Hotel on Broadway! We'll pay
for your flight, your hotel—even a Broadway show!

Available in December at your favorite retail outlet.

NEW YORK
Marriott.
MARQUIS

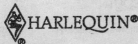 

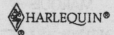

HARLEQUIN ®

Scandals

A passionate story of romance, where bold, daring characters set out to defy their world of propriety and strict social codes.

"Scandals—a story that will make your heart race and your pulse pound. Spectacular!"
—Suzanne Forster

"Devon is daring, dangerous and altogether delicious."
—Amanda Quick

Don't miss this wonderful full-length novel from Regency favorite Georgina Devon.

Available in December, wherever Harlequin books are sold.

SCAN

You're About to Become a
Privileged Woman

Reap the rewards of fabulous free gifts and
benefits with proofs-of-purchase from
Harlequin and Silhouette books

Pages & Privileges™

It's our way of thanking you for
buying our books at your
favorite retail stores.

**Harlequin and Silhouette—
the most privileged readers in the world!**

For more information about Harlequin and
Silhouette's PAGES & PRIVILEGES program call the
Pages & Privileges Benefits Desk: 1-503-794-2499

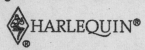

HARLEQUIN®

WBD-PP19